HER RELUCTANT HIGHLANDER HUSBAND

CLAN MACKINLAY SERIES

HER RELUCTANT HIGHLANDER HUSBAND

CLAN MACKINLAY SERIES

ALLISON B. HANSON

This book is a work of fiction. Names, characters, places, and incidents are the product of the author's imagination or are used fictitiously. Any resemblance to actual events, locales, or persons, living or dead, is coincidental.

Copyright © 2020 by Allison B. Hanson. All rights reserved, including the right to reproduce, distribute, or transmit in any form or by any means. For information regarding subsidiary rights, please contact the Publisher.

Entangled Publishing, LLC
10940 S Parker Rd
Suite 327
Parker, CO 80134
rights@entangledpublishing.com

Amara is an imprint of Entangled Publishing, LLC.

Edited by Nina Bruhns
Cover design by Mayhem Cover Creations
Cover photography by Period Images
Background by kamchatka/Deposit Photos

Manufactured in the United States of America

First Edition November 2020

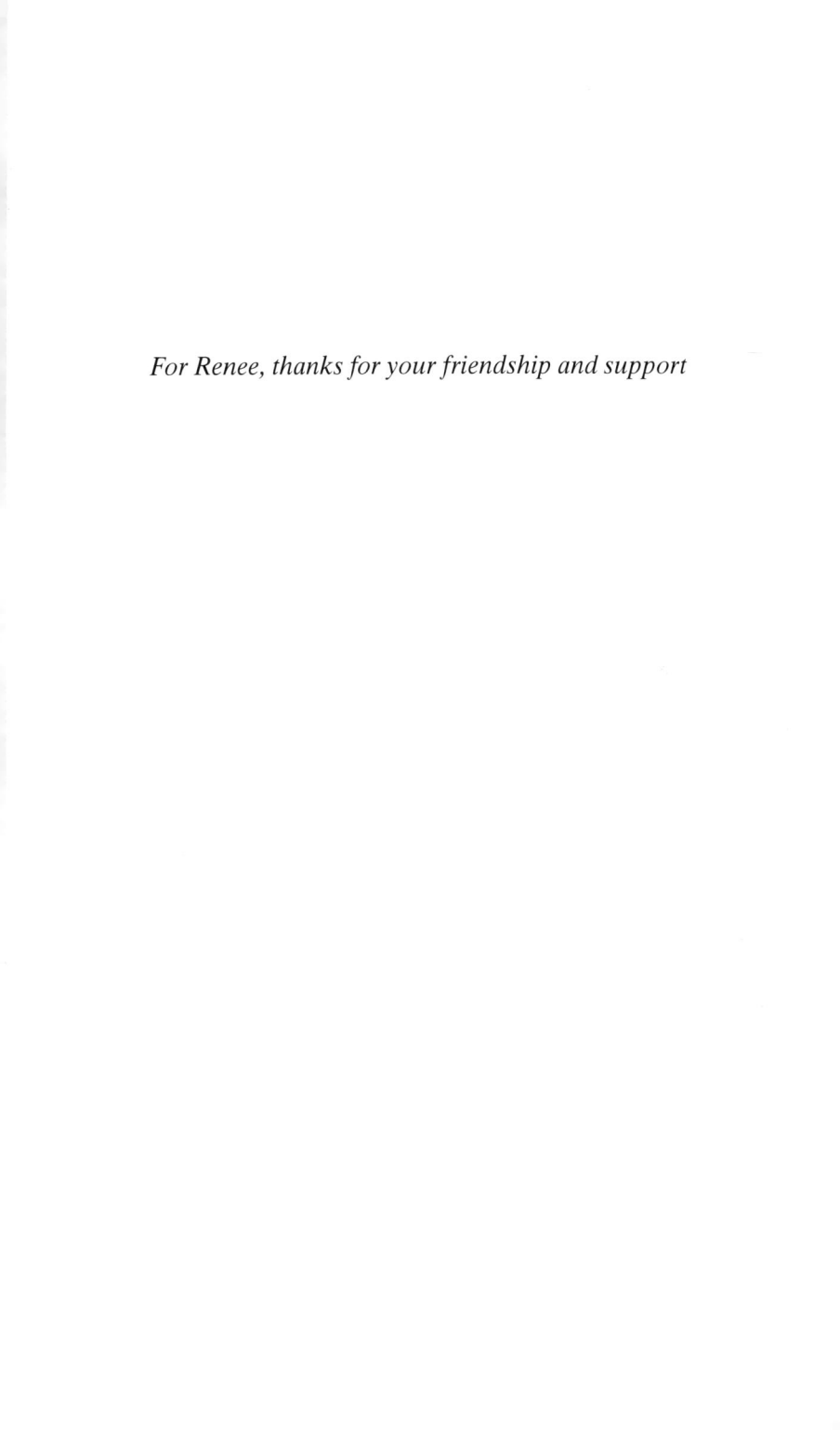

For Renee, thanks for your friendship and support

Chapter One

SEPTEMBER, 1662 SCOTLAND

If he could only take that final step, it would all be over. Bryce MacKinlay Campbell, war chief of Clan MacKinlay, balanced himself on the edge of the battlements for a few seconds longer before stepping back to safety.

He'd been here many times over the ten years since he'd lost his wife and child, and each time he'd been unable to take that fatal action. While the grief still haunted him, he couldn't force fate's hand and join them.

Kicking the immovable buttress, he slid to the stones and let his head hang. Letting his misery wash over him.

"You think it's weakness that keeps you from ending it, but it's not. It takes strength to stay and do what needs done." Lachlan MacKinlay, laird of Clan MacKinlay, was the last person Bryce wanted to see at the moment.

"Only if what needs doing is at your order," Bryce grumbled.

Lach was his younger cousin, though they'd been like

brothers. He'd thought the man would always have his back, but it turned out Bryce was wrong about that. They'd not always agreed on how things should be, but there had always been respect between them.

Bryce's respect had faltered when his laird had ordered him to wed. Bryce had considered for a time returning to the Campbells where his father still lived. His mother had been a MacKinlay, and when she'd passed he'd come to Dunardry to live with his uncle. He'd never regretted his decision to stay. Until now.

"I know ye think I only have one motive for forcing this marriage on you, but you're wrong. It's more than a simple alliance with the McCurdy clan to gain access to a port. I do it for you as well."

"Please don't offer me any favors, laird. You know well enough, I dinna want to marry ever again. I had a wife I loved. Making me take another is a sure way to promise two people are miserable for the rest of their lives."

"Or…it could be a new start. You may have lost Maggie and Isabel, but you're still alive. Perhaps it's time for ye to start living."

"I'm alive, yes, but without a heart to give to another. It's not fair to this McCurdy lass to strap her to a husband who's hollow and broken inside."

"I would ask you not to be cruel to her because you're angry at me."

Bryce's head snapped up at the insult. "I may not be able to toss myself over the battlements, but I'll give you a mighty shove if you dare suggest I would do such a thing to an innocent girl."

"I know you wouldn't intentionally. But I also know well what can happen when one is not happy about being wed."

"*You're* the one I'm unhappy with," Bryce reminded his cousin.

"Fair enough." He held up his hands in surrender. "Then if you can see to treat her decent, I don't think she'll ask for much else. You can be sure it would take a lot for her new home to be as unpleasant as living with the McCurdys."

"Mayhap she's just as horrible as her kin." The McCurdys were known across the Highlands as the worst that man had to offer.

Lach shook his head and held his hand out to assist Bryce to his feet. "I was told she is a quiet lass."

Bryce snorted at the word *lass*. He knew she'd come of the age to marry two years ago when Lach had planned to marry her to Cameron, only to have their other cousin wiggle his way free of the arrangement. It meant Bryce's new bride had only recently turned eighteen. Making him thirteen years older than she.

"She's a child," Bryce complained, though she was the same age he'd been when he'd married an even younger Maggie. It wasn't that his intended was so young, but that Bryce felt so terribly old. It had been a lifetime ago that he'd been a happy groom looking down at his bride's shy smile.

"She's a woman," Lach argued. "She'll cause you no problems. Will you not give her a chance?"

That was the problem. If he allowed someone the chance, they might break through the walls he'd built to protect himself from feeling such pain ever again.

He cared for his cousins and their growing families. Lach's three boys and Cam's wee lass were blessings that brought a smile to his face whenever he had the occasion to be around them.

Though he made sure that occasion came rarely.

Bryce's attention was drawn below by the sound of a wagon and horses entering the bailey. The man in the front carried a banner with the McCurdy arms.

"I must go greet our guests," Lach said. "If you're not

planning to throw yourself to your death, perhaps you'll come with me."

"I'll never forgive you for this."

"I didn't expect forgiveness." Lach frowned. "I carry many burdens for the sake of my clan. One more is not so much. Though I do hope it turns out well for you."

Lach couldn't understand how Bryce felt. His wife, Kenna, was healthy. His children hearty and full of energy. He'd never lost those who were most precious to him. He'd never been broken the way Bryce had.

When Bryce had come home to find Maggie and Isabel in their beds, dead for days from a fever, his heart had been shattered into pieces so small there was no way to mend it.

He hated to chain Dorie McCurdy to the impossible task of finding happiness as his wife.

With another longing look over the edge, he turned to go face his future.

. . .

When the wagon stopped, Dorie's brother, Wallace, grabbed her ankle to yank her down. His efforts tore her already ratty dress. She winced more at having her bare leg exposed to the cool morning air than any worry over the dress. What was another rip in the tattered hem anyway?

She was certain whoever she was here to marry would take one look at her and send her away. She couldn't wait to see her father thwarted at whatever foul plan he was attempting with this clan. Not that he'd know immediately since he hadn't deigned to come to her ill-fated wedding.

Two days ago, she'd been pulled from her prison of a room and scrubbed clean by maids who had dressed her in this sorry excuse for a gown. Her brother had thrown her in the wagon after her uncle appraised her with a frown and a grunt.

She hadn't expected anything different. The McCurdys hated her. So much so that she'd been kept in her room for the last nine years. The windows of her makeshift prison had been boarded up after her first attempt to escape.

Her life had consisted of the few books she owned and the single visit per day by a silent maid who brought her meals and tidied her room. Neither of them spoke, but a few times they'd exchanged a smile.

Twice over the years, men had entered her room with the purpose of doing her harm, but her brother had stopped them. Not out of brotherly regard, but with the reminder that she was to remain chaste so she could be bartered at some point.

Apparently the time had come. She had heard her brother and cousins speaking of a wedding during the journey. She had no idea what clan she was to be married off to or who her husband would be. But surely her life couldn't be any worse than it had been these last nine years since her mother passed.

Thoughts of her mother brought a strained smile to her face. She might not look like much in the ragged dress, but her mother had always said a smile was all she needed to be beautiful. Perhaps her smile would enchant her new husband into keeping her so she wouldn't be sent back to Baehaven Castle and that small room with no windows.

"Stop that. You look a fool," Wallace said, giving her a firm shake.

Her smile fell along with her hope of any chance for a better life. Whatever husband waited for her here did so because of an arrangement her father would surely default on.

It wouldn't be long before her unsuspecting groom realized he'd been tricked and would punish her for her father's crimes. Of which there were many.

Dorie might have spared the man this fate, but she knew she would remain silent.

Silence was safe.

• • •

When Bryce entered the hall in his best shirt and his hair combed, he found the small gathering waiting by the hearth. Other than two servants there were no other women with their group.

For a moment his chest relaxed. Perhaps his bride had abandoned him. He'd be glad to be spared this duty. It would save them both a lot of misery.

Lach might be able to force him to marry for an alliance, but the laird couldn't force Bryce to live with her or get a bairn on her. It would be a marriage contract in name only. A binding to gain access to a seaport from the McCurdys and nothing more.

Lach, Cam, and the priest were frowning when he arrived.

"What's the matter? Did the lass flee?" Bryce couldn't help a slight smile.

"Nay. She's there with her maid."

Bryce glanced over at the woman young enough to be Dorie McCurdy. A tall stick of a girl who looked as if she hadn't eaten a good meal in ages. Her midnight hair longed for a comb, and her blue eyes darted around as if ready for an attack. He'd noticed her as he'd approached, but thought her a maid for how poorly she was dressed.

He knew the McCurdys were hurting for coin, but surely they could spend the money on a clean dress for the laird's daughter on her wedding day. The gown wasn't even made for her, as evidenced by the way the hem fell well above her thin ankles. He groaned when he noticed her bare feet. A twitch of sympathy coiled in his stomach before he reined it in. *No emotions. None but anger.*

"For the love of all that's holy, what is going on here?" Bryce asked, quickly murmuring an apology when the priest gave him a look for his blasphemy. "She's no shoes."

"Aye." Lach frowned and pulled him aside to whisper, "She's got nothing except the dress on her back, and I don't think that's hers, either."

"My Mari wasn't better dressed when I married her," Cam offered. "In fact, she had no shoes, either. Perhaps it's a good omen."

"Marian had been on the run from the British for months. This lass is being delivered to her planned wedding by her family," Lach said with a wave. "Kenna offered to find her a better dress and shoes, but her brother won't have it. He wants the wedding done with as quickly as possible."

"And you don't think that speaks of something underhanded?" Cam asked.

Before Lach could answer, the McCurdy heir, Wallace, stepped up with his two cousins behind him.

"Is this the groom?" the man bellowed. "Let's get on with it. Before the MacKinlay breaches another arrangement like the last time." The younger men with him chuckled at the man's snide comment.

Cam took a step toward the strangers, but Lach put out his arm to stop his progress. "Father," Lach said to the priest. "Let's commence with the service so our guests can return home as soon as possible."

A few moments later everyone was sorted out and Bryce stood in front of his bride, who stared back at him openly with wide eyes.

Eyes the color of the perfect September sky he'd observed earlier while standing on the battlements. He swallowed and looked away. The lass was pretty enough despite her condition. A few good meals and a bath and she'd be much improved. Not that he cared.

He planned to see her to his cottage in the village and be done with her. He'd stay in his small room in the keep. He'd give her enough of his pay to care for her better than she was currently, but she would be on her own.

His duty to his clan ended with him speaking the words, "I do."

Chapter Two

Dorie blinked up at the man who would be her husband.

At her height, she was taller than many of the men in her clan. And nearly as tall as her brother. But she had to look up at Bryce MacKinlay Campbell.

Even frowning at her the way he was now, he was incredibly handsome. There were so many shades of blond in his long hair she didn't think any two strands were the same color. Honey, wheat, gold…there was a different name for each hue. And she found she wanted to spend hours assigning each one.

His green eyes glittered even though it was clear he was unhappy. She wondered how bright they would be if he smiled or laughed. Not that he seemed the sort for such frivolous things.

Her new husband was a serious man. He'd hardly said two words as they stood in front of the priest to be married. The words he did say sounded less than happy about their arrangement.

She hadn't expected him to want to marry her. Looking at

the servants in the hall, she knew she was lacking. She didn't even have shoes. There was no need for shoes or new dresses when she'd spent her life in one room with a few books and a lumpy bed.

She'd never cared about such things. Until now.

Swallowing, she turned toward the priest as he began the ceremony. She'd never been to a wedding before so she didn't know what to expect. When the priest told her to repeat his words and waited expectantly for her to do so, she could only blink.

"Go ahead, lass," her groom prompted when she remained silent.

She shook her head, hoping the gesture would explain the problem, but her brother strode forward and grabbed her by the arm.

"You'll say the goddamn words, ye fool. Don't play with me. I've no patience for it today," Wallace snapped and gave her a hearty shake.

If she did speak, it might be to point out that her brother had no patience any day. *Ever*. But she didn't have the chance for he was shaking her again.

"Stop it," Bryce said, pulling her brother back. "What's the matter?" he asked, his glowing green gaze on her. "Are you being forced to marry me?"

Again she shook her head; though she hadn't a say in marrying, it wasn't that she didn't want to. Now that she was here before him, she felt that tingle of hope under her breastbone. How much worse could she be here where the servants were better cared for than she?

"She doesn't speak," Rory, her younger cousin, explained. A year younger than her, Rory was a gangly lad who had been kind to her when no one was around. When others were close by, he joined in so as not to be teased by the older men.

Bryce's eyes went wide as the priest mumbled in

dissatisfaction. "I canna perform the service if the bride doesna say her vows."

"She can nod. Then you know she wants to do it," Wallace suggested while leaning forward to tap her chin.

The priest shook his head. "There's no proof she has the capacity to understand what she's agreeing to without her speaking the vows."

Her brother reached for her, this time smacking her in the back of the head. The force caused her to bite the tip of her tongue. Even if she'd wanted to, it would be difficult to speak now.

"Enough," Bryce said, drawing his knife. "Touch her again, and I'll drop you here where we eat our meals. I'd rather not have your bloody carcass sully our hall."

Her older cousin, Desmond, and Rory were at her brother's side in a second with their own daggers drawn.

She swallowed and opened her mouth to say something, but before she had the chance the MacKinlay laird shouted that everyone was to put their weapons away.

Her groom was the first to follow the order, slipping his knife in the sheath and putting up both hands in a non-threatening way.

The other men backed away, glaring. "You better say your vows if you know what's good for you. If we have to take ye back with us to Baehaven, you might not make the trip," her brother whispered before stepping away.

...

Bryce didn't hear what the McCurdy arse said to Dorie, but her already pale skin went a shade or two lighter, and fear clouded those clear blue eyes.

He didn't want a wife, but he couldn't make this woman go back to her family. Not that they acted like family. These were her brother and cousins and they treated her like less than a worm. Even as mad as he was at Lach, he regarded his cousin with more respect than this.

"There must be another way," Bryce said. He looked around at the other people and spotted Cam and Mari, recalling the way they'd been wed by accident. "We can be handfasted."

"Handfasting still requires a verbal declaration of intent," the unhelpful priest replied. It figured they would find the one priest in all the Highlands who was also fluent in the ways of the law.

"Do you know what a promise is, lass?"

Dorie nodded immediately, intelligence clear in her eyes.

"Can ye do this when you want to promise something?" Using his index finger, he drew a cross over his heart.

Another nod and she mimicked the motion.

"Does that make her intent clear, Father?"

The priest frowned and let out a huff before agreeing. "Aye. It will do." He went on to murmur something about the bride having no shoes, but Bryce paid him no mind. Instead he took Dorie's hand in his.

"Go on then with the vows," Bryce said, wanting it to be done.

After dealing with the issue of his bride's silence, things went rather quickly. In no time at all, the priest pronounced them wed. Bryce watched his new wife's eyes go wide as Lach came forward with his dirk. He nicked Bryce's skin first and then took her wrist.

When she fought, Bryce reached out to place his hand on her shoulder. She steadied when he gave her a nod.

For all she couldn't speak, she definitely understood him. And he found he could understand her as well. Mayhap everything they needed to communicate in the short time they'd be together could be accomplished with their eyes.

When her hand was open and seeping, Bryce placed his own to hers as their hands were bound. He said the words alone as she watched. When he gave her hand a squeeze, she tightened her grip in reply.

"It's done," Lach said as he untied them. Bryce flexed his hand, feeling the sting from the binding ceremony.

"Nay." Wallace stepped forward. "The MacKinlays have weaseled out of the agreement too many times for me to leave without consummation. Once you've marked your sheets with her blood, I'll take what's owed and be on my way, our agreement secured."

Dorie's eyes went wide at the mention of blood.

"Don't be skittish, girl. Go do your duty." Her brother gave her a shove as Bryce held on to her hand.

Skittish was the proper word. Bryce held on tighter to her hand in an effort to keep her from running off, but she panicked. One moment he was watching as her eyes darted in all directions, most likely looking for escape. The next, she had bitten his hand, causing him to let go.

Once released, his wife tore out of the hall toward the bailey with her brother and cousin on her trail.

"Christ almighty," Bryce cursed, and followed behind them with blood seeping from both wounds.

Dorie hadn't made it far before Wallace gripped her hair and tugged her back to him. A sharp slap on her cheek would have knocked her down if he weren't still holding her up by her hair.

She whimpered as he yelled at her. "Where do you think you're going, you stupid bitch? Get back in there and let him take you so I can be done with this place."

The lout raised his hand to strike her again. Bryce saw her wince in anticipation of a blow that didn't come. Bryce grabbed the man's arm and twisted it back, ready to break it if the arse gave him a reason to.

"She's *my* wife now. And I'll thank you to not touch her again, or feel the wrath of my blade on your neck. Do ye ken?" Bryce's words were deadly calm.

The woman hadn't been his wife for more than ten minutes and already he was being called on to protect her.

"Aye. Just take her. I wish to leave before the stench of this place becomes permanent," Wallace sneered.

Wanting to get the man away from her, Bryce turned to lead the oaf back inside.

"You can't leave her. She'll run," her older cousin warned.

"She'll not run. Where will she go?" Bryce held out his hands.

"She's daft. She'll run."

"You'll wait here for me?" Bryce asked her.

Dorie swallowed then nodded, swiping her finger over her heart in a promise.

"Let's go." Bryce gave the man a shove back inside. Once he'd secured him with the rest of his likewise oafish kin, Bryce hurried to the kitchen to gather food and drink. Swiping a plaid from the hall, he went back to the bailey to find his new wife was gone. "Blast and damn."

• • •

Dorie heard the puppy before she saw him. He was a matted mess of fur whining under an empty wagon.

Moving slowly so not to frighten the animal, she reached under the wagon and scratched him on the head. A few moments later she had coaxed him out, and he crawled into her lap, licking her face and wagging his tail.

It was then she heard a man curse and turned to see her new husband was standing where he'd left her. He was looking around unhappily.

With a gasp, she ran across the courtyard to the place

she'd promised to be. When she stood in front of him she cringed, bracing herself for his displeasure, but nothing happened.

The snuffling at her leg caused her to open her eyes. She attempted to wave the dog away, but he wouldn't go. Instead he thought she was playing a game and snagged a piece of her gown, ripping it.

"It looks like you've made a new friend," Bryce said drily.

He reached for the dog, and she jumped in front of the animal, pushing him away so it wouldn't be beaten. Once again she expected a punishment, but Bryce leaned around her to get to the dog. Picking him up, he scratched the dog affectionately behind the ears.

When she summoned the courage to look at him, it was to see an amused smile on his face instead of the anger she expected.

"Aren't you a wee rascal?" her new husband said to the dog. "You need to be cleaned up, but you have a gentle spirit. Would you like him, Dorie?" he asked.

Her eyes went wide and she nodded, though still wary it could be a trick.

Two women who had been present at the wedding came out of the castle and headed in their direction. The taller redhead was the laird's wife. While the women were different in coloring and stature, Dorie was sure they were related. It was there in their eyes.

"Are you well, dear? Your brother is a beast," the shorter blonde said in a cultured English accent as she rubbed her rounded belly. "Did he hurt you?"

Dorie shook her head, but it was her husband who spoke. "I stopped him before he was able to cause any damage."

"He's blustering about not leaving until he's seen proof of the consummation," Kenna said with a frown. "While I wouldn't want ye to rush things, mayhap you can see to your duty so the bastard can leave my castle as quickly as possible."

Dorie might have laughed for hearing the laird's wife call her brother a bastard, but she was stuck on the first part. The consummation part, to be exact.

In truth, she didn't know what it entailed beyond what her mother had told her when she was a child. That a man lies with a woman and she has a baby. Surely that wasn't all there was to it.

"I planned to take her for a ride and have a bite to eat. Are you hungry?"

Dorie nodded.

"When we return, I'll have the proof and they can be on their way."

He reached for her, and she stepped back. He didn't move to grab her, and after a few seconds she realized he intended to take her hand. Allowing it, she let him lead her toward the stables.

She turned to wave to the women as they went back inside. The dog followed Dorie into the dim stables. She loved the sweet smell of hay and the snuffling sounds the horses made.

"Do you ride?" he asked.

She shrugged. She'd ridden as a child, but she barely remembered that life.

He helped her onto his horse and slid up behind her, his body pressed against hers. They headed for the gate and the dog followed along. Occasionally she would twist back to check.

"He'll not lose sight of you, lass," Bryce assured. "He's well smitten."

He said nothing else as they traveled. She didn't mind the silence. It gave her time to enjoy the beauty that was the MacKinlay lands. The leaves were still green, though she could smell a hint of autumn in the air.

She was certain the lands at Baehaven were just as lovely,

but she'd rarely seen them. When they'd left to come to Dunardry for her wedding, it had been dark, so she hadn't had the chance on her exit, either. It didn't bother her much. Everything that had made it a home was long gone. As a child, she'd loved Baehaven Castle. But then her mother had been there to give it light and happiness. What little she'd seen of it since that time was dark and daunting.

Bryce stopped by a stream and dismounted before helping her down. The dog came over as soon as she was on her feet. Her still bare feet. Fortunately it was warm. As best she could tell, it was probably early September. Being barefoot in the cool grass by the stream was a lovely experience.

She smiled and spun in a circle while looking up at the trees above her. It felt wonderful to be free of her small, dark room. The warmth of the sunshine as they'd ridden had warmed her through.

Bryce set out a blanket and settled on the edge of it. She was quick to join him so he wouldn't be frustrated by her delay.

"Under normal circumstances, we would get to know each other," he said as he handed her a piece of bread and a hunk of cheese. "But I don't see the point in it."

She thought maybe he meant that it would be one-sided since she didn't talk. She almost opened her mouth to ask him a question, to prompt the discussion he was so quick to brush away, but she remained silent. He seemed nice enough, but she wasn't certain of him yet.

"The only thing ye really need to know is that I'll not hurt you. I'll give you a home and food. I'll get you some bloody shoes. You'll be provided for. As war chief, I earn decent pay. I have a cottage. It's not overly fancy, but you'll have what you need within reason. That's what I can offer you."

He opened his mouth as if to say something else but tossed in a bite of food instead.

"It's a nice enough day," he said, and she nodded.

"I'm not a man of many words. It's odd having to carry on the conversation by myself. I'm happy to have others do the talking. You're probably tired of hearing me rambling."

She shook her head and reached out to touch him, so he'd know how much she enjoyed hearing his voice. He hissed in pain and drew his hand away. She looked down to see her teeth marks in his skin. Wincing, she tried to convey her regret and apology with her expression.

"Don't worry, lass. I'm not angry at you for defending yourself. Only a person with no hope left allows themselves to be mistreated without fighting back."

She was grateful he understood, but still wished she'd not lashed out and injured him. She knew him better now. Trusted him.

"Have you always been mute?"

She shook her head.

"I've heard of people losing their ability to speak after a tragic event. Is that what happened?"

She nodded slowly. Her words had gotten her mother killed. She'd vowed to herself never to be so reckless again. Staying silent ensured she wouldn't say anything wrong. Not that many people had bothered to speak to her over the years...

Bryce looked out over the stream as the pup came up to be petted.

"Och. You need a bath, you wee beast." He turned to her, still wincing. "Will ye help me clean him so he can come home with you?"

A smile pulled up on her lips. It felt strange, having not done it for so long. Maybe it would be the first of many to come.

Perhaps she could be happy here, with this man.

Chapter Three

When Bryce's new wife smiled, she was beautiful. She was fairly pretty when not smiling, but he'd not noticed until the moment Dorie showed her pleasure at being able to keep her new four-legged friend.

It didn't matter if he found her lovely or not; nothing would come of it. He'd already had a lovely, beautiful wife and lost her. He would not allow himself to get close to another woman. Even one he was now wed to. There was only one woman whose memory he kept in his broken heart.

Dorie wasn't smiling as they packed mud on the flea-ridden mutt. Bryce wasn't sure what kind of dog he was. Maybe a mixture of many kinds. His feet and ears were of a size. It made him look lanky and clumsy.

"Shall we name him Rags?" he asked.

Dorie was quick to shake her head. She pointed toward the castle and then to him. He didn't understand. Apparently their ability to communicate had been short lived.

Just then the dog shook the mud and water all over them, spattering them with filth. "Be still, you wee rascal," he commanded and, amazingly, the dog obeyed. At least for the moment.

Dorie grabbed his arm and nodded.

"What is it, lass?" he asked, as if she could explain herself.

In answer she pointed to his lips. Then tapped her own. For a moment he thought she was requesting he kiss her, but then she pointed to the dog.

Hmm. Something he'd just said? "Wee rascal?" he repeated, thinking that must be what she meant.

She nodded enthusiastically and pointed to the dog again. He finally understood, though how he did, he wasn't sure.

"You want to call the dog Rascal?"

Another nod and another blasted smile that stirred something he'd thought had died years ago. He cleared his throat, trying to force down the lump that had formed there, then looked away from her.

"Very well, Rascal he is. At least until he flings mud all over us again. Then he'll be called the late Rascal."

At Dorie's gasp, he tempered his words with a grin so she'd know he didn't mean the dog any real harm. As if on cue, Rascal shook, spraying them again with mud and water. Bryce let out a curse and looked up at Dorie when she laughed.

She pointed at his face, no doubt spattered with mud, and laughed again. The sound made him smile, something he'd not done in so long it felt tight and unnatural on his lips.

When she covered her mouth to hide her laughter, she smeared mud across her face, which had him laughing and pointing at her. She splashed him with water, probably to clean the mud from his face. He splashed her back, his only intention to get her wet and make her squeal in protest.

She was quick to oblige and used both hands to throw water at him.

Before long they were both soaked, water dripping from

the ends of her hair.

He'd been having fun, and when he realized it, the smile slid from his lips. His temporary giddiness faded back into solemnity. Nodding toward the blanket in the sun, he let out a breath.

"Enough. Let's dry off. We'll need to get back soon." She gave a nod and he was sad to see the smile die from her face. Like the sun setting on a perfect day you didn't want to end.

He'd had many perfect days in his life, but the sun had set, never to rise again.

• • •

When Rascal was bathed and they'd dried from the ordeal, Bryce looked up at the sky and let out a sigh. Dorie knew what he was going to say next and wished she could keep him from voicing their need to return. Here in their quiet piece of the world, it was easy to pretend things would be fine.

Bryce's smile had faded and he was the serious man she'd married, but she trusted him already. Seeing the kindness he'd shown an animal told her the type of man he was. She was safe with him. She couldn't be sure of the rest of the MacKinlays waiting back at the castle.

"It's time we get home," he said, sealing her fate.

She stiffened, knowing what awaited them. The McCurdys wouldn't leave until the marriage was consummated with her blood. It was clear by the frown on her husband's face that it wouldn't be as fun as bathing the dog.

"I feel like maybe we've made some ground between us. I hope you can trust me. What I have to do now will not be pleasant, but it must be done."

She remembered her brother's words. Bloodying his sheets. She had no idea what he'd meant by that, but it sounded painful. She stood, ready to run if needed.

"I'll not hurt you. You have my word."

She settled, even when he pulled his dirk. He lifted his kilt enough to reveal a muscled thigh. He drew his blade across the flesh and hissed as blood welled along the line of the cut.

She gasped and stepped closer to stop him, but he'd already wiped the blade clean and sheathed it. Using a wet cloth, he smeared the blood around and wiped it on the blanket.

He looked at her. "Forgive me, but I need to mark you with blood. Your devil of a brother will probably check."

She stood still as he lifted her skirt and smeared the blood on the inside of her thighs. And higher to the place between her legs. When she tensed, he apologized again and huffed. "Let's get this over with."

After cleaning his wound, he gathered the blanket and handed it to her so he could lift her to his horse. She was prepared for his hands on her waist, but not for the thrill she felt sizzle through her at his touch.

As they rode back, she held on to him tighter than before. She breathed in the scent of him. Earth, clean water, and sun. She probably smelled the same now since their time in the river.

The sway of the horse and the heat of his body nearly put her to sleep. She thought of the place he'd touched between her legs and the warmth that pooled there now. She'd never felt so at ease to be close to a man. She knew it wasn't some huge change in her, but the difference between this man and the ones she knew.

At the castle, Rory winced as she dismounted from the horse and stumbled on shaky legs. The brow over his left eye—bisected by a scar she thought might have been her fault—rose and she noticed the glare he gave Bryce.

Her brother and Desmond came out to meet them,

grumbling their displeasure over the delay.

"It took ye long enough," Wallace spat as Bryce handed off his horse to a groom.

"Mayhap you McCurdys like to force yourselves on your women. We MacKinlays like to see to their pleasure," Bryce taunted and took her hand. She didn't understand the exchange, but it was clear his words irritated her brother, so she smiled. She was awestruck by the man beside her. The way he didn't cower under her brother's glare. The way he stood at her side as if ready to protect her, his hand casually resting on the sword at his side.

Any man who stood up to her family was a hero to her.

"Pleasure or no, I'll see that it's been done proper so we can take our fee and go."

Bryce and Lach shared a look of unease. Lach cleared his throat. "Just remember that money is payment to book room for cargo on the next ship that comes to port. Make certain it gets back to the laird as part of our arrangement."

"Aye. I remember. But there'll be no agreement if he didn't do the deed."

Bryce handed over the soiled blanket. Wallace and Rory opened it to reveal the bloodstain.

Her brother turned to Bryce and nodded toward the binding on his wrist from the wedding. "I'll see that your wounds haven't been reopened."

Glaring, Bryce unwound the cloth and held up his cut. Wallace turned on her and roughly tore her bandage off as well. Turning to the maid, he pointed to Dorie. "Check her. See that she's no longer a virgin."

When the maid reached for her skirt, Dorie pulled away. "Hold her," her brother ordered. Desmond came forward, but Bryce held them off with a wave of his hand.

"I told you what would happen if you touched my wife again." His words were low and filled with menace. Turning to her, he winked. "It's okay. She's just looking. She willna touch you."

Dorie relaxed and the woman lifted her skirt high enough to see the blood Bryce had smeared on her thighs.

"It's been done," the woman announced.

Tension left the group and Wallace turned to Lachlan expectantly. The laird held out a leather purse, and her brother grabbed it up. "Let's be away," the man announced loudly.

"Someone will send word the next time a ship is expected so we can have goods ready to trade?" Lachlan said.

"Aye. We'll let ye know." They rode through the gate.

Rory waited a moment before mounting. "Goodbye, Dorie. I wish you well."

She nodded and he was away. When they were gone, Dorie felt her body relax in a way it hadn't since her mother had been alive.

She was free.

Chapter Four

Lach was the first to come up and shake Bryce's arm. "Thank you for what you did for your clan today."

Bryce glanced over at Dorie, who was petting the dog. "I would have been happier to take over their stronghold by force. The McCurdys are a blight on the Highlands."

"I don't disagree. But at least this way it ends with no one's blood spilled."

"That's not true." He nodded toward his bride.

Lach snorted. "I know ye did not take the lass in the woods. Where did you cut yourself to supply the blood?"

"My leg," he admitted with a smirk. It was good to know Lach didn't think him coarse with his new wife.

"I hope you'll find some happiness with the lass," Lach said, serious now.

Bryce walked away, knowing that wasn't going to happen. He wouldn't allow it. Other men—men like his father—were able to move on to the next wife as if the first didn't matter. As if they were interchangeable. One warm body for the next. But Bryce wasn't that kind of man.

There'd only ever been one woman for him. And that was all there'd ever be. Dorie would never take the place of Maggie.

"Let's go," he said to his bride as she waited at the edge of the group.

He led her out of the bailey toward the village. His cottage sat on a rise looking out over the rest of the houses, in the same spot his old home had been.

He'd burned the first cottage after finding his wife and child inside dead. He couldn't imagine living where they'd died. While they'd been gone for nearly ten years, his new cottage was only built last fall, in preparation for this possibility.

He opened the door and waited for her to go in. When she didn't, he went first. The dog came in with her.

"This is your home now," he said, holding his hands out. "It's not a castle, but it has what you need." He pointed to the large pots and stores of food on the shelves. "Food." Then he pointed to the bed in the side room. "Bed."

In the main area there was a large stone hearth and two chairs. A small bookcase held a few books he'd acquired from his aunt. Dorie went to them and touched their spines reverently.

"There are plenty of windows to let in light and air. You catch a nice breeze up on this hill."

She nodded and stepped into the bedchamber. There was a trunk at the end of the bed to hold her things. Not that she had any things. He'd best remedy that.

"I'll see that you get shoes and new gowns. A brush, I suppose. If there's anything else you need, you can let me know and I'll see to it." Though he wasn't exactly sure how she would let him know since she didn't speak. "I hope you'll be happy here," he said and turned to leave.

When he stepped out of the cottage and closed the

door behind him, he heard a screech, similar to the sound an animal makes when in pain. A moment later there was banging on the door from the inside.

He opened it to find Dorie throwing herself against it. As soon as she saw it was open she rushed outside and stood in the dying sun, her chest heaving and eyes wide with terror.

"What the bloody hell?" he muttered as he went inside to see what had scared her. Perhaps a mouse or a spider. The dog was stretched out on the rug by the hearth making himself at home. "What is it? What scared you?" he asked, but of course she didn't answer.

Her silence was fast becoming an inconvenience. When he tried to get her back inside she wouldn't go. He thought she might resort to biting him again so he backed off.

"This is your home now. I'm sorry if you don't like it, but it's where ye must stay."

He thought his words would reassure her, but instead she looked all the more panicked. She didn't want to stay inside? Perhaps she was daft as her brother had said. But he'd seen intelligence in her eyes. He'd been able to communicate with her, without words.

For the life of him, he didn't understand what she was trying to convey now. He just wanted her to go inside so he could go back to the castle and find his bed. Getting married and spending time with Dorie had opened his wounds. He needed to be alone for a time.

He walked inside again, and eventually she came in. She propped the door open and stood close by it. He passed her and made to leave, but she quickly ran out of the cottage before he could close the door to keep her in.

"Bloody hell," he whispered when realization dawned. She was afraid of being trapped in the cottage. "Did the bastard keep you locked up?" he asked.

She didn't nod, but the way she looked away told him the

truth of it. She was afraid of being imprisoned in her new home.

"Look here," he said, going to the door. "It locks from the *inside*. You canna be locked in. See?" She watched but stayed back. "I'm going to go inside, and you try to lock me in."

He heard her try the latches, but he opened the door and walked out. "I promise you'll not be locked inside. Can you trust me?" he asked.

She clearly struggled with the thought of trusting him on this, but eventually she went inside. He waited for her to close the door herself and then he waited. She opened the door and came out. Calmer this time.

"You can come and go as ye please. I would suggest you keep the door closed so you don't get pests inside, but you can open it at any time."

She nodded and pointed to him. Then pointed inside. Their silent communication was working again.

"Nay. I stay at the castle. I'm the war chief so I have to be close if I'm needed." This wasn't exactly true. Lachlan would have let him live with his wife if Bryce had wanted to. His cottage was not far from the castle; he'd be able to get there quickly if called. But the excuse was handy so he used it.

She pointed to herself and then toward the castle.

"You stay here. I'll check in. You'll be fine." With that, he turned and walked away, leaving his new wife alone.

He'd done his duty. He'd married her. He'd provided a home for her as well as food and anything else she might need. He wouldn't feel guilty that he was leaving her.

He wouldn't.

"Damn it to hell." Instead of going up to the castle, he stopped at the cottage where one of their guards lived. His young son was always looking for things to do.

"Chief," Gordon greeted him upon opening the door.

"What brings ye here?"

"I wondered if your lad might be up for a job."

"Of course." He pushed the boy toward the door. He was a thin lad, his face spotted with youth. He'd reached thirteen years last fall.

"I'd like you to deliver wood to my house for my new wife so she has it to cook. Check in on her and let me know if she's running low in anything."

The boy nodded, not a big talker. He'd get on fine with Dorie.

Satisfied that he'd done his duty, he continued to the castle without the burden of guilt.

...

Dorie took in her new home. From the farthest room where a large comfy bed sat, it was only eleven steps to the door. She'd taken those eleven steps four times since Bryce left.

Just to be sure the door still opened.

She stopped by each of the windows. They were small, but they opened and she would fit out through the openings. She'd tried that only once. After falling on her backside with a heavy *plop*, she decided to leave that route for an emergency.

From the far window she could see the castle. She wondered if Bryce could see the cottage from the battlements. She supposed he could if he wanted to, but why would he?

When the sun was gone, she made a fire in the hearth, then went to the storage area to see what she had to eat. Most of the sacks held ingredients, but she didn't know what they were used for.

She'd never cooked in her life. As a child, she'd been the laird's daughter and above any form of labor. But then things changed and she was a prisoner. Less than a servant. She'd been fed gruel and stale bannocks.

"Cheese," she said upon finding it in one of the sacks. Now that she was alone, she was free to speak aloud.

Rascal barked and came over to share her treat.

"Don't tell anyone I can talk. It shall be our secret."

She and Rascal shared the cheese. Her companion lay at her feet while she sat by the fire reading aloud to him. The books on the shelves were meant for an adult, rather than a child, as were the books she'd had at her room in Baehaven Castle. Some of the words were difficult to make out, though she was certain the dog didn't mind when she stumbled over a word here and there.

Soon he fell asleep, his legs twitching as dreams of chasing rabbits filled his scruffy head.

When she could not hold her head up any longer, she gave in and went to the bed. Taking off the straggly dress, she hung it on a peg and slipped under the covers in nothing but her shift. After lying there a few minutes, she got up and went to the door to make sure it opened and she could leave if she wished.

The night chill made her shiver, and she closed the door again. As soon as she snuggled back in her bed, Rascal decided he wanted to go out.

That was fine. It gave her another opportunity to check the door. It still opened.

She opened it a few more times while waiting for Rascal to return. When he didn't, she got in bed and closed her eyes.

Rascal barked at the door.

She grumbled while getting up once again to let the dog inside. When he jumped up on the bed she told him to get down. Giving up with a whine, he curled up on the rug next to her bed and she tried again to settle for the night.

She was nearly asleep when she felt the bed shift as the dog returned to his spot by her feet. Enjoying his warmth and company, she didn't protest.

What a different life this was from the one she'd had before this morning. She now had a home of her own and could come and go as she pleased. Her husband said he would provide her new dresses and even a brush.

She hadn't expected to be pampered, but she looked forward to it.

She also looked forward to spending more time with Bryce. Perhaps this could be a real marriage someday. She hadn't ever bothered to hope for such things as the love of a husband and children of her own.

But it was still too soon to wish for more. For now she'd just enjoy the freedom and peace.

Her freedom and peace were interrupted the next day when she received visitors from the castle. Rascal barked twice before Dorie heard a knock. She hurried for the door, assuming it wouldn't be Bryce. This was his house; he had no need to knock or wait outside. Still, she hoped.

She hated the twinge of disappointment she felt as she opened the door and didn't see her husband. Why would she give a thought to a man who had left her here without another word? Her little cottage felt oddly similar to her room at Baehaven despite being able to walk outside whenever she wished.

However, she was excited to have guests and smiled in greeting as Kenna and Mari came inside. They looked around and she pulled out chairs for them to sit.

"This is lovely," Mari said. "It looks like you've already settled in."

Dorie nodded, though the cottage was mostly the same as it had been when Bryce had left her the day before. She'd not had anything to add to the furnishings, though a young boy had brought her wood that morning and she piled it in the corner by the hearth.

She looked over her shoulder at the table where she was

attempting to make something edible from the stores Bryce had left for her. So far, it hadn't turned out well.

Mari and Kenna kept the conversation going with little input from Dorie, which was a relief. The sisters were easy to be with. She liked them both and hoped her smiles spoke of her appreciation.

"We'll leave you now, but we'll be back to check on you tomorrow," Kenna promised. That promise turned into fear the next day after Dorie had burned her third attempt at making bannocks.

The smoke caused her eyes to water. She dumped the hardened lumps out in the grass and opened all the windows to air out her home. She couldn't have the laird's wife and a former duchess see her failure. They would think her unworthy. Instead she watched, and when the women were approaching, she met them at the bottom of the hill with a basket as if she was going down into the village to make a purchase.

They joined her without coming to the cottage, and Dorie was spared the humiliation. This became her habit each day for the next few weeks.

...

Bryce's life was back to normal. He woke in his bed alone. He ate the morning meal, trained with his men, rode the borders, and came back in time for the evening meal before going to bed. Alone.

His life was just the way he liked it. He spent his meals conversing with his cousins and their wives just as he always had. When they went off with their families, he was alone once again.

It had been three weeks since he'd left Dorie in her new home and he hadn't seen her since. He'd hired a woman in the village to make her a few dresses and paid for shoes.

According to wee Gordon, she had plenty of wood with which to cook. Bryce had done his duty.

Oftentimes he was able to forget he was even married. That would have been fine with him, except everyone kept asking him how his wife fared.

"She's fine," Bryce answered Abagail, the latest person to ask while stitching a gash he'd earned during drills.

"Are you sure?" the healer pushed.

"I haven't heard that she wasn't." If the woman knew something, she should get on with it.

Instead of pushing further, she simply nodded and jabbed him deeper than she had on the last stitch. Surely it was a coincidence.

Later at supper, Lach asked after Dorie as well.

Bryce shrugged and focused on his food. "She's fine."

"I haven't seen her up at the castle since ye wed her."

If Lachlan wanted some form of answer, he would need to ask a question. Bryce kept eating until the laird tried again.

"I know you weren't pleased to wed, but it's not like you to be cruel to a woman."

This earned Bryce's ire, and not because he felt guilty. "Ye think me cruel because I did what you asked of me? Provided her a home? Clothing, shoes, food? Saw to her comforts? Mayhap you thought to make a love match. I'm sorry to disappoint you in your matchmaking. I didna ken you had turned into an old woman."

"I thought you might grow to be friends with her at least."

"That was not what you ordered me to do. You said it was my duty to wed her. Ye said nothing of being friends."

Lachlan frowned but gave up when Cameron and their women joined them at the table.

Bryce wouldn't be made to feel guilty. Especially when he knew Dorie was better off without him in her life. He was miserable; there was no sense making her miserable as well.

Chapter Five

Dorie muttered a few curses at her latest attempt to make bread. It hadn't turned into anything remotely close to bread. Again.

In fact, nothing she'd attempted so far had been edible. The cheese was gone and she'd eaten the vegetables raw. She would never complain, though. She'd eaten much worse when she lived with the McCurdys, but her stomach growled at the thought of the meals they must enjoy up at Dunardry Castle.

Even Rascal had taken to begging up at the castle for his meals rather than rely on her. Which was why she hadn't been given proper notice that visitors were on their way until they'd reached the door and knocked.

A few more curses whispered across Dorie's lips as she answered the door with a smile. Once inside, Mari and Kenna looked around.

"What are ye baking?" Kenna asked as she stepped closer to the mess on the table. Her brows pulled together while Mari frowned. She set down a basket filled with bannocks and preserves, and Dorie's mouth watered.

Dorie let out a sigh and shrugged. Not just because she didn't speak, but because even if she did, she wouldn't have a name for whatever the mess should be called. Except failure.

Tears filled her eyes and she sat on one of the chairs with her head in her hands. She hadn't had high hopes for her life when she came here, but she'd hoped not to be hungry for the rest of her days.

"Oh, dear," Mari said, coming to pat her shoulder in a comforting way. "It's no shame if you don't know how to cook or bake. I didn't know either when I arrived. I was a duchess, after all, and duchesses are forbidden to enter the kitchens. But I've learned a bit since I've been here helping the women prepare the meals."

"Aye." Kenna held up the basket. "We brought something to share for now. And mayhap you'd like to join us in the morning? We'll be making tarts and stew."

Dorie wiped her tears and nodded enthusiastically. She remembered the rare occasions when there were tarts at Baehaven, back when her mother was alive.

But it wasn't just the tarts that caused excitement to settle in her stomach. Being invited to the kitchens meant she'd be with people. She was bored to misery in her little cottage. Even though the door didn't lock her in, she'd felt like a prisoner just the same.

Rascal was growing like a weed and offered companionship, but he didn't offer much in the way of robust conversation.

She wiped her tears away when there was another knock at the door. She opened it so wee Gordon could enter with an armload of wood to put with the growing pile in the corner. He asked if she was well. She nodded as she had each day he'd come. He bowed to them and turned to take his leave.

"Has Bryce sent you to check on Dorie?" Kenna asked the lad as Dorie poured them all a bit of ale to go with their light meal.

"Aye. I come every day to bring wood and see that she is well."

"Yes, I see that." Mari frowned as the boy took his leave.

"Bryce should be ashamed of himself for leaving you here and not checking on you himself."

Dorie appreciated Kenna's ire on her behalf, but she didn't begrudge Bryce for not coming to visit. He'd hired the boy to check in. Bryce didn't want her. That was clear. But he'd provided for her. That was all that could be expected. And she was grateful. It was more than she'd had in recent years.

"Fear not," Mari said with a smile. "We'll see that you're cared for." The woman looked Dorie over and frowned yet again. "Is this the dress he had made for you?"

Dorie nodded and crossed her arms. The woman who'd come to measure her complained about the extra fabric needed because of Dorie's height and skimped on the length and other places that made Dorie uncomfortable.

"This looks like the work of Sarah. The stingy old crow. She probably charged him for a full gown and had enough material left over to make a second."

Dorie tugged at the garment in an effort to cover more of herself and the seam ripped.

Kenna let out a breath. "Tomorrow when we're done in the kitchen, we'll go to the solar and start sewing you something decent to wear. Do you sew?"

Dorie nodded, though her skills were more functional than fashionable. She knew how to darn a sock and mend her ill-fitted gowns, but she wasn't able to embroider or create any embellishments. Life at Baehaven had lacked embellishment of any kind.

"Then it's settled. We'll see you in the morning."

She squeezed the women's hands as they prepared to

leave, hoping to convey her gratitude. Mari and Kenna had treated her as a friend. Dorie couldn't thank them enough.

"Everything will be fine soon," Kenna promised. "We'll see to that."

The look the sisters exchanged gave Dorie a moment of worry. They were smiling pleasantly, but even Dorie—who didn't spend much time with people—heard an undertone of threat in the woman's voice.

Dorie pitied anyone who was unfortunate enough to upset Kenna MacKinlay.

• • •

Bryce had just sat at the table when the two ladies next to him turned to glare. He swiveled to see who they were casting their scowls at but saw no one beside him.

That could only mean…

Bloody hell.

"What did I do?" It was best to get clarification first before launching into a defense.

"We went to visit Dorie today. She's been in her new home for a few weeks now. Have you stopped by to visit?"

"Nay. That is to say, *not yet*," he quickly revised when their eyes narrowed on him. "I haven't had the chance." He winced at the lie and ducked his head when it was clear the women didn't believe him. "But I hired a lad to check in daily, and I provided more than a month's worth of food. She should be fine for another week or so until I can visit."

"He provided *food*," Kenna said to Mari in a deceptively pleasant tone. He knew the sisters were working up to a good dressing down. He wasn't yet sure if it was deserved. Chances were good he was guilty of whatever fault they found in him.

He glanced at Lach and Cam, who simply shook their heads in pity. *Bollocks.* There was no saving him.

Mari, usually kinder than Kenna, smiled indulgently and tilted her head. "We did notice you provided ample ingredients."

"Kind of you, it was," Kenna added, her eyes snapping with fire.

He was clearly in trouble. He still couldn't quite figure out why...

"It seems..." Mari continued with her index finger poised at her lip in thought. The woman seemed polite and demure, but those hands had killed a duke with a fireplace poker, so Bryce was wise to be wary. "...you might have forgotten to make sure she knew how to use the supplies properly, in order to feed herself."

"Or might you have just dumped her there and run off without seeing if she needed anything more?" Kenna accused. "And before ye even think of blaming poor Gordon, he did exactly as you asked. He brought wood and asked if she was well. It wasn't for the lad to notice she'd hardly *used* the wood. And even if she nodded in answer to his question, she most certainly isn't *well*."

Bugger. Bryce frowned and let out a breath, realizing he deserved their anger. He was a piss-poor excuse for a husband—but he'd admitted to such before he took her to wife. Still, he should have done better by her. He'd practically shoved her into the cottage and run back to his old life. His life with no responsibilities save feeding himself and seeing to his own needs. Christ, he truly was the selfish bastard they accused him of being.

In his defense, he had gone to check on her once, but he'd seen her walking in the village with Mari and Kenna and turned back before he was noticed. He'd seen enough to know she was clothed and had shoes.

"I'll go check on her tomorrow," he said quickly.

"No need. We've already invited her up to the castle

tomorrow to teach her to cook and to help sew some new gowns for her," Mari informed him.

"But I bought her gowns." In this he could not be judged. He'd even seen her wearing one of them that day in the village.

"You ordered her gowns from Shifty Sarah McNaub. Those dresses are nothing but stingy scraps, and so thin they'll never get her through winter. She needs something decent that actually fits."

"I bought her shoes," he noted quietly, but stopped when their glare settled on him yet again. He'd had her shoes delivered instead of taking them to her himself to make sure they would fit.

Shame turned the tips of his ears hot. He looked at the food on his tray and let out a breath. He couldn't very well eat it now. Not knowing Dorie might be going hungry. What kind of man had he become? Letting his wife fend for herself in the cottage. Hadn't he left Maggie and wee Isabel alone only to come home and find them dead? Was that what he wanted to happen to Dorie? He shuddered at the thought.

She was not to blame for any of Bryce's pain.

He gathered some food and lurched to his feet. He gave them a nod before heading out of the hall toward the gate. As he strolled through the village, he remembered the feeling of excitement he used to experience when walking this path.

Back then, he'd been returning home to Maggie. Even if he'd only been up at the castle for a day of drills she would grace him with a wide smile when he entered their home.

If her hands were busy, he would walk up behind her and wrap his arms around her waist, bending to kiss her neck until she squirmed. By then Isabel would be fretting for him to pick her up. He'd bend down and scoop her up, throwing her in the air to make her laugh until Maggie scolded him.

It was a happy memory, one that twisted his stomach into

knots when he remembered he wasn't going to live it ever again.

He reached the new cottage and paused outside to collect himself from the pain the memory had brought on. It was there, standing by the open window, that he heard an angel's song. The female voice lifted and dropped fluidly with the notes of a happy tune. A dog barked and the singing stopped on a laugh.

"You naughty boy. You are indeed a rascal. No more meat for ye. Sorry, I need to save it so we won't starve."

Bryce gasped when he peeked through the window to see the only person in the cottage was his new wife. The woman who couldn't speak.

Or...*didn't* speak.

Rather than go inside and confront her, he turned and headed back toward the castle. He didn't know how to manage the feeling in his chest that came from hearing her sing. For a moment, his spirits had lifted and he'd felt at peace.

But when he realized the sound had come from Dorie, the weight of his duty came back tenfold. Not only was he married, despite his wish to never wed again, but it appeared he was bound for life to a liar.

Dorie *could* speak. And not just speak, she could sing beautifully as well.

Why had she lied?

What was she up to?

A frown creased his forehead as several possibilities flooded his mind.

He hurried away from the cottage. She'd spoken of having meat, so he was assured she'd not go hungry today.

Meanwhile, he would watch her to see what she was up to before confronting her. If she had been brought to Dunardry to report information back to the McCurdys, his marriage might be over before it could become an even bigger nuisance.

...

Dorie tossed and turned, her stomach hurting from whatever she'd eaten that wasn't fit. Sweat ran from her brow into her hair. She sat up when the dog ran to the door barking and growling.

Perhaps she'd poisoned her faithful friend as well. Stumbling to the door, she opened it and stepped out into the cool night air.

A chill ran up her spine where her damp skin met the cold.

Having moved too quickly, she bent to be sick in the weeds next to the cottage. The dog continued to bark savagely and took off into the trees.

"And I'd thought you faithful," she muttered as she went back inside. With her stomach empty, she felt better, if not a bit hungry. Rather than climb back into her sweat-dampened bed, she settled in a chair by the fire to wait for Rascal to return.

Next she knew, it was morning and Rascal was barking to be let in. She stretched her aching back as she went to the door to let him in. When she gave him a pat he whimpered and her hand came back damp with blood.

"What's happened to you?" she asked. When she knelt next to him her balance went off. She felt weak from her sickness in the night. She shook off the dizziness and looked to the scrape on the back of her dog's neck. The dog was no longer a puppy and seemed to grow a few inches per day. His head was as high as her hip. There was hardly another dog in the village bigger than Rascal.

"Were you scrapping with some beast who got the best of you?" she asked. "Let's clean you up. I've been invited to the castle today."

The dog let out a whine.

"I know. I'll miss you. Truth be told, I'm not feeling much up to it, but I don't want them to think I'm ungrateful and don't need their help."

She skipped the morning meal, unsure of what she'd eaten that had made her ill. Her appetite had not returned yet. Nothing she'd consumed had tasted bad, but she knew that wasn't always the case. She settled on a few sips of water and left the cottage.

Wincing up at the morning sun, she put a hand to her throbbing temple. The short walk to the castle felt like a tiring journey. Rascal followed along by her side until they got inside the bailey, and then he ran off after a cat. By the time Dorie arrived outside the kitchen, she needed to sit down.

"Dorie? Are you not well?" The voice belonged to the one person she'd wished to see every moment in the last few weeks. Well, except for right now.

Bryce came to stand before her, fear and worry in his eyes. "You're sick?"

She shook her head, making the pain worse. She groaned, feeling nauseous again.

"Why didn't you send for me if you are ill? I would have sent a healer. Come with me."

He lifted her into his arms and carried her inside, stopping to speak to a young man her age. "Liam, go find Abagail and send her to my chamber."

Despite the embarrassment of needing to be carried, Dorie knew it would have taken a good day to make it to Bryce's room in her current state.

He laid her in his bed and slipped off her new shoes. The movement was too much, and she jumped from the bed just in time to grab a basin and be sick. She coughed, and Bryce wiped her brow with a wet cloth, then helped her back into bed. She was almost too ill to be mortified that he'd seen her cast up her accounts.

Kenna rushed into the room. "What's wrong?"

"I don't know. I sent for Abagail."

"She's gone to Fletcher Castle to see to my brother's wife."

"Do they not have a healer?" His words snapped with frustration, causing Dorie to worry that she looked even worse than she felt. Why else would he be so frantic to have a healer see her?

"Aye," Kenna said. "But not one I trust as much as Abagail. I can see to Dorie. Don't worry."

Bryce let out a sound of impatience and turned away from Dorie while running his hand roughly through his hair. She realized then that Kenna was right. He was worried over her. She had to admit, she rather liked the thought of it. Even as much as she wished she hadn't given him reason to be concerned.

"She's weak and I think her head pains her."

She looked up at her husband in surprise. How observant he was to have known that from the short time he'd been with her this morning.

"How long have you been ill?" Kenna asked as she sat on the edge of the bed.

"She can't talk," Bryce was quick to say. He paced once and shook his head. "She *doesn't* talk," he amended.

His gaze was intent on hers. Perhaps he was even more observant than she'd realized. Had she spoken aloud since leaving her cottage? She didn't think so. But it was clear he questioned whether her silence was not an inability but rather a desire to stay quiet.

She looked away first, proving her guilt. She might as well have spoken up right then and told him he was right.

Her heart pounded, though in truth it had been pounding hard already. Rather than address Bryce's accusation, she looked to Kenna and motioned in a way to communicate that she'd gotten sick only the night before.

"Did you eat something that tasted bad?" Kenna asked.

Dorie gave it a moment of thought, though she'd been considering it since the night before when she'd fallen ill. She shook her head now, after coming to the same conclusion.

She rubbed her chest as her heart continued to beat uneasily.

Kenna noticed the motion and came closer to put her hand in the same place. "Your heart is beating rapidly. Did that start last night as well?"

Dorie nodded.

Kenna frowned. "Did your beast eat the same thing you ate?"

Dorie paused before nodding again. She didn't want Bryce to know she'd fed the food he'd purchased for her to the dog, but she couldn't let Rascal go hungry. And she didn't want him leaving to go looking for scraps.

"Did he get ill?" Kenna continued her questions.

Dorie shook her head. She couldn't be sure, of course. But he'd had enough energy to get into a fight the night before, so he wasn't as bad off as she.

"Was there anything you ate or drank that burned your tongue? Something the dog didn't have?"

Dorie's thoughts piqued at that specific question. She'd found a small skin of ale with her stores she hadn't noticed before and had some with her meal. But it had tasted bitter and burned her tongue. She'd only had a swallow before tossing it out. She motioned a gesture for drink and nodded.

Kenna frowned and let out a sigh.

"What is it? What ails her?" Bryce asked with a scowl.

"I think your wife has been poisoned."

Chapter Six

Poisoned? Bryce stared down at the woman lying in his bed with clammy skin and wide eyes. She surely didn't look well, but poisoned? Who would want Dorie dead?

"Why do you think it's poison?" he asked. He didn't want to doubt Kenna. She'd become a fine healer in the years since coming to Dunardry, but still, she wasn't Abagail.

"If it had just been a queasy stomach, I might have thought she'd eaten something spoiled. Even the weakness and the headache could speak to such. But her heartbeat—quickened and irregular as it is—is a telltale sign of foxglove poisoning."

He led Kenna quickly from the room so they could speak in private. There was no reason to make his wife panic with such silly ideas.

"What are ye talking about?" Bryce accused.

Before Kenna could open her mouth to answer, a deep voice sounded close behind him.

"I love you like a brother, Bryce," Lach thundered. "But if you don't unhand my wife and stop hissing at her, I'll take your arm off without blinking."

Bryce hadn't realized he'd grasped Kenna's arm so tightly, or at all, for that matter.

"Forgive me," he said, with genuine remorse, removing his hand. He'd been tense since seeing Dorie, but the thought of poison had his own heart racing erratically.

"I think she'll be fine. If I understood her correctly, she threw out the ale after a sip, so she couldn't have taken in much of the poison."

Bryce understood that as well from Dorie's gestures. The woman had a knack for communicating in every way but her voice.

"*What?* Who was poisoned?" Lach stepped closer and looked over Bryce's shoulder to see Dorie lying in the bed. His brows came down in a menacing way. Lach took responsibility for everyone in the clan. It made him a great laird, but it was an impossible task for one man to take on.

"Have you angered someone?" Lach asked Bryce, as if the line of his enemies wrapped around the castle. Bryce winced. Perhaps just to the gate.

"Nay. No more than you have." Bryce thought briefly of his altercation with Wallace McCurdy and the threat Bryce had made, but brushed it off. The man had wanted to be free of his sister, and he was indeed free of her now. What reason would he have to kill her?

"What about jealous lovers?" the laird reasoned, making Bryce laugh.

"You know well enough I've no one wanting to keep me warm at night."

"True. Who would want to be stuck with a miserable old goat like ye?" The man scraped his fingers over his whiskers in thought.

Bryce wasn't insulted by the comment, for it was true enough. He felt much older than his years. "Could it have been an accident?" Bryce asked.

Kenna shrugged. "I suppose so, but I'm not sure who would have made such a mistake."

Lach's eyes narrowed. Bryce recognized it as an idea.

"What are you thinking?" Bryce pushed.

Lachlan shook his head. "I was just wondering if mayhap it wasn't an accident. You say she didn't take enough to be permanently harmed. What if that was intentional? Maybe she only took enough for this." He waved at Dorie lying in Bryce's bed.

Bryce knew he should mention that he'd heard her speaking to the dog. How he'd heard her singing while in the cottage. It was proof she'd misrepresented herself. If she'd taken poison to gain access to the castle, she might truly be a threat.

The sound of a hand smacking Lach's arm brought Bryce's attention to Kenna and her unhappy scowl.

"Lachlan MacKinlay, how dare ye accuse the poor girl of such a thing? You saw well enough how the McCurdys treated her. She's happy to be here, anyone can see it."

"She could be a good actress," Lach defended himself. "The tattered dress and no shoes could have been part of a ruse."

Bryce gave the idea a moment or two to spin around his mind but eventually he shook his head. "Nay. Her fear of Wallace was real enough. As was her fear when he'd demanded her blood on a sheet. It wasn't her idea to fake the consummation, and I doubt she would have been willing to give up her maidenhead for a bastard like Dougal McCurdy."

Lach nodded, obviously agreeing with Bryce's assessment. He frowned again and ran his hand over the back of his head. "Do you think she might be so unhappy she wished to do away with herself? You left her alone. Perhaps she doesna want to go on being cast aside."

"I don't see that kind of misery in her eyes," Kenna said. "She cried yesterday when we went to visit her, but it was with frustration more than hopelessness. She was excited to come to the castle today to learn to cook. If she wanted to gain access to the castle, she had that already. If she was lonely, she had plans to be with us today."

Lach nodded again. "For now we'll keep watch over her. Either for her protection or for ours."

Bryce nodded and kept silent about his wife's ability to speak. For some reason it felt like something to be addressed privately.

But soon enough, he'd get an answer.

• • •

Dorie wasn't sure what the group outside Bryce's room was discussing. They were too far away for her to hear, and she was distracted by trying to figure out how she might have come to be poisoned. Perhaps her new husband had enemies and mistook her for an opportunity to hurt him.

She might have laughed at such a thought if it weren't for the seriousness of the attempt on her life.

Eventually Kenna came back into the room and smiled down at her. "I'm going to have food sent up."

Dorie winced.

"I know you don't have much of an appetite, but you need to eat something to get your strength back."

Dorie nodded. She would try her best.

A serving girl brought broth and bread. Dorie had only managed a few bites of both before Bryce walked in.

"You must eat all of your food." He frowned at the barely touched broth. "I'm told it's the only way you'll be strong enough to get out of my bed."

Of course he wouldn't appreciate her taking up space in

his room. She gasped and sat up, planning to leave, but the room spun around her.

"Rest easy. It was but a jest." He winked at her, and she relaxed when she realized he was teasing her. He closed the door and came to sit next to her on the bed.

"How do you feel?" he asked. It wasn't an empty question as most people asked. It was as if he truly expected her to answer him. Aloud.

She might have considered it if Mari hadn't knocked just then and come in.

"Do you need anything?" she asked.

Dorie shook her head and offered her friend a smile.

"Who would do something like this?" Her question was directed toward Bryce.

"We can't think of a reason for anyone to want to hurt Dorie. So it must have been an accident," Bryce answered.

"An accident?" Mari didn't seem any more convinced of that possibility than Dorie felt. Mari turned her question to Dorie. "Your brother Wallace was a monster. Do you suppose he had something to do with this?"

Dorie shrugged. It had crossed her mind more than once in the time since she'd found out she was poisoned. But why would he bother? She was no longer his responsibility. If he'd wanted her dead, he could have done so long before now. It would have been easy to poison her when she still lived at Baehaven.

"We're not sure," Bryce said. "What we do know is she needs to finish her meal and rest."

Mari took the hint and patted Dorie's hand. "I'll be back later to visit after you've rested."

A rest sounded good. Dorie was exhausted. Plus it would keep Bryce from pressing her to speak. It was clear he was waiting for a chance to bring it up again. However, he waited until she finished her food, then he took the tray and left.

She tried to sleep, but her mind continued to conjure up possible enemies. Who would want to be rid of her? She swallowed when she realized Bryce was the one person who truly didn't want her around. He'd done his duty and married her. But now they were wed, could he be trying to get rid of her?

He'd married her only to make an alliance. He'd said so himself. What did he need her for now?

Not a thing.

...

Bryce checked on Dorie a few times throughout the day. Each time she was resting peacefully. Kenna assured him she would be fine. Her heartbeat had evened out and her appetite had returned.

"I'll have Liam guard her."

"Do ye really think that's necessary?" Kenna asked.

Bryce remembered how much Kenna hated being looked after when Lach had posted guards to protect her. He didn't imagine Dorie would like it overmuch, either, but he'd rather have an irritated wife than a dead one.

"Aye. For now. I'd rather be safe."

"So you care for her?" Kenna cocked her head, a small smile pulling up her lips.

Bryce frowned at the woman. It figured Kenna would try to make this arrangement into a love match. She, being quite fond of her husband, wanted every marriage in the clan to be a loving one.

He growled at her. "I have a duty to her and nothing more. Don't try to make this into something it's not."

Kenna pouted, though Bryce knew her well enough to know she wasn't even close to giving up. Kenna didn't know the meaning of defeat. Bryce was in store for meddling. That was for certain.

"I'll have her protected, though I don't need to be the one to do it. Let me know when she's well enough that I may have my bed back."

"There's plenty of room…"

He gave Kenna another scowl and rushed off. He knew well enough the bed was big enough for the two of them. Especially since his wife was so thin. Though he'd noticed briefly as Kenna and Mari had stripped off her gown that the lass wasn't without lush curves.

He'd pushed away thoughts of those curves while she was sick, but now that she was on the mend, he recalled the swell of bosom he'd seen when her shift fell open a few days ago.

In a foul mood, he was fit for a fight when he reached the bailey and found his men standing around doing nothing.

"What's this? Did you all wake up lazy today?"

Galen was the unlucky one to speak first. "We are awaiting a wagon to go out to Cam's house. We were told we're to be working there this afternoon."

"And who told you that?"

"The laird," Galen answered.

This news didn't make Bryce any happier. Bryce was the war chief, but Lach, as laird, was the only person in the clan who could overrule Bryce's command. Once again he and his cousin didn't agree on orders.

As usual when he was fed up with the way Lach did things, he thought of his father's letter last year, inviting him to take his rightful place within clan Campbell.

He pushed the thought away.

"Fine. But Liam, ye will stay behind. I have another job for ye."

Liam frowned but voiced no complaint. The lad was smart and rarely objected to any task. He'd been an orphan when the old laird brought him to the castle and gave him small jobs. He grew up in the shadow of the castle, helping to clean weapons and run messages until he was big enough to carry his own sword.

The other men loaded their tools into the wagon and left for Cam's manor house.

"What do you wish me to do?" Liam asked.

"You'll stay with my wife and see her safe. You'll also watch to make sure she doesna speak to anyone in private."

Liam's brows creased and he leaned in closer. "But she doesn't speak."

"Aye. She *doesn't* speak," he repeated. "That doesna mean she *can't* speak if she wanted to."

Liam's eyes went wide and he looked toward the castle, clearly understanding Bryce's accusation. After a moment, Liam asked, "Do you think she's a spy for the McCurdys?" He was a sharp lad, his second in command.

"I've no idea. If she is, I don't ken what information she would be passing to them since she's not privy to any great knowledge. But for now, we'll watch to make certain of it."

"Shouldn't *you* be watching her? You'd be able to do so without her knowing."

"True." Bryce swallowed, not wanting to tell the boy the real reason he didn't want to watch over his wife himself. Instead he crossed his arms and went on attack. "Do ye question my decision?"

"Of course not," the lad was quick to say. With a nod, he was off to follow Bryce's orders, sparing Bryce from having to explain that the longer he was near his wife, the more intriguing she became.

He couldn't allow her to undermine his protective walls. Especially if she turned out to be a spy.

He went to the cottage, thinking he might find something to prove his allegations. Instead he found it exactly as it had been the day he'd brought her there weeks ago.

Other than the dwindling food stores, it hadn't changed a bit. The floor was clean. Everything neatly arranged. A book lay on the stand next to the bed. It was as if a ghost lived here.

He winced. He knew well enough about living with ghosts.

Chapter Seven

Dorie met Mari and Kenna in the kitchen the next morning. She felt much better, having slept most of the day before and the whole night in her husband's bed. Bryce hadn't returned, but she'd enjoyed the comfort of the large bed and the way it smelled of her husband.

In the kitchen, Mari introduced her to the other women who worked there and explained to them that she didn't talk.

Dorie almost wished she had already spoken to Bryce and her new friends rather than let the deception go on so long. She hadn't ever considered the idea of having someone to talk to when she'd first come here. By the time she had, she was too embarrassed to explain why she'd deceived them. They all seemed so kind and understanding. None of them acted like the kind of person who would use her words against her, to cause harm to another, or worse, death.

She prayed there would be no danger in communicating with the people in her new home. But she didn't dare try. Not yet. Not until she was certain.

Also, it was best to remain silent so they didn't know

what a fraud she was. Keeping silent ensured she'd never be expected to tell her story…and confess her terrible sin.

An older woman named Millie welcomed Dorie to help with rolling dough. Millie was patient on the occasions when Dorie pushed too hard and needed to start over.

It wasn't long before the talk in the kitchen turned from food to husbands. And what they did with their husbands at night in their beds… Dorie felt her face heat when they spoke of such things, though she couldn't help but be curious.

She'd felt urges and tingles the few times Bryce had touched her. She'd never experienced such things before but wasn't surprised. For the past nine years she'd been isolated in her room with no company but a maid and random unpleasant visits by her brother. Being touched was…nice.

She'd never been interested in the ways between men and women. Until now. According to these women, there were many, many ways in which a couple could be joined. Some seemed impossible, and she occasionally thought they were making up these tales to cause a reaction from her. She couldn't fathom how some of their suggestions were even possible.

But as she listened to their advice and comments to one another, she understood they didn't speak of such outlandish things for her benefit. Though she had to admit, she was benefitting from the education.

She remained silent except for the occasional gasp of shock. And her face must be as red as a setting sun. Surely a man would never put his lips…*there.*

When the conversation wound down, Millie directed a question to Kenna. "I couldn't help but notice one of you has a shadow. What have you done this time, mistress?"

Dorie had also noticed the young man, Liam, following them to the kitchen. The laird's wife was a bit rebellious, and Dorie agreed she would be the most likely cause for protection.

Kenna laughed off the accusation. "Nay, it's not me who

has Liam sitting outside the kitchen working on his carving. It would be Dorie this time."

Dorie's eyes went wide in surprise. She was being followed by a guard? Did that mean she was in more danger than she'd thought? She'd hoped the poisoning had been an accident, as Kenna suggested.

"Does Lachlan think she's in more danger?" Mari asked. Dorie was grateful to the woman for asking the question Dorie most wanted answered. "I'll be ready to help if needed."

"Relax, sister. We don't need you to grab up a fireplace poker yet. Bryce thinks she might be a spy and wants her watched." Kenna rolled her eyes, showing what she thought of that idea.

The women all laughed, but Dorie was shocked by the fireplace poker comment. She'd heard whispers about Mari having killed her first husband. Apparently it was true!

Mari leaned over to pat her shoulder. "Not to worry. I only resort to murder when there's no other option."

Good to know, Dorie thought. Then her mind focused in on what Kenna had said.

Her mouth dropped open. Bryce thought she was a *spy*?

Kenna smiled with a hint of mischief. "Don't fash. We can help you teach him a lesson."

Dorie blinked. She had no doubt that whatever Kenna had in mind would not please her husband.

...

Bryce was exhausted as he walked through the gates with the other men. The only thing he wanted to do was eat a good meal and fall into his bed.

He wondered if his wife was still tucked under his covers wearing nothing but a shift.

His body declared its interest in something other than

food and sleep, but Bryce brushed the thought away quickly.

When Liam met him in the hall looking anxious and confused, Bryce knew his plans for the evening had changed. "You're supposed to be looking after my wife. Why are you here?"

"Your wife is a bloody ghost, I swear it. She's vanished on me three times today, and this last time I haven't been able to find her anywhere."

"Did ye ask the other women where she may be?" Bryce nodded at Kenna and Mari sitting at the head table looking for all the world as if they were up to no good.

"Aye. I did. They told me they saw her in six different places. I went to all six and didn't find head nor hair of your lass. I think they're mocking me." Liam gave them a disgruntled look and they burst into giggles.

"I'll take care of it. Go find a meal." Bryce frowned as he approached the table. Lach and Cam hadn't arrived yet so he was on his own.

"Good evening, Bryce," Mari said sweetly.

He wasn't falling for her feigned innocence.

"Aye. Good evening to you as well." He rubbed his forehead, not hiding his exhaustion. "I'm almost too tired to eat after having spent the day working on building your new home. I surely hope my efforts please you, Mari." He held out his blistered hands casually.

The smile slipped from her face as a guilty expression seeped in.

"I didn't mind spending my day doing hard labor for you...though I might have used the time to check in with my sick wife. I asked the lad to watch over her and keep her safe, and it seems she's missing. I hope she hasn't been kidnapped."

He turned to a serving lass to address her with a grim look. "Lass, please bring food for my men. Despite our exhaustion from the day's labors we must go back out and search for my wife, who's been stolen away from the security of the castle. I hate to think who else might be in danger if someone was so bold as to—"

"Stop," Kenna said and shook her head. "She's well and safe," she added when the serving lass looked startled. Kenna sized up Bryce with a glare. "Your wife is back in her home. If you're as worried over her as you say, I expect you'll want to go check on her immediately."

"Why would you not want her to be protected?" he couldn't help but ask.

"Your men apparently do not understand the difference between protecting someone and keeping them prisoner in their own home. Dorie's beast will protect her from any direct threat, and she has food and drink from the kitchen that's safe enough."

Bryce sniffed at the thought of the small dog protecting her. But before he could point out their error, she went on.

"We even have Millie's sister and brother-in-law keeping an eye on her. Their cottage is just below Dorie's. She's safe."

Bryce couldn't argue with that logic. It seemed they'd taken care of things.

"Having a person looked after like a sheep being herded is humiliating," Mari added. "It might make you feel better, but it obviously makes Dorie uneasy to be confined."

Another point he couldn't argue. He'd seen it the first day he'd taken her to the cottage—her terror of being locked inside.

He bowed. "Thank you for your counsel and for looking after my wife."

Bryce blew out a breath as he made his way to the cottage. The women had chastened him into shame over the way he was treating his wife. They'd made it quite clear what they thought of his having her guarded. Especially by someone other than himself.

However, it was his duty as war chief to make sure no danger came to anyone in the clan. And it was also his duty as Dorie's husband to make sure no danger came to her.

He couldn't help but think his day just kept getting worse.

As he turned up the lane to the cottage, he tried to rein in his frustration. While he knew he was wrong, and he even knew Dorie had done nothing to earn his hostility, he couldn't change his heart.

He was angry at life and the way things had worked out.

Many people would agree he had a right to his anger. However, the ladies who'd married his cousins weren't among them. They encouraged him to give Dorie a chance. Both women had found love in their marriages and thus believed the world was full of the sentiment. All a person had to do was reach out and pluck the feeling of love from the air and one would be happy to the end of one's bloody days.

He paused, fearing he might wretch, and not from the trek down the hill. He could have lost Dorie. And missed the opportunity to get to know her better.

When he reached the cottage he waited outside, even ducked under the open window for a moment, listening for Dorie's singing, but all was silent today.

His fist hovered for a moment at the door before he dropped it to the latch and went inside. It was his own cottage, after all, why should he have to knock?

Dorie turned toward his invasion and a smile pulled up her lips a second before two large paws slammed into his shoulders.

"Ye gads!" He pushed the dog off and gaped at the furry monster as he snuffled around Bryce's feet. "Rascal?" He had to be at least two feet taller than he'd been when they washed him at the creek.

Dorie laughed and the sound caused a twisting pain in his chest.

He was struck with the vision of another woman smiling

and laughing when he'd entered their home. The memory was so strong he even looked around on the floor for a wee lass crawling toward him. But Isabel wasn't there. Neither was Maggie.

They were both gone.

This was no longer the home he had shared with them.

He wouldn't be able to scoop up his daughter and hear her giggle. He wouldn't be able to kiss his wife and whisper promises of what he'd do to her later in the darkness when their child was asleep.

That life was gone along with the cottage he'd deliberately burned down, though it all continued to haunt his memories.

He swallowed back the pain, and Dorie's smile faltered. As if she understood what had happened in his mind.

Rubbing a hand over his face, he schooled his features into his normal scowl. He expected her to let it go. Of course, Dorie never did what he expected. Instead she came closer and took his hand. Tugging on his arm, she led him to a chair and motioned that he should sit.

She poured him a cup of ale and set it before him. When he frowned at it, she shook her head and pointed toward the castle to let him know it was safe.

Taking the other seat at the small table, she pointed to her lips and then to him. She cocked her head and pointed to her ear.

Even though she hadn't spoken a word, he knew exactly what she meant. He was supposed to tell her what was wrong, and she would listen.

He wanted to explain why he'd had her followed and apologize for not trusting her. He'd planned to use guilt to earn her compliance, but to his surprise he opened his mouth and began speaking of something else entirely.

"When I walked in and you smiled at me, you reminded me of my wife. That is, my first wife. Not that ye look like her at all. She was beautiful." He took another sip of his drink and realized what he said. "You're beautiful, too, don't get me wrong. Just in a different way."

She smiled and put her hand on top of his. Her cool skin offered comfort from the blaze of embarrassment burning through his body. When had he lost his ability to charm a woman? He used to have a silver tongue that made ladies smile. Now words bumbled out of his mouth without a care.

"I'm sorry you got stuck with me, Dorie. I'm sorry I don't have more to give you."

Her fingers brushed his cheek and he glanced up to see her shake her head. She pointed to herself then at her lips as she smiled. She was happy to be married to him.

He didn't know how he knew what she meant from her few gestures, but they were able to communicate on a level without words. He found it easier this way and knew it was the reason he hadn't told her he knew she could speak.

She pointed to his chest, in the vicinity of his heart, and then picked up a bannock from the plate and broke it into two pieces.

When he nodded that, yes, his heart was indeed broken, she offered one piece to him while she nibbled on the other. He could only hope the analogy of his heart to the bannock had ended by that point.

He smiled at the thought and watched her eyes light up. She was lovely when she smiled. Her blue eyes danced with a joy that drew him in. Before he knew what was happening, he leaned across the table and pressed his lips to hers.

She didn't move away, but she didn't kiss him back. Not at first. He'd probably shocked her. Hell, he'd shocked himself as well. He was a breath away from pulling back when she wrapped her arms around his neck to hold him there. Her lips moved against his in a way that told of her inexperience.

He wanted to teach her the way of kissing. Show her

how great it could be when she opened to him, but he knew he wouldn't stop there. He could already feel his body responding.

It wasn't fair to satisfy his lust when he wasn't able to give her anything deeper. Rather than run away, as he had done before, he slowed the kiss and pulled back.

She smiled, her lips shiny from their kiss.

"You're beautiful, Dorie. I wish I could be a real husband to you."

The smile faded and she touched her lips with two fingers as if to hold the feeling in place. She gave a small nod and lowered her gaze to her hands. He'd hurt her again without meaning to.

He cleared his throat and got to the point of his visit. "The reason I stopped by was to make sure you are well. I'm sorry I put Liam to watching you without talking to you first. I'm used to having my orders followed, but you're not one of my soldiers. I was worried whoever tried to poison you might try something else, and I want you to be safe." He cleared his throat. "You're my wife and it's my duty to protect ye."

She nodded, still not looking at him. It was time to change the subject.

"I also wanted to make sure you have enough supplies. I was told you visited the kitchen. I hope you learned more from the ladies than just bawdy talk."

Her cheeks turned a lovely rose, and he knew it was now a different reason that kept her from looking at him. He stood to go, and she jumped up and reached for him but let her hand fall back to her side without touching him.

He wished she would have made contact as much as he wished she wouldn't have tried.

"Did you need something before I go?"

She turned quickly and looked from one place to the next. A low sound of frustration came from her throat. He wasn't sure, but he thought maybe she was frantic to find some reason for him to stay.

Maybe if she'd talk to him, he could sit with her and they'd chat about the situation and how to move forward.

"Dorie, I know you don't talk, but…I think maybe it's more that you don't want to, rather than you aren't able to."

She froze.

"I'm not going to push you if you don't feel comfortable, but know I'll listen if you want to tell me about it."

A quick nod was her only answer. She wrapped her arms around her waist and he could tell she wasn't going to talk to him today.

Maybe someday soon. If only he could stop being such an arse.

"If you need anything, let me know. It's my duty to take care of you, and I mean to do it." He opened the door and the dog ran after him. It was obvious now Rascal hadn't been a small dog but only a puppy when Dorie found him. He was already huge, and who knew how much larger he'd get. Bryce might need to build a bigger cottage.

He held the door open and the mutt ran back to his mistress, his huge tail wagging. Bryce felt something akin to jealousy when Dorie smiled at the dog and kissed his head. He shook off the ridiculous feeling. He couldn't make Dorie happy, so why should he resent the person—or creature—that could?

"If you'll allow it, I'd like to send a guard to walk you to the castle tomorrow."

She nodded.

"Thank you. Lock the door behind me when I leave."

He waited until he heard the proof of her compliance as the bar slid in place. She was safe for the night.

He went back to the castle, feeling the loneliness surround him once again.

Chapter Eight

It was still dark when Dorie was licked awake by Rascal. She made a disgruntled noise of protest, having been disrupted from a particularly nice dream.

She'd been with Bryce. He'd been smiling and laughing. He'd kissed her, as he had earlier that day.

Another lick and a whine. Fine. She would get up and let the dog out. It would be better than him having an accident in the house. He was getting so large now she might have to get a shovel from the stables to clean up after him like they did a horse.

She sat up and blinked. Then rubbed her eyes when they stung and tried to focus again. She smelled the smoke and jumped up to go out to the main room.

A fire blazed in the middle of the room. The rug was in flames along with the back wall, cutting off her escape to the front door.

She gasped, which only pulled in more smoke, causing her to cough and wheeze. She needed to get out. Already she felt dizzy.

"Rascal, come," she said, bringing him back to the alcove with her bed. She pushed the curtain away and tried to open the window, but it wouldn't budge.

It couldn't possibly have gotten stuck in the few days since she'd had it open last. Looking out at the main room, she knew that route was hopeless. That window was her only way out. She hurried over to the fireplace, grabbed a piece of wood, and used the log to break the window. She swiped up a thick blanket to clear away the rest of the jagged glass so it wouldn't cut them.

"Okay, boy. Out you go."

She wrapped her arms around Rascal's chest and heaved, but the beast's feet only came off the floor a few inches.

"Please. I can't leave you in here. You have to go out the window. Go." She pointed, but Rascal just sat whining at her.

Panic started creeping in. She couldn't leave him behind! But how to get him to move?

The fire was licking at the shelves that held her food, but she managed to dart in long enough to grab the cheese.

"Here we go." She tore off a chunk and held it out, getting his attention. "Go get it," she said and tossed the piece out the window. Rascal whined and put his paws up on the edge of the window. "That's it, jump out. Go get the cheese. Go get it." She tossed another piece and he leaped through the window like a stallion taking a hedge.

She thought she heard cursing and a growl, but a beam came loose from the ceiling just then and crashed into the room. She had to get out now or she'd die.

Scrambling up the wall, she leaned out and fell onto the ground headfirst, then rolled away under a bush where she closed her eyes.

Thank God.

For the second time in a matter of days, she gave in to the darkness.

• • •

Bryce had no sooner fallen asleep than someone was beating at his door.

He'd lain awake for hours remembering the kiss he'd shared with Dorie. Wondering what had made him do it. He decided it had been fear. His worries over her safety and wanting to win her trust so he could keep her safe. But he knew that wasn't all it was.

He'd felt something. Something more than just the need to keep her safe. A different need. Not purely physical, but intimate. She'd understood his pain, and he'd needed her closeness. Instead, he'd left.

"What is it?" he grumbled when the pounding came again.

"Your cottage is on fire. Come quick," Liam called.

For a second, still in a fog from sleep, Bryce pictured his old cottage. The one where he'd lived with Maggie and their little one. But if that home had still existed, he wouldn't be sleeping in a room at the castle. Yet there was something else important that had him jumping out of bed to get dressed.

Dorie.

He hurried out of his room, still buckling his belt.

Following the other men out the gate, he looked toward the village and saw flames.

"Dorie," he whispered when he saw the fire. Even from here he could see how far the flames rose from his cottage.

His wife was in that house.

He tore off at a dead run. He hadn't so much as grabbed a bucket to help put out the fire. He didn't know what he'd do when he got there, he just needed to get there. He ran the whole way.

"Dorie!" he yelled—a fierce cry that carried over the crackle and hiss of the cottage as it gave in to the flames.

Rascal came up to him. His bark was hoarse as he nudged Bryce in the leg with his big head. He barked again and turned toward the back of the house.

When Bryce didn't move fast enough he came back, barked, and tugged at Bryce's kilt.

"Where is she?" he asked the dog in desperation.

In answer, Rascal led him over to a bush. Bryce was about to leave him to start searching when the bush moaned.

"Dorie?" he cried, bending down to feel around in the shadows. Sure enough, his wife was under the bush asleep. No, not asleep. Unconscious. She was bleeding at her temple.

"Good boy." Bryce patted the dog before lifting Dorie into his arms to carry her back to the castle. He left the other men to put out the fire. It was clear there was no hope for saving the cottage.

It didn't matter. He'd not leave her there alone again anyway.

All that mattered was that his wife was alive. He'd promised to take care of her and had failed. *Again*. He'd keep her close now, so he could watch over her better.

The dog followed after, occasionally brushing Bryce's leg. The maids might have something to say about him allowing the beast into the hall, but Bryce would deal with them. He couldn't put Rascal out, and not just because he wasn't sure he'd win that battle.

"How is she?" Lach asked as soon as he made it into the hall. Kenna was at his heels.

"She's hit her head. She hasn't woken up, even with the bouncing on the way up here. Can you help her?" Bryce asked Kenna.

She frowned and came closer, carrying a lamp. "Let's see."

Bryce stood close by as she felt around Dorie's head and neck, then moved to her arms, legs, and the rest of her body.

"It looks like there are no other injuries. She just bumped her head. Let's try some cold water. I'll clear away the blood. It's already stopped bleeding. That's a good sign."

Bryce wasn't sure if she was talking to him or herself, but he relaxed because she didn't seem frantic.

"How can I help?" Mari asked as she stepped up to offer her sister assistance. The more the better, Bryce thought, and stepped back to let them get closer.

Cam strode into the hall looking grim. "It's gone."

Bryce didn't care about the cottage. It was just a building. He'd burned the last one down on purpose and rebuilt. He could rebuild again. People were different. They were irreplaceable.

"Will she be all right?" he asked Kenna as soon as the blood was washed away.

"I think so. It will depend on how much smoke she breathed in and for how long."

Before she'd finished talking, Dorie began to cough. Her eyes fluttered open and darted from face to face until she found him. He stepped closer and took her hand as she began crying.

He didn't know how, but he knew she was upset over the cottage. He was only upset about her.

"It's all right. The cottage doesn't matter as long as you're safe. Are you well? Does anything hurt?"

She shook her head too quickly to have done a thorough assessment first.

"Dorie, look at me," he insisted, raising her head. "What hurts?"

She blinked and he could tell she was cataloging and prioritizing her injuries. After a moment she pointed to her head. Then her wrist. Her eyes went wide and she turned in his arms, looking for something on the ground.

Again, he knew what she needed.

"He's under the table. He wouldn't let you get far from his sight," Bryce said, pointing. Rascal lumbered out from under the table and she hugged the dog.

Bryce was standing close enough to hear her whisper, "Thank you," to her furry protector.

"Bryce," Lach called, and he stepped away from the reunion to speak to the laird. Cam followed.

Bryce expected his cousins to encourage him to have Dorie stay with him at the castle. He'd already planned to do so and didn't need a lecture from them.

"We've a problem," Lach said with a frown and took a few steps farther from the group. "Cam thinks the fire was intentional."

"Why do you think that?" Bryce turned to the larger of the men. He hadn't had time to consider such a thing, but given the poisoning, it made sense someone might try again if they'd failed with the first attempt on her life.

"There were footprints leading off to the forest. Blood drops. And this." He held out a scrap of cloth. A tartan in the McCurdy colors. "There were paw prints. It looks like the dog gave chase. He might have gotten a bite of one of the bastards."

"A McCurdy bastard," Bryce said, keeping his voice low. "Why would they want to hurt her? They didn't seem to care for her much, but to risk getting caught at murder..." He shook his head.

Lach ran his hand over his face with a curse. "I should have suspected the blighter was up to something."

"What is it?" Cam asked.

"The contract. It said we had to wait a full year to build a ship to moor at their port. I was fine with that, since we weren't prepared to build our own ship yet. But it also said if anything happened to Dorie within that year, the alliance was void."

Cam scowled. "And you agreed?"

"I thought he was worried we wouldna care for her. He was her da. I'm a father, and it would be something I might have negotiated if I had a daughter. Though he must not have cared so much for her since he didn't come to the wedding. But at the time, it seemed easy enough to agree since we'd not harm her and she appeared hearty enough. It wasn't much of a risk. I didn't think more of it. I should have."

Anger and outrage pricked up Bryce's spine. "They're trying to get out of the contract by killing my wife," he said, then slashed a hand through the air. "We've dealt with them long enough. It's time we take Baehaven and end them for good."

Lach remained silent, his brow raised. No doubt he didn't like Bryce giving orders, but surely the man had to agree. Now was the time to put a stop to their treachery.

Finally the laird spoke. "Aye. We tried to do things the honorable way, but they are not honorable. We'll need more men. I think we may be able to get the Stewarts to help. I can send Liam with a message. Bryce, you'll need to speak to your father's family and see if the Campbells will join us."

Bryce frowned. He didn't want to visit the Campbells, let alone ask for their help. He'd been sent to Dunardry a year after his mother died. She'd been the sister of Lachlan and Cameron's fathers. As the laird's daughter, she'd married far beneath her status when she took Thomas Campbell, a lazy soldier, as her husband.

Bryce's father had remarried a young lass only a month after his mother died. His stepmother was soon expecting a babe and they didn't have enough room or coin to feed Bryce, so he was sent off to live with his uncles at Dunardry.

It had been for the best. The MacKinlays had welcomed him, and he'd been able to grow up with Lach and Cam. Their fathers were honorable men and had taught Bryce to be honorable as well.

As much he had no desire to face his wastrel of a father, he'd do it if it meant putting an end to the McCurdys and keeping Dorie safe.

"Aye. Once I'm certain Dorie has recovered, I'll approach the Campbells. And the McCurdys will pay for this."

Chapter Nine

Dorie's chest and throat burned and her head throbbed, but she was happy to be alive. She would see that Rascal received a juicy reward for his heroism, for she might have succumbed to the smoke and not had the chance to escape if not for her loyal friend waking her.

Tears sprang to her eyes when she thought of the cottage she'd lost. It hadn't been grand, but she'd made it her home. It was safe, and most important, she'd been able to go outside whenever she wished.

She tugged at the soiled shift she still wore and pointed in the direction of the cottage with a frown.

"You lost your new dresses," Mari said, patting her on the shoulder. "Not to worry. We'll get to work on making you new ones tomorrow."

"And you can wear one of mine until we get one ready. It will be a bit short, but it will do in a pinch." Kenna offered a smile and Dorie squeezed their hands in thanks. She'd never had friends before, but she had to think these two ladies were the very best possible.

"For now, we must all go to our beds and get some rest. We'll have a busy day tomorrow, and it will be here in just a few hours."

Nodding, Dorie slid off the table and stumbled when the large hall spun around her. Bryce was there in an instant, putting an arm around her waist to steady her.

"Up you go," he said, scooping her into his arms.

She didn't know where she would sleep. She assumed she would stay on one of the benches in the hall. Some of the soldiers slept there. She didn't mind. The room was large enough she wouldn't feel trapped.

But instead Bryce carried her upstairs, stopping at the very end of the corridor. He set her down in front of the last door and opened it. His chamber. "You'll stay with me until we come up with something else."

She'd been in his room for a few days after she was poisoned but hadn't noticed how small it was. Perhaps it was the fire that had her panicked. She still felt like she was suffocating.

She whimpered when he closed the door after Rascal came in. The large dog and man seemed to make the room shrink even more. The walls were coming closer. She opened the door and stepped out into the corridor, desperate for breath. There wasn't enough air in the room. She couldn't survive in there.

"We can prop the door open, if it helps," her husband offered, and she wanted to hug him for his kindness. She didn't know how he always seemed to know what she was thinking, even when she didn't speak the words.

So many times since she married him, she'd wanted to talk with him, but she was still keenly aware of the dangers of saying the wrong thing. Of spilling secrets and putting those she loved at risk. Silence was better. Silence was safe.

"I'm afraid we'll have to share the bed. Don't worry,

you're safe with me," he reassured her. "I'll not touch ye."

She hoped she hid her disappointment. While she wasn't up for touching tonight, filthy and sore as she was, she might welcome it another time.

She simply nodded and looked around the room.

The bed—bigger than the one at the cottage—would hold them both without risk of touching.

He poured water for her to wash up and then offered her a clean shirt. He turned around as she changed into it. She felt so much better without the layer of smoke and ash covering her.

Bryce settled in on the side of the bed facing the door. She had to climb in from the bottom of the bed since her side was against the wall. She frowned at the closed-in feeling as she slid under the covers.

When Rascal jumped up on the foot of the bed, cutting off her only escape, she was glad when Bryce shooed him off.

"You may be the hero, but you stay on the floor." He turned to her. "Did he sleep with you at the cottage?"

Not sure if the truth would make him angry, she shrugged. After all, she hadn't *allowed* it. It had just happened. Bryce didn't press for more details.

His breath evened out in sleep almost immediately. She envied the way he was able to let the worries of the day drift off so quickly. Being in a strange place plus the excitement of the day had her tossing and turning.

She noticed he wasn't the least bit bothered by her movements, so she placed a hand on his arm, testing her theory. When he didn't wake, she slid her hand across his chest and pressed her body up against his. If anything, he seemed to relax deeper into sleep.

She knew she shouldn't take advantage of his slumber, but being close to him like this made it easier for her to calm down, and soon she was dreaming of her husband.

...

Despite his attempt to be quiet, Dorie woke when Bryce slipped out of bed the next morning and wrapped his kilt around his waist. Rascal stirred as well, hurried to the door, and turned his head as if asking permission to go out despite it being open. Bryce waved him out and thought to follow behind immediately but decided he should offer his wife a greeting of some sort.

He was out of practice with such things. He'd woken hard and aching with his body wrapped around hers. When he'd pressed his hips closer, she'd made a sound of pleasure and pushed back against him.

It wasn't until that moment he'd recalled who was in bed with him and froze.

"Good morning," he mumbled as she slid off the bed and offered him a shy smile.

She probably didn't realize how the sun at her back filtered through his thin shirt, highlighting the curves of her body. She probably didn't notice that, because of her height, his shirt fell just above her knee, giving him a glance at her thigh. Nor did she know the chill of the floor caused her nipples to harden and push at the fabric in subtle invitation. And she definitely didn't realize how standing there with her bed-mussed hair and soft smile made his body hard and his kilt tent.

She was innocent.

While it was his right to change that, he wouldn't touch her. Well, he wouldn't touch her *again*.

"I need to go," he offered before rushing out of the room to escape. Innocent or not, she was tempting as hell. It had been too long since he'd taken a woman to his bed.

Even then, it had been a quick thing. Lust and need. He'd not fully sated his desires with a woman since his wife was alive. He enjoyed the act itself, but he longed for the other things that came with bedding a woman he thoroughly desired. The laughter and play that went with it. The thrill of discovering something new she liked and doing it over and over until she was pleased and gasping.

That feeling of utter contentment when he could lie next to her running his fingers through her hair and listening to her breathe.

He could have relations. He could slake his lust. He could tend to his physical needs. But he'd never have the connection that came with making love to someone who truly belonged with him.

"How do you fare?" Lach asked as he took a seat at the head table.

"I'm fine."

Nay. He wasn't fine. He was never fine. And even less so today when he was restless and needy. Despite having slept better than he had in years, he was irritable.

They turned the discussion to clan affairs. Specifically, the issue regarding the McCurdys on their land trying to kill his wife.

Bryce had just finished his meal when Dorie entered the hall looking as disheveled as the day she'd arrived at Dunardry. Her hair was a mess of tangles and the ill-fitting dress she'd found was both too short and too big. It didn't help her appearance when her four-legged beast sidled up next to her looking like a hellhound ready to fetch someone's soul for his mistress. And like on that first day, she had no shoes.

"The poor girl," Mari said from his side. "My dresses were much too short for her. But even Kenna's don't fit properly. She has nothing. Not even a way to brush her hair."

Kenna let out a sigh. "I don't have a spare brush set, but I'll see that she gets one. Until then—"

"I can take care of my own wife," Bryce snapped,

cutting off Kenna's offer of assistance. He didn't know why it bothered him, but it did.

Kenna and Mari weren't trying to make him feel guilty—at least not this time—but he felt the shame nonetheless.

"I appreciate you helping her with a dress. I'll see to her shoes and the rest today," he offered, feeling bad for snapping at them when they were only trying to help.

"You've done a poor job of it so far," Cam said with a brow raised. He didn't even have the grace to lower it when Bryce glared at him. The big oaf wasn't threatened by his smaller cousins.

Leaving the hall, Bryce went out to find his wife something decent to wear.

He *would* take care of her, and he would damn well keep her safe, too.

...

It was clear to Dorie by the way Bryce ran out of the chamber that morning he hadn't liked sharing a bed with her. And now he had also raced out of the hall the minute she arrived to break her fast.

Perhaps he didn't want to have to see her, ever.

She couldn't blame him. She was certain she looked a fright. She'd used her fingers to smooth her hair, but she could feel it sticking out. Some of the singed parts were impossible to tame. She didn't even have a hair ribbon to secure it as she normally did.

Kenna waved for her to join them, so Dorie made her way to the front table. Rascal loped along beside her. At least he didn't mind the way she looked. She couldn't be sure if the stares from the other people in the hall were due to her state of disorder or because she'd run her husband from the room. It didn't matter. She was getting used to the looks and whispers. She sat and smiled at the serving girl who brought her food.

"As soon as we've eaten, we'll get to work straight away on some new dresses for you," Kenna said.

"I'm quite good with hair," Mari suggested. "I can trim off the scorched bits if you like."

Dorie gave them a grateful smile and touched each of them. As a girl, she'd often hoped a prince would come rescue her from her prison, like in the ballads the bards sang. But she now realized that a few good friends would do just as well.

"I believe Bryce has gone to the village to get you shoes and a gift."

"Kenna! Why must you spoil the surprise?" Mari gave Kenna a sisterly shove.

"I'm sorry." Kenna looked embarrassed but her excitement returned. "I canna help it. When I know something that will make someone happy, it just spills out."

A gift? For her? Why would Bryce get her a gift after she'd burned down his cottage? Although for the life of her, she couldn't remember leaving anything out that might have caused the blaze.

As they spent the day making new dresses, Dorie was often distracted with thoughts of Bryce showing up with some trinket of affection.

She touched her lips, remembering the sizzle she'd felt when he'd kissed her. She also recalled the warmth of his body against hers this morning. The hard muscles in his arms as they wrapped around her. His hand so close to her breast she'd shifted, hoping he'd touch her there.

She would gladly give up any possession for another touch.

It was ridiculous she should want him so much. Especially after he'd made it clear he couldn't care for her in that way. But something caused her to yearn for her husband.

Something she didn't quite understand.

Chapter Ten

Having failed in his mission to secure a brush for his wife, Bryce returned to the castle and handed off the shoes to a maid to be taken to Dorie straight away. Then he returned to the bailey to run drills with his men. The troops had a visitor—their previous war chief, his cousin Cameron.

Cam slapped his shoulder as he came closer. The man had been busy working on a new house for his family. It was coming along nicely, but there was still work to be done.

"You're joining us today, you sluggard?" Bryce asked.

Cam looked insulted. "To prepare for the battle to take Baehaven Castle and put an end to the McCurdys? Of course I'm here. I may not be war chief any longer, but I'm a MacKinlay."

"And I'm not," Bryce reminded him, earning a sound of dismissal from his cousin.

"That isna true, Bryce Thomas *MacKinlay* Campbell."

Bryce laughed it off and drew his sword to start their practice. The men were energized, and the sound of clashing steel filled the crisp morning air. Everyone was excited to end the McCurdys.

"I need to go speak with the Campbells about getting more men to aid our cause," Bryce said with a frown.

Cam misunderstood what was bothering him. "Do you think you'll not get their support?"

"I understand my da has moved up the ranks since marrying the laird's daughter," Bryce said.

"Is that his fourth wife?"

"Nay, fifth. I hope this one is of fair health. And that she has provided enough influence I may use to my advantage."

"Influence is one thing. Connection is another. You've not spoken to your father in many years."

"I visited a year or so after…" He didn't need to speak of the event out loud. Cam would know what that pause meant. "I have seven half brothers and sisters. They write."

He moved out from under Cam's heavy strike and twisted to offer his own blow, but Cam blocked him.

"Did you wish me to join you when you go see him?" Cam asked when they took a break.

"Nay. You have your own duties here with your house. Your wife is increasing and will need your help."

"I'll still be able to run the men through their drills every morning in your absence."

Bryce turned to eye Liam. He was eighteen now, a man, and Bryce would have put him in charge if not for the fact Lach was sending him on an errand soon as well.

"If you could manage that, I'd be obliged," he told Cam. "I don't want them getting soft while I'm away."

"I'll see it done," Cam promised.

"Tomorrow I'll be leaving to check the borders. I'll leave for the Campbells when I return. I would already have been off if not for needing to see Dorie settled. She slept like a rock last night, no doubt exhausted after her ordeal."

"She's definitely had her share of struggles lately."

"I think the lass is used to struggles. It's obvious she hasn't had the best life thus far." And then she'd married the likes of him. After becoming his wife, she'd been poisoned and nearly killed in a fire. Dorie McCurdy MacKinlay was not high on luck. Though she was still alive, when his Maggie was not.

Cam shook his head. "You mean because it's possible her own father planned to kill her to get out of an accord with us?"

"Aye. But I don't want her to know about that." Bryce might not be the best husband, but he would do what he could to protect her. That meant sparing her additional grief. He'd keep her safe.

"But she'll need to be guarded in case there's another attempt."

"I understand, but I can have her guarded without telling her the why of it." He didn't think it would come as a surprise to Dorie, but there was a matter of expecting such a thing and knowing it to be true. "She's my wife. She'll do as I say."

Cam laughed at this. "If you've found a wife who listens to ye, you are blessed indeed."

Bryce knew Dorie was strong, she'd proven that by her very existence— She'd survived life with the McCurdys. But he couldn't hurt her in that way. To know that her own father would rather kill her than honor his agreement. It would break the lass's heart.

He'd never been one to push his men to alleviate his anger, but as he snapped orders to the lower ranks he had to admit it did make him feel slightly better.

But whatever relief he'd gained during drills was short lived, and by dinner he was restless again. Dorie entered the hall in her borrowed gown and new shoes. Her hair had been brushed. He took in her slender ankles which were revealed by the dress that was too short for someone of her height. He swallowed as he noticed the curve of her hips. She'd been so thin when she arrived, but those new curves were enticing.

She smiled at something Mari said and he felt his stomach flip in excitement. Nay. Surely it was just hunger. He hadn't eaten since the morning meal. That was all.

"Doesn't Dorie look lovely?" Mari encouraged when they arrived at the table.

"She looks better than she did this morning," Bryce agreed, earning a glare from Kenna and a sad frown from Mari. Dorie continued to smile as if she'd taken his rude comment as a compliment. He should have done better. It seemed his wife was as unused to receiving compliments as he was at giving them.

"The three of ye ladies do our clan proud. We don't deserve such lovely brides," Cam said. Mari fluttered her lashes at him and offered a smile that foretold of an early departure to their chamber.

Bryce had always been a flirt in the past. Charming women was an amusing way to pass the time. Especially since it never led anywhere. A few sweet words here and there didn't cause any harm. But he'd grown rusty.

He drew on the skill that seemed to have abandoned him since he'd been forced into marriage. "You look fetching," he said quietly, just for Dorie.

Her blue eyes went wide with surprise as a blush stole over her creamy skin. How would he survive another night lying next to her without touching her?

As expected, Cam and Mari slinked off to the stairs as soon as the meal was over. Lach and Kenna didn't remain much longer, leaving him alone with Dorie.

Rather than sit awkwardly in the hall, he asked her to join him on a walk. Her excited agreement never ceased to surprise him. No matter how awful he'd been, she still seemed happy to be with him.

His invitation was completely selfish. His plan was simply to tire her out so she'd fall asleep instantly when they returned to their room.

Not that she was some grand seductress, but in the low light, with her eyes luring him to tell her all his secrets, he was weak. The warmth of her body would be too close for him to resist. Fortunately his plan worked, and after returning to their room and slipping off that delicious gown, she slid under the covers in her equally delectable shift.

He spent the night tossing and turning. At the first light of morning he sat up, eager to flee. She slept on, so he paused in his escape to look at her.

As the day before, her black hair stuck out at all angles and points. He remembered his failure to offer her even the simplest necessities.

He slipped from the bed and moved to his trunk, silently lifting the lid to peer at the memories that lurked inside. The scent of Maggie had faded, but he still caught a slight whiff of something familiar.

Moving aside a few of her garments, he found what he was looking for. A brush and comb set she'd been given by her parents when she and Bryce married. He recalled the way she sat in their home stroking the brush through her heavy blond locks until they crackled and lifted from the heat of the fire.

He breathed in the pain and let out a breath before he tucked the ivory brush and comb set back in his trunk. He knew Dorie needed them—she had nothing when she arrived, and even less since the fire—but he wasn't strong enough to offer them to her. They belonged to Maggie.

He glanced over his shoulder to make sure she hadn't seen him. She was still asleep, her hands folded under her cheek like an angel.

If he'd been a different man, he might have thought she

was sent to him as recompense for everything he'd lost. But he didn't believe in such things. He'd not have anything to do with a god who took innocent women and children while leaving him alive covered with the blood of his enemies on the battlefield. It made no sense. Maggie and Isabel had done nothing wrong.

He dressed and left the room before his new wife woke.

Knowing that he cared even a bit for Dorie annoyed him enough that he was glad to be off to check the far borders. Being away for a few days would give him the distance he needed.

He didn't want to care.

...

Dorie looked for Bryce at the morning meal but figured he was already out with his men when she didn't see him. It wasn't until the evening meal when she heard Cam mention Bryce had left the castle that she became concerned.

When Cam gave no details, she reached across Mari to touch his arm. Her brows pulled together.

"Of course he dinna tell you where he was going." Cam shook his head and looked at Mari, who only shrugged. "I hope I was never such an arse to you."

"You'll recall you didn't want a wife when we wed any more than Bryce did."

Dorie was surprised to hear this. Especially seeing how much Cameron clearly loved his family. Even now his hand rested protectively on Mari's round belly.

"You see, it's not the worst thing to have a man leave you for a bit. So long as he realizes he cannot live without you," Cam said. "When Mari left me, I dinna think I'd survive it."

With the couples chatting to one another, Dorie finished her meal and went to help the women in the kitchen. There was no refuge to be found there. Millie and the other women were speaking of the romantic things their men did for them.

She made a hasty escape as they began to delve into the subject of other services their husbands provided.

Rascal was waiting outside the kitchen for her. Dorie fed him and led him out of the gates toward the stream where she and Bryce had sat and talked the day they were married. Well, he'd talked. She'd been too afraid to speak. Many times since, she wished she hadn't continued this deception. There were so many things she wanted to say to him now. But what would he think when he found out she'd lied to him all this time?

"Do you think his leaving could be a good thing?" she asked Rascal, who loped along beside her. "I don't know the ways of husbands and wives. I have to think it shouldn't be this difficult."

She was about to tell her dog the confusing things she'd learned from the women in the kitchen when he went on alert, the fur rising on his back. A low growl rumbled in his chest as he ducked down and slipped away from her.

She trusted Rascal. He'd already saved her once before, so she took his warning seriously and wedged herself between a dense bush and a large rock.

"Where did she go? She was just standing here talking with that demon hound," Desmond said as he pointed to the ground far too close to her. She could just make him out through the leaves of the bush where she hid.

"You lie. My sister doesn't speak," Wallace snapped.

"Nay, it's true. I even heard her singing when I was watching her at her cottage. Look, there's the dog over there. She must have crossed the creek." It was Rory who spoke, but she couldn't see him.

The men's heavy footsteps faded away but she remained crouched in her hiding place. Good lord. Her brother and cousins were here. What did they want? Had they been responsible for the fire at the cottage?

She couldn't see what was happening. She shook with worry for her dog. What if they killed him because he was protecting her? But to jump from the bushes would mean certain death for both of them.

She pressed her forehead harder into the rock and jumped when she felt a stick poke her in the foot. She looked up at Rory. She almost smiled in relief, but then she remembered the danger.

Rory had once brought her a meal and had been beaten for it. No doubt he hated her now. It wouldn't surprise her if he called for her brother and turned her over to him so he could earn their praise and respect.

She stared at him, begging him with her eyes not to call her out. Slowly he raised his index finger to his lips, bidding her to be quiet. She nodded at once. He tapped her foot again, silently telling her to move it beneath the bush.

Tucking her long legs in as tightly as possible, she looked up to thank him, but he had moved on without a word.

She remained in her hiding spot until the sun set and the noises from her hungry stomach drowned out the night sounds of the darkening forest around her.

Rascal had returned to her hours ago. He'd left twice again but hadn't growled or seemed alert to any danger. Still, she wasn't willing to risk exposure. Not when her brother was out there.

...

Bryce had seen enough to know Clan MacKinlay had an issue with intruders. He'd found at least ten separate tracks coming from the McCurdy land onto theirs. Most were fresh, which meant they could have been made when the buggers had come to set the fire at the cottage.

They'd found a piece of McCurdy plaid then, clear evidence they had been there.

But confronting the McCurdy would do no good. He was no doubt behind the intrusion and would defend his men. A mere scrap of fabric wouldn't be enough. Bryce would need irrefutable proof the McCurdy clan had come unwelcome onto MacKinlay lands. Not that they needed yet another reason for war.

Settling in to wait, he set up a small fireless camp and thought of how his clan might win a war against the McCurdys. Bryce wasn't looking forward to visiting the Campbell clan to ask for assistance.

It wasn't that his father was a horrible man. It was the opposite, actually. Nothing seemed to get the man down. Not the death of Bryce's dear mother. Definitely not that. Every time he lost a wife, he was quick to replace her with a new and younger version.

To his father, marriage seemed to be nothing more than a state to keep oneself cared for. And…as evident by the number of half brothers and half sisters Bryce had, their father also took fair advantage of the marriage bed.

Bryce thought more of marriage. It went beyond having a place to put his cock and someone to mend his shirts. Marriage was reserved for the person one wanted to give their heart. A partner. The person who made life complete.

When one loved someone like that, the person was not so easily exchanged, if ever replaced.

His mother had once told him lightning didn't strike the same place twice. She would probably be saddened to see how many times lightning had struck his father.

In the dark, surrounded by the sounds of the woods and the animals that lived there, it was easy to feel as if his mother could be there with him. Or Maggie. Perhaps it was the magic of the forest, but he also imagined Dorie looking up at the star-filled sky, noticing the same patterns as he. From there it was easy to recall sharing a bed with her.

He'd been able to pull Dorie against him and breathe in the scent of her hair, feel the softness of her skin. His cock grew hard at the memory and he scowled up at the night sky.

He had the ability to conjure up any fantasy he wished here in the dark. Why would he think of Dorie instead of his beloved Maggie? Dorie had been forced on him, so his reality was filled with her. His thoughts should still be loyal to his first wife.

The wife of his heart.

Except as he lay there, he couldn't recall the smell of her. Couldn't hear the sound of her laughter or her voice. He remembered things they'd said to one another, but the timbre of her whisper in the dark eluded him. When he envisioned touching her, her features transformed into those of Dorie.

"Christ." He was losing Maggie.

When he'd been numb with the pain of Maggie's death, everyone had told him it would get easier. Time would heal his pain. But it was no more than an illusion. Nothing healed the pain. Time was a bastard who stole away his memories so he could no longer summon enough details to feel that level of pain anymore. It was nothing but a cruel trick.

Despite his irritation, he must have drifted off. A twig snapped, waking Bryce fully. He blinked, trying to recall where he was and why he was sleeping rough in the woods. The events from the day before filled in and soon he was crouched in the bushes watching as three men wearing McCurdy plaid trudged by. It was difficult to see their features clearly, but they were the same size of the men who had brought Dorie to Dunardry.

"I can't believe you let her get away again," Wallace McCurdy barked at his cousins.

"Ye were there, too. It wasna only my doing. That blasted dog. If we have any chance of getting to her, we need to kill the dog."

"I don't kill dogs. I'm not a monster."

"You plan to kill your own sister, but not her dog?" Rory pointed out the hypocrisy.

"She's not my sister now, is she? Not by blood anyway. Besides, this would have been done already if you'd used all the poison as I said to."

The men continued their grumbling as they passed, but Bryce could no longer hear their words as they trudged back onto their own lands. He didn't need to hear any more. He might not have proof, but he'd heard the truth from their own lips.

They had tried to kill his wife and failed. Which meant they'd probably try again.

Chapter Eleven

When Dorie made it back to the castle, it was nearly midnight and the hall was abuzz with activity. But the commotion ceased the moment they noticed her enter with Rascal by her side. She thought for a moment the looks of frustration were because of the dog, but one by one the warriors disbanded and walked away, muttering to themselves.

"You're back." Kenna came over, a worried look pulling at her brows. "Everyone was worried about you. The men were going to start searching."

Dorie's eyes went wide at the thought of anyone caring that she was missing. She hadn't even considered the idea that people would worry over her. While it was a lovely feeling, she also felt guilt tug at her for making them lose their rest.

She pulled Kenna into a hug and offered a strained smile of apology.

"Are you injured?"

Dorie shook her head.

"Did someone bother ye?" Cam asked, looking gruff.

Again Dorie shook her head. Not just because she didn't

know how to communicate what had happened without speaking, but also because she didn't want to cause them any more worry.

She'd made it back to the castle without any issue. From what she'd overheard, her brother and his men were only looking to hurt *her*, so the others were safe enough. He couldn't get to her while she was in the castle. If she stayed within the walls of Dunardry, he would grow bored and leave, if he hadn't already.

There was no need to make her new friends concerned, even though it was a wonderful feeling to know someone cared.

After everyone went off to their beds, Dorie kept the door to her bedchamber propped open. She knew she was at risk of having an unwanted guest in the middle of the night, but so far she'd not seen many drunken men stumbling through the halls at Dunardry. It was worth the risk to know she wasn't locked in the small room alone. In the dark it was too easy to confuse Bryce's chamber with the room at Baehaven Castle that had been her prison.

She slept restlessly, plagued with nightmares of her brother chasing her into a room and locking her inside. She woke too early to be about and decided to look around for a place to put her few things. The new dress Kenna and Mari had helped her with was her most treasured possession, and she opened the first trunk in the room, hoping to find a safe place for it.

The trunk held a number of items. None of them looked like they belonged to her husband. A gown or two. Some other clothing that would have fit a babe. An ivory brush and comb set.

Dorie picked them up, stroking the elaborate design etched into the handles.

For a moment she thought of using them, but if they had

been placed in the trunk it was because they were special. Most likely all of these things had belonged to Bryce's late wife, his treasures and memories of the woman who had won his heart, even unto death. Dorie knew well enough she'd never be that important to him.

When she grew hungry, she went down to break her fast with the other ladies, then they gathered in the solar to work on more dresses for her. She tried to protest that the two she had were plenty, but they insisted on another.

Mari sucked in a breath and rubbed her large belly. "The little one is active today. I believe he's doing flips."

Kenna placed her hand on her sister's belly and smiled. "That is a large foot." Dorie saw the bond between the sisters and wished she'd been blessed with siblings. Wallace didn't count.

"Please, don't speak the word *large* to me," Mari said worriedly. "I was blessed with a small child when Lizzy was born. She took after me. If this one takes after his father, I'll be split in two."

"You'll be fine. I'm sure of it," Kenna said, though Dorie detected an edge of concern.

Mari caught Dorie watching them. "Would you like to feel the babe moving?"

Dorie shook her head, thinking it was too intimate.

"Come now. I don't mind. Besides, your time will come and it's better to have an idea as to what it feels like."

After a brief hesitation, Dorie reached out tentatively, and Mari guided her hand to a place where she felt a bit of fluttering. Then two hard kicks. Dorie jerked her hand back and smiled.

"Stop that, you ruffian. You'll have to do with the space you have for a few more weeks."

Dorie looked down at her palm where she'd felt the babe move. It was almost magical. She blinked and the feeling of wonder faded when she remembered she would never have that experience.

She'd gained an education during her time in the kitchen, and while she didn't know all of it, she knew enough to be certain she'd never have a child if her husband refused to lie with her.

When she'd first slept next to him she thought it might happen, but then she learned he had to—

She closed her eyes, unwilling to think of such things, but longing for it all the same. That was yet another experience she'd never have. She remembered the trunk of memories in her room and felt the first stirrings of jealousy for a woman who no longer lived.

The sisters were still chatting away about babies when the dowager entered the room—the Dowager Duchess of Endsmere. Dorie had learned that Mari had once been a duchess, and the dowager was the mother of Mari's late husband, who had moved to Scotland after her son's death. The formidable older lady was now living at Dunardry with Mari and her second husband, Cam.

The dowager walked into the room carrying Mari's daughter, Lizzy. Mari's smile lit up the room upon seeing her daughter, and Dorie again felt a yearning as the child reached for her mother.

All the years Dorie had lived in that single room at the castle she'd remembered a fairy tale her mother had told her of a princess who'd been locked away until one day a handsome prince came to save her. They fell in love and lived happily ever after. But in all those stories her mother had told, she'd never said anything about the prince being disinterested enough to put the princess in a cottage and never come to see her again.

"What are you working on?" the dowager asked them.

"A third dress for Dorie. Won't this look lovely with her

coloring?" Mari pointed to the yellow fabric and settled Lizzy on what was left of her lap.

"It will." The dowager inspected Dorie with her head cocked and Dorie felt the need to squirm—like what a worm must feel when in the gaze of a bird. "I suppose your brush was destroyed in the fire and that is why your hair is a trifle unkempt?"

Dorie knew from listening to the other women that the dowager had a hard edge but generally meant well. Something about living alone for so long had made her abrupt. Dorie had been told to ignore it, but her face burned with shame at the woman's words. Dorie had done her best, using her fingers to sweep her hair back into a knot, but without a brush she wasn't able to duplicate the smooth styles of the other women.

She'd appreciated Mari and Kenna's help in fixing her hair the night before. She had hoped Bryce would find her to his liking and maybe he would grow to feel something for her.

Instead, he'd left.

She nodded in answer to the dowager's question, unwilling to admit she'd not had such luxuries as a brush and comb even before the fire. The dowager was confident and intimidating. Doubtless, in this woman's eyes Dorie would forever be found lacking.

Without a word the older woman spun out of the room.

"Don't mind her," Mari said quietly. "She doesn't mean anything by it. Your hair is lovely."

It was nice of Mari to say so, even if it wasn't true.

Kenna, the more blatantly honest sister, nodded. "Your hair *is* lovely. It just needs a good brushing. Mayhap we'll work on that when we're done with this gown."

Before she'd finished the sentence, the dowager was back and handed Dorie a beautiful brush and comb set, very much like the one she'd seen in the trunk in her room that had belonged to Bryce's late wife.

She looked at the woman holding them out, not understanding.

"Take them. You may have these. I have another set."

Dorie's eyes went wide in surprise. She was being given these elegant things? Surely she must have misunderstood.

"Go on." The dowager placed the comb and brush in Dorie's hands.

Pointing to herself, she held them out, questioning.

"Yes. For you." The dowager turned to Kenna and Mari. "It's as if she's never been given anything before."

Small wonder. Because she hadn't. Not until she'd met the generous people here in Dunardry.

Tears of gratitude welled in her eyes. Perhaps with these and the help of her new friends, she might be made pretty by the time her husband returned. And if so, maybe he would come to like her. Eventually.

In a flurry of excitement she hurried out of the room to go and find the perfect place for them in their chamber.

...

Rascal was sleeping next to Bryce when he woke on the last morning of his border patrol. The pup was a welcome sight, despite the stench of the animal's breath. Bryce knew the beast would not have left Dorie's side if she were in danger.

"We'll be seeing her today," he said with a surprising bit of pleasure at the knowledge. The truth was, he'd been thinking of her each night of his journey. Each dream of her had been more explicit than the one before.

His new wife was beautiful. He'd known it the morning he wed her, despite her rumpled appearance. He'd only found her more alluring when forced to lie next to her.

He'd run away to be free of his lust before he betrayed

Maggie. He'd not been a monk since her death, but when he'd succumbed, he'd made sure it was nothing more than relieving a physical necessity. His heart and mind had stayed firmly loyal. If he were to bed Dorie, he knew in his heart it would be different.

He couldn't tup her and walk away. She would expect something from him. The kindness and consideration of a lover. A husband. She deserved no less. In fact, she deserved so much more.

He'd wanted to stay clear of her so as not to be pulled in by her charms. But even in the short time he'd been with her since they wed, he could tell she was kind. And she wasn't a spy. Even before hearing the McCurdy's comments, he'd trusted her.

It would have been much easier if she truly were a spy. Then he could easily cast her aside and not think of her. It would have been far better. Better than this wanting and longing for someone he couldn't give himself to.

Surely now that he'd spent a few days away from her he would be better prepared. And if not…well, perhaps there was a way to embrace the things a wife offered without hurting her.

Perhaps he would be able to perform the duties of a husband after all, even while keeping his heart secured. He knew the things women liked to hear from a lover. He could say them to Dorie even if there was no real sentiment behind the words. She'd never had a lover before, she'd not know the difference. And as long as she was happy, he could take pleasure in her pleasure.

Aye, he'd have to carefully consider doing that.

For it would solve all their problems.

Chapter Twelve

Thinking of bedding Dorie made Bryce give his horse another nudge to hasten his trip. He'd been in a hurry to get away from her, and now he was equally eager to get back so he could report to Lach and then go and find his wife.

He arrived late in the afternoon after stopping at the loch to bathe.

He was glad to be back inside the walls of Dunardry. Normally he would have seen to his own horse, but as hungry as he was—for both food and company—he passed his beast off to a groom and headed for the hall.

Everyone was just gathering for the evening meal, so he went to the head table to speak to Lach and Cam about what he'd encountered on the McCurdy border. He was deep in conversation when the hall went quiet. He looked up to see what had caught everyone's attention, and stared at the vision coming toward him, stunned.

'Twas his wife.

The new gown she wore was blue and called notice to the blue of her eyes.

Her gaze was focused on the floor as if she were afraid of making a misstep. Or perhaps she was focused on her breasts—as he was—for they were practically popping out of her bodice. This dress was cut low and her breasts were pushed up, giving the illusion of escape. Perhaps she couldn't see past them.

Her gaze moved up for a moment and she stopped there in the middle of the hall, gazing at him in surprise.

"Bloody hell," he whispered to the smiling women beside him.

"Aye. We thought you would be pleased."

"Pleased?" *Was* he pleased? She was lovely, it was true. Her midnight hair had been brushed to a high shine and piled on top her head. A few wisps touched her elegant neck.

He'd known attraction before. But this was more than attraction, this was full-on lust. When he'd dreamed of her, she'd come to him rumpled and uncertain as he was used to seeing her. Not this graceful vixen.

The knowledge that he could actually have her because they were wed took his excitement to a higher level than he'd experienced in ages.

Not since—

"Bloody hell," he repeated. "What did you do to her?"

Instead of answering, Kenna frowned and nodded at Dorie, who was still motionless in the hall. "Go to her and lead her to the table as your mother taught you, Bryce Thomas."

Jumping up, he hurried to his wife's side and led her to the table.

"You look beautiful," he said, gazing down at her breasts. They were even more glorious up close. What spell had she placed on him?

When she smiled back at him, his earlier plan to offer meaningless words went to hell. For when he leaned over and said, "The gown is lovely, but I can't wait to have you out of it," he meant every word.

...

Dorie's hands trembled as they approached the chamber she would be sharing with her husband. Tonight was different from the last time they'd entered his chamber together. She could walk under her own power for one thing, but that wasn't the only difference. The air between them practically sizzled with attraction.

She wondered what had caused his reaction. Surprisingly, it wasn't just the new gown and having her hair done. He'd hardly looked at her dress or her hair. His gaze had been on her face.

And her breasts.

The women in the kitchen had mentioned how enthralled men were with breasts. It was the reason Kenna and Mari had designed this gown with such a low neckline, despite Dorie's protests. They just smiled and told her to trust them.

So she had. And look what had happened.

She swallowed. Exactly what she'd wanted to happen. The way Bryce was looking at her—as though she were a gooseberry tart—made her heart pound. She'd never felt like this before—nervous and hot and cold and shivery all at the same time—but she knew from listening to Kenna's bawdy talk that it would all end in enjoyment. Or so the other women had made it seem. Dorie now wished she had asked for more details.

So far, all she knew was she was supposed to put her mouth…somewhere…and he would fall helpless to her wishes. Surely Bryce would be able to instruct her in the ways a wife was supposed to please her husband.

She whimpered when he shut the door behind him,

leaving the dog on the other side. He slid the bar into place and turned toward her. Pushing away the fear of being trapped, she forced a smile to her lips. The door was locked from the inside. She could get out if she needed to.

And at the moment, she didn't want to go anywhere. Because Bryce was here with her.

"Would you like help unlacing your gown?" he asked. The suggestion was politely helpful, but the tone of his voice and the way he watched her sent a thrill through her whole being.

She nodded and lit another lamp by the bed.

He came closer and bent his head right by her neck. She could feel his breath on her skin and closed her eyes, letting the warmth settle over her. He'd just untied her laces and had loosened the strings when his hands stilled.

She felt his tension and turned to see what was amiss. He was standing and staring at the nightstand where she'd set out her things. His eyes, filled with hunger just a moment ago, were hard and angry.

She stepped away, holding her gown in front of her.

Was he angry that she'd put her things out to be seen? Perhaps he liked things to be tidy and put away.

"Why do you have these? They're not yours," he snapped. "I will see you get what you need. Put these back where you got them this instant."

Jumping, she lurched forward and picked up the brush and comb set. She spun toward the door. She'd managed to get the bar off while still holding up her dress, but Bryce was there again, even angrier.

"Where do you think you're going? Give them to me." He snatched them from her hands and marched to the trunk at the end of the bed. Throwing open the lid, he stopped abruptly. He must have seen the brush and comb set she'd found there before. The set that looked so similar to the one the dowager had given her.

He turned to Dorie, confusion on his face. "These aren't Maggie's."

She shook her head quickly.

"I thought you—" He stopped and took a step toward her.

She jumped back and winced, expecting pain.

"I'm sorry," he said quietly.

She would have liked to see the expression on his face, but tears had blurred her vision and were now streaming down her cheeks.

"Lass…" He took the set and returned them to the small table by the bed. "I'm so sorry."

She wiped at her eyes with the back of her hand and stood uncertainly in the middle of the room. She could see clearly enough to take in the pain in his eyes. She didn't know what she'd done to cause him such agony, but she didn't want him to hurt. He'd been hurting for so long.

When she reached out, he turned sharply and went to the door. Her hand dropped as he opened it, and she braced herself for the door to close and the suffocating feeling of being trapped to grip her. But it didn't come.

Instead of leaving the room as she expected, he paused there for a long moment, then closed the door again and slid the bar back in place.

He came to stand before her, lifting his gaze to meet hers. "I used to run away when I'd upset Maggie, to give us time to calm down and speak without angry words between us." He ran his hand over his hair. "I deserve your angry words. I deserve to have you yell and call me horrible names. But you won't, because you won't talk to me."

He looked toward the door and then back to her. Gazing at her intently, he said, "I know you can speak. I heard you talk to your dog. I even heard ye singing one day when I came to see you."

She gasped, eyes going wide with distress. He'd been at the cottage? He'd heard her when she thought she was alone?

He took her hand and guided her closer. She let him, though she was trembling inwardly.

"I'm sorry for yelling, for accusing you of something you didn't do. In truth, I should have given you those things in the trunk. They aren't doing anyone any good in there. I'm sorry I've been a bastard to you. I've been so intent on keeping everyone at a distance, I hadn't realized what an arse I've become."

He took her other hand and rubbed circles on the back with his thumbs. It was a pleasant feeling and she relaxed, moving toward him slightly. When he released her hand, it was to place his fingers gently on her cheek. She watched his eyes, waiting for his mood to shift again. She didn't expect him to lean in closer.

"Can you forgive me for yelling?"

She nodded. Forgiving him was an easy thing to do.

It wasn't until his warm lips were pressed to hers that she realized his plan had been to kiss her.

A small sound left her throat. If he hadn't already known she could speak, it might have given her away. He made an answering noise, as if they were creating their own form of communication.

She enjoyed the way his mouth fit against hers. The way his lips moved over hers. Small nibbles at the edges of her mouth. Then his tongue teased at the seam of her lips and she parted them.

The small opening she offered was breached by his tongue, and it searched her mouth. His actions startled her at first, not knowing the ways of kissing since this was only the second time in her life, but when it seemed as though he wanted her to participate, she reached out with her own tongue and stroked his.

The sound he made this time was much louder and filled

with need.

His arms wrapped around her waist, pulling her against him. Her hands had still been holding up her gown, but she dropped it and trailed her fingers up over his large shoulders to his neck so she could twine them in his hair. Her dress slipped dangerously low on her breasts.

She was lost. She'd seen people kissing before, but it hadn't looked like this. She'd seen men and women as they slipped away to their rooms or to the darkness of the forest.

She'd been too young to want to know what happened when they were alone. But now she wished she'd had someone to tell her the way of things so she knew what to expect.

"Have you lain with a man?" he asked, pulling away.

She shook her head, her breath coming fast as if she'd been running or hiding.

"I know you were supposed to be a virgin when we were wed, but it wouldn't matter to me if you were or were not. I only ask to be sure you know what is done."

She shook her head again but held on to his arm, hoping he wouldn't leave.

He rested his forehead against hers and offered a soft smile. "Very well. We'll go slow," he whispered.

Slow? She might not know what she wanted, but she was fairly certain it wasn't to go slow. Not with the way her heart pounded and her breath quickened. She felt jittery, ready for something amazing to happen.

But she allowed him to do as he wished, since he had more experience with such things. Slowly, he peeled her dress from her body and helped her out of her boots. Then he took her hair down, running his fingers through it.

Something deep inside her throbbed and ached. What was he doing to her? She was as terrified as she was intrigued. Whatever being a real wife entailed, she wanted it. Very much.

She leaned closer and kissed him. She felt his lips pull up

against hers and enjoyed the feeling of knowing she'd brought a smile to the face of this normally stoic man.

When he pulled away she made a sound of complaint, and the smile grew, causing a small dimple to form on the left side of his mouth.

She'd thought her husband attractive, formidable, and handsome. But now she also thought him incredibly adorable. He looked almost boyish when he grinned like that.

Then he moved away from her. She reached for him, wanting him in her arms again, but he reached behind his neck and tugged his shirt over his head. He took a step closer when she held out her hand and allowed her to run her palm down his chest, over the hard ridges of his stomach.

Her hand was stopped by his belt. She frowned down at the fabric of his kilt that was keeping her from seeing and touching every part of him.

With a wink he reached past her hand and unfastened his belt. "Don't be afraid when you see me. It will be all right, I promise."

She nodded that she understood, but when his kilt dropped to his feet, she did not understand at all.

A hard length of flesh shot up toward her, causing her to yelp with surprise. She'd never seen such a thing. Her own body surely wasn't built like that.

Her confusion must have shown on her face. After another laugh, he took her hand and placed it on the part of him that was so different from her.

He groaned, but the smile remained on his face, proving he enjoyed the torment. She looked down at the odd thing, noticing how smooth it was, as if the skin had never been touched by the sun or any harshness the world had to offer.

She gasped when she recalled something similar Millie had said about her husband's cock.

So, this was a cock.

And she was touching it. If she remembered correctly, he would be putting it inside her.

Inside? Nay. That wasn't possible.

And another thing... Millie had said she was to put her mouth on it. Good lord. How would she ever fit this into her mouth?

Her breath, which had already been coming quickly, picked up speed until she felt she might faint with panic.

"Calm down," he said softly. "I'm not sure what you've heard about what happens next, but I promise you, all will be well."

She didn't see how. She needed to leave. Her body might enjoy his touch—more than enjoy it, to be honest—but what was to happen next would be too much.

But before she could flee, he reached up and cupped one of her breasts. She froze and made another sound as the ache she'd been feeling in her heavy breasts eased slightly.

"Do you like when I touch you here?"

She did. She nodded quickly so he would know how very much she liked it. He bent and placed his mouth over the peak, using his tongue to rasp a particularly sensitive area. Blissful sensation shivered through her. She whimpered and nearly lost her balance.

His arms found her and held her steady, somehow without releasing his mouth. He walked toward the bed and she suddenly realized her feet were off the floor. She had a feeling of floating, and then he leaned her over the edge of the bed and fell on top of her. But she didn't feel smashed by his weight, she felt only the warmth of his skin on hers as he held himself above her.

He moved to her other breast, and she wiggled on the bed, unsure how to ask for what she wanted, even if she were willing to speak. There were no words for what she needed. At least none that she knew.

She'd been so focused on what his mouth was doing, she hadn't realized his hand had moved down her body. She sucked in a breath when he pushed one of his fingers inside her, filling a place she hadn't known existed. The pleasure made her cry out in surprise.

"Do ye like that?"

Another nod.

"When you're ready, I'm going to put this part of me here in this spot," he said as he took her hand and pressed it against the hard bulge.

She had no idea how mating worked. Being locked in her room, she'd never even had the opportunity to see animals doing it. His explanation seemed a bit preposterous, but she trusted him, and she did like the way he'd made her feel thus far.

She was sure she would like whatever came next as well. Certainly the women in the kitchen seemed to like it.

He shifted and slid a second finger inside her. He waited and she relaxed as her body acclimated to the feeling. When he still didn't move, she pressed down, relying on instincts to direct her. She pulled her hips back and pushed forward again, moaning at the pleasure building deep inside her.

He whispered words, but she didn't hear all of them. The ones she was able to focus on told her to seek out what felt good. To enjoy the moment.

In truth, she hadn't a clue what was happening. She was simply dizzy with the sensations. Something unfamiliar was building inside her, and every thrust of his hand brought her closer to whatever it was.

He moved his fingers.

It was the slightest change in angle, but it was enough to push her all the way over whatever mountain she'd been climbing.

But instead of falling, she flew.

Chapter Thirteen

Bryce felt as if he'd been caught in a whirlwind. He'd kissed Dorie as a means of apology. As a way to let her know he was sorry for jumping to the wrong conclusions.

To be honest, the only reason he'd been mad was because he'd felt weak for not giving her the brush and comb from the trunk right away. It had been selfish of him to withhold something she'd needed when he had it to offer. Worse, he wasn't even certain he was still thinking of the blasted brush and comb.

He'd wanted Dorie to know he did care about her. At least as much as he was able to. But it hadn't taken long for him to get caught up in the kiss, and he'd found himself removing her clothes and easing her back on their bed.

Now he was lying between her thighs, his cock lined up to her hot center as he prepared her to become his wife in every way.

He'd not felt like this since…Maggie. He could remember it now, at least. Though now was mayhap not the time he should remember such things. But he could think about what it had been like with Maggie and still enjoy kissing Dorie, knowing it was different.

Good. Better than good, but still different.

Dorie was tall, which meant she lined up with him perfectly. He could press himself against her warmth and look into her blue eyes at the same time. He hooked her legs around his waist and placed his forehead against hers in an effort to calm himself.

It wouldn't do to rush the moment. There was no way to avoid hurting her briefly, but he could control himself so he didn't make it worse than it needed to be.

He was shocked when she used her long legs to pull herself up, sinking him farther into her. She wiggled impatiently, driving him mad with wanting to plunge into her heat in one thrust.

The way she responded to every touch made him want to touch her more, just to see her reactions.

"There will be a bit of pain when I push into you all the way, but it will be over quickly. If you don't want to, we don't have to."

She looked at him with her wide blue eyes and he saw the trust there. She moved against him again.

He pulled away in preparation, and she made a noise of protest.

"I'm not going anywhere, lass." He wouldn't have been able to leave her if the castle were under attack.

"Before we go any further, I need something from you," he said.

She looked up at him, waiting.

"I need you to speak to me. I need you to tell me you want this."

She was quick to reach between them and make a cross over her heart. It was a valiant effort, but he shook his head. "Can you speak, love?"

She glanced away and then back to face him. She nodded.

"I'm sure there's a reason you've chosen not to for all this time, but I'll not have silence any longer between us. Do you understand?"

"I do," she whispered. It was as if they were starting over with the first words she should have spoken at their wedding. Her voice was low and husky, either from lack of use or from passion. Whichever reason, hearing those two words made him burn.

He kissed her again, a reward for trusting him enough to break her silence. "I know you just started to use your voice, but I'm planning to have you scream with desire before the night is over," he promised with a smile.

Her wide eyes went even wider as he nudged closer between her legs, but passion overtook her fear. She moaned and gripped him tighter.

Maggie had also been a virgin when he'd bedded her. At the time he'd thought it best to go slow, but later he'd thought maybe that wasn't the best way. It had just taken longer to get past it.

He decided to go about things differently with Dorie. He waited for her to open her eyes and look at him. He smiled, hoping to reassure her.

"I'm going to make it quick." He paused to clarify. "The painful part. Not the good part."

She gave a slight nod and then a more determined, "Aye."

He kissed her hard, at the same time pushing inside her the whole way, claiming her as his wife.

Softening the kiss, he held still to give her a moment to relax and took that time to caress her mouth with his tongue. Her fingers clutched his hair, holding him to her. But it was unnecessary. He had no plans to leave. Instead, he continued to kiss her until she shifted restlessly. He knew she was ready for more when she whimpered in frustration and pushed up from the bed as if to ease a need.

"Are you ready for the good part?" he asked, and she nodded.

When he waited, she swallowed and answered, "Please." The yearning in her voice nearly did him in, but he'd promised it would be good.

He'd told her the good part wouldn't be quick. Why had he made such a foolish promise? It had been so long since he'd lain with a woman he'd probably spend in less than a minute. She was so tight around him he could barely stand it.

He moved out of her, watching for any sign of pain. When he saw none, he pushed forward again. She groaned in pleasure, saying his name.

He murmured her name as well and was surprised when it didn't bring the usual guilt and sadness with it. Building on the welcome freedom, he whispered other words of praise and encouragement. He told her how wonderful she felt under him, how lovely it sounded when she moaned. How he would never tire of hearing his name spoken in her sweet voice.

Her breathing came faster, and when she tensed in pleasure, he thrust deep inside her, feeling the pulses of her body drawing him to his own release. He hadn't made it last all that long, but thankfully it had been long enough.

He collapsed next to her afterward, tossing his damp hair out of his face so he could watch her reaction to what had just happened between them. When she tilted her head to smile up at him, he allowed the joy he felt to pull his lips up into an answering smile.

Unfortunately, his happiness was short lived. It didn't take long for the guilt and pain to return in a rush. He pulled her against him so she wouldn't see the hurt in his eyes.

What had he done? This was not at all what he'd planned for. He'd wanted the act to be cool and devoid of tender feelings. It had been anything but that.

Worse, all he could think of as he lay next to her was, what if he'd planted a babe in her belly? Of course he was aware of the possibility. It was the reason for the act in the first place. But he worried what would happen if Dorie had a child. It was unfair that he wasn't able to love Dorie the way she deserved; he wouldn't be able to stand it if he disappointed an innocent child as well.

He took a shaky breath and forced himself to calm down. He would decide how to handle the situation if it came to that. For now, he wanted to know more about the woman in his arms.

"Will you tell me why you chose not to speak?"

...

Despite Dorie's exhaustion, she felt something stir in her core. How could she still want Bryce after all they'd done already? It was probably the way he looked at her while tracing his fingers down her arm. So...meltingly open and warm.

Her cheeks heated from the memories as she cleared her throat to answer his question.

It felt strange to speak so openly. She'd used her voice over the years, but never in front of anyone. Except her dog.

She didn't want her husband to know what she'd done. She didn't want him to hate her. But she was tired of carrying around this terrible secret. The weight of her guilt labored every breath she took. It was time to confess.

"The last time I spoke, I killed my mother," she said quietly.

As expected, his face showed his shock and confusion.

She swallowed and explained. "I was nine when I overheard my mother and my aunt—her sister—talking one day. I'd been playing under a shrub and they didn't know I was there. My aunt told my mother she could no longer send letters for her. That the affair had gone on long enough, and that nothing was ever to come of it. Of course, I had no idea what they were speaking about. But then my mother pointed toward the castle. And she said, aye, something *had* come of it. *Me*."

Bryce sat up, looking at her more intently, but didn't interrupt.

She couldn't stop now. She had to get it out. She'd had it all bottled up inside of her for too long. She brushed tears aside and pressed on. "My aunt told my mother that it didn't matter that I was Captain Dorien Sutherland's daughter. No one could ever know. And there was no use in staying in contact with the man. He lived in London and was to marry another woman. My mother began to weep then, and even as a child I knew it was because she was brokenhearted."

Bryce didn't touch her; he simply sat there, silently listening.

She'd reached the hard part of the story. She looked him in the eyes and went on. "Later that same day my father—the McCurdy laird—scolded me. He took away my doll, and I was very upset with him." As an adult she saw that punishment as nothing compared with what came later. "I opened my mouth and words flew out. Angry words."

She twisted her fingers together, remembering the rage she'd felt.

"Go on," Bryce urged quietly.

"I told him he wasn't my father," she blurted out. "I told him my real father was a brave captain and that my mother loved him and didn't love the laird. I kept talking, spewing fantastical stories, as children often do. I told him my mother and I were going to move to London to be with my real father, and that he would buy me new dolls and never scold me."

Bryce gazed at her with an expression torn between sympathy and horror.

She took in a deep breath, preparing herself for the final part of the awful tale.

"The laird was enraged. He hauled me up by the arm and dragged me to my room, tossing me roughly to the floor and locking me inside. I hammered my fists on the door, demanding to be let out. I only stopped when I heard my mother's screams."

Bryce reached for her, but she shook her head as tears pooled in her eyes and leaked out.

"Her cries went on for hours. It grew dark, and eventually they fell silent. The next morning, a maid came in to bring me food. I asked about my mother, and she told me she'd had an accident and had died."

"It was no accident," Bryce said, his voice rough with emotion.

"Nay. The laird had killed her because of my words. That's when I vowed never to speak again. I wouldn't risk saying something that could cause anyone pain or death ever again."

Bryce brushed a finger across her cheek, wiping away the tears. "You were just a child. You didn't know what you were saying. Or how he would respond. It wasn't your fault."

She appreciated his words, but she knew the truth of it. She'd spilled a secret that wasn't hers to tell. She'd released a truth that never should have been told.

Her aunt had been wrong. The truth of who her father was *had* mattered.

It had mattered a great deal.

...

Bryce watched his wife as she wept bitterly over her part in her mother's death. He knew well the weight of guilt, how exhausting it was to carry day after day. He also knew that the words of friends and family did nothing to ease it. He'd been told many times it wasn't his fault that Maggie and Isabel had died. He was away doing his duty. They would have died even if he'd been there. And he might have died as well.

It didn't matter. It made no difference if the words they spoke made sense. In his heart, he was to blame. He might have been able to do something if he'd been there. Even if only to make sure they hadn't died alone and frightened.

He didn't even know which of them had passed first. Had wee Isabel been abandoned and afraid, alone with her mother's lifeless body? How many days had it taken?

He shook the thoughts away, knowing he'd never have answers, no matter how many sleepless nights he pondered their demise. He would always wonder if they'd hated him and blamed him in their final moments.

He held Dorie close and let her cry. It was the only thing he could think to do.

He found it strange that some words held so much power—like the ones she'd spoken in anger to the man she'd thought was her father—while other words were meaningless. Like offering absolution to someone who vowed never to forgive him- or herself.

"I understand," he said, knowing it was naught but more meaningless noise escaping his lips. He couldn't understand her pain any more than she could understand his.

But perhaps that was what understanding was truly about. Knowing you couldn't possibly know the other person's sorrows, and yet feeling for them deeply.

"It is over and done," he said. "There's nothing you can do for your mother now by looking back and blaming yourself for her death. Would your mother have wanted you to carry this grief and guilt for years, or would she have demanded you let it go and be happy?" he asked.

A question he dared not think about too closely.

He wouldn't ponder how much Maggie would have hated the way he still mourned for her. She would have snapped at him in irritation and told him to stop moping about.

"When I was a child locked in my room, I wished my real father would come to take me away," she said in a shaky voice. "But I secretly feared it as well. Because when he found out what I'd done, he'd surely punish me even worse than Dougal McCurdy."

"I was a father, and I can tell ye there is nothing I wouldn't have forgiven my Isabel for. It's just the way of fathers."

"Is it the way of husbands and wives to forgive each other?" she asked softly.

At first he thought she wanted him to forgive her for something, but then he realized she was speaking of Maggie and how his first wife would have forgiven him for leaving her to face death alone.

"Aye. Sometimes," he said with a sigh. "But not always."

Some things were unforgivable.

...

As she had the day before and the day before that, Dorie sneaked out through the bailey gate while Bryce worked with his men in the bailey.

He'd asked her to stay inside the castle walls, but her dog was too large now to be content with that small area. He loved to run in the fields and hunt along the edge of the forest.

And she liked to visit Cam and Mari at their new house. It was still being constructed, but one wing was complete and they were able to live there. It made Dorie feel better to help Mari with curtains for her home after her friend had been so kind to take time to help with Dorie's gowns.

It was no coincidence that Dorie timed her walks for when the women convened in the kitchen. Their lurid discussions had given her thoughts that frustrated her. They spoke of things she wished to do and feel with Bryce. But unfortunately, after their one splendid night of making love, he remained distant. Despite lying next to her each night, he hadn't touched her again.

She thought he felt the same tension and longing she felt, but they didn't talk of it. In fact, he hardly talked to her at all. He'd claimed what had happened to her mother was not her fault, but did he secretly despise her for causing it nonetheless?

Or mayhap he simply felt guilty over what they'd done. He still loved his first wife, and he probably thought making love with Dorie was wrong. But she had never felt so right in all her days.

The tension between them continued to grow night after night until Dorie thought she might explode.

Her only solace was being able to press up against him once he fell asleep. She enjoyed touching him until he pulled away in the mornings to go train with his men.

Slipping out through the gate today, she let out a breath and raised her face to the morning sun as Rascal tore off to expend his energy. She wished she could do the same—run across the meadow and plunge into the cool stream. Maybe it would help.

She had almost worked up to giving it a try when she heard a *whoosh* and was knocked to the ground. She found herself staring up at the sun again, only this time her view was obscured by a grouping of feathers at the end of an arrow that was sticking out of her chest. She choked in terror as fire burned through her body and darkness descended.

She woke in flashes, unable to move but able to hear.

A shadow fell over her as she gasped in shallow breaths. "She's done for," a familiar voice said. *Wallace.* "Finish her off."

"I thought it was supposed to look like an accident," Desmond complained.

"We haven't had luck with that. We'll just tell my father they killed her. We'll not need to worry any longer about this truce."

"Maybe if you'd just told the laird what you'd arranged, he would have gone along with it."

"Then I would have had to give him the money the MacKinlay paid me."

"You could have left that part out."

"It would have come up eventually, you lout. Now cut her throat, and let's go."

Oh, God.

She tensed, expecting more pain and a terrible death. Instead, the sound of growling filled her ears, turning into a buzzing sound.

Pain, intense and overwhelming, brought her abruptly back to harsh reality. She wasn't dead, but from the sound of her own screaming it was clear that she wished for it intensely.

"Be careful with her," a woman's anxious voice said in a cultured accent. *Mari.* "We need to get her back to the house. Send for Abagail and Kenna. I'll need their help to remove the arrow. Be still, Dorie. You're safe now."

"Angus, bring the dog and send for Bryce," Cam ordered.

Dorie whimpered and reached out, hitting a wall of muscled chest. "Shhh. Be still, lass," she was told again before the voices around her faded.

This time she wasn't able to bring them back into focus.

Chapter Fourteen

Bryce pushed the horses to go faster and only slowed when Kenna and Abagail nearly flew out of the wagon. It wouldn't do Dorie any good if he arrived at Cam's house alone. He was not a healer. He needed the women with him if there was to be any chance of saving his wife.

Angus said she'd been shot with an arrow. In the chest. Such a wound sounded fatal. Even now he could be too late.

"I don't know why she left the castle. I told her to stay inside," he complained, allowing his anger to fend off the worry and pain.

"Did you tell her *why* you wished her to stay put?" Kenna asked.

"Nay. I'm her husband. I don't need to explain myself to my wife."

Kenna harrumphed. "Strange, I haven't seen you act like a husband to the lass."

"I've taken her to my bed." He didn't know why he'd blurted that out. It was a slippery defense to be sure.

"Oh! Well, then. In that case, I'm surprised she wasn't

following at your heels begging for more of your attentions." Kenna rolled her eyes as she clenched her fingers around the seat.

Ignoring her taunts, he gritted his teeth. "She's supposed to obey me."

Kenna laughed. "Men think wives must obey them, but if you truly want us to listen, you need to tell us why you insist on this or that. Ordering us about with no good reason won't do it."

"That doesn't help me now." He assisted the two women down when they arrived in front of Cam and Mari's half-finished manor house. "Please hurry."

Before his request was out, Mari appeared at the door, covered in blood.

"Dear God," Bryce choked out.

Abagail, Kenna, and Mari had already surrounded his wife when Bryce woodenly strode into the room. He couldn't see Dorie past the flurry of females tending her, but he saw a pale hand hanging over the edge of the table, blood dripping from her fingertips.

He couldn't breathe.

He was going to lose her, and he'd not had the chance to make things right. He knew how fickle life could be. He knew nothing was promised, yet he'd treated her as if she hadn't mattered.

"Drink this," Cam said. Bryce hadn't noticed the man standing next to him but reached for the offered cup. Cam's hands and clothes were also stained with blood.

Bryce wasn't able to drink. He knew he'd not be able to swallow past the lump in his throat.

"The arrow is stuck in her breastbone. It didn't go into her heart. She's not choking up blood, though her breathing is raspy. If they can get the bleeding stopped and remove the arrow, she'll have a chance."

A chance.

It wasn't enough, but it was all he had to hold on to. He would grasp any hope with both hands.

The sound of a low growl had him turning to look behind him. Rascal was laid out on the floor. Angus the stable hand was cleaning a wound while a young boy held the dog's thrashing head.

"Hold him tight. I don't want him to bite me," Angus ordered.

"The beast saved her life," Cam explained. "Tore the throat out of one of the attackers. The older cousin, from the looks of him. From the trail leading away, the other one was sent off unhappy. Rascal made it here to me and led us to Dorie before he finally collapsed."

Anger and gratitude welled up in Bryce in equal measure. "Will he live?" He would treat the beast like a king from now on for saving her life.

"Most likely. He'd be better if he didn't keep trying to get up to go to her."

Bryce went over to the dog and knelt down. "Shhh. Settle yourself. There's a good lad." He scratched the dog behind the ear, and the mutt relaxed a bit. "Thank you for looking after her. I've got it now. You rest." With a pat, he stood to go see his wife. He would hold her good hand and stand next to her through whatever came next.

He wouldn't stand off to the side like a coward.

· · ·

Dorie noticed the chill first. She wanted to get another blanket or light a fire, but she was too exhausted to move. The only warmth resided in one of her hands.

She focused on that heat, hoping it would spread to the rest of her body. She felt a pulse against her palm that didn't match her own. Her own heartbeat pounded loudly in her temples. She tried to slow it to match the one in her hand.

Fingers twitched against hers and visions of Bryce flitted through her groggy thoughts. Bryce kissing her, holding her. She held on to that thought tightly. It was a nice memory.

Bryce scowling. That memory wasn't so great, so she skipped to the next. Bryce sleeping next to her, lying on top of her. In her. She remembered the heat of his body pressed against hers and wished he'd offer his heat to her now.

"Shhh," Bryce murmured from somewhere close by. "Rest now."

But she couldn't rest. Not without knowing if her dog was well. Not without warning Bryce that McCurdys had attacked her and might harm him. Not without telling him she was sorry for sneaking out of the castle.

"Shhh," he urged. "Everything is fine. Rascal is sleeping at the foot of your bed. He's a bit ruffled but he'll mend. We're both keeping watch. You're safe now. We won't let the McCurdys get to you."

She thought maybe she had actually spoken her worries out loud, but she didn't think so. And there was still one concern he hadn't addressed.

Trying her best, she squeezed his hand. Though it felt as if she'd hardly made an impression, she felt the warm wetness of a kiss against the back of her hand.

"I'm sorry, I failed ye," he said quietly. "I should have told you of the danger. I should have explained why I wanted you to stay within the castle walls instead of barking orders at you and expecting you to obey. I've given you no reason to do what I say. Please forgive me."

Since she couldn't get her throat and lips to work, she relied on her only method of communication and squeezed his hand again.

"They were able to get the arrow out without causing

more damage, but you've lost a lot of blood. Abagail says it's why you're shivering. I was concerned of fever, but your skin is much too cool for a fever."

He said more, but now that she knew everything was well, she was able to focus on the sound of his voice rather than the words, and she slipped into a comfortable sleep.

Bryce was here.

Everything would be fine.

...

It was an excruciating three days before Dorie finally opened her eyes and looked at Bryce. *Thank God*, he thought. *At last!* He smiled at her. But it didn't help.

She gasped in fear and tried to back away, wincing when the action pulled at her wound.

"It's me. Bryce," he assured her. "You're safe, lass."

She blinked and he figured he understood her concern. No doubt he was a dismal sight. He'd rarely left her side since arriving at Cam's house. He'd not taken time to bathe or shave. He'd only changed clothes because his cousins and their wives forced him to out of shame.

They brought him food and ale.

"It's so nice to see your beautiful eyes open again," he told her, and leaned over to kiss her forehead. When he pulled away she smiled up at him. "Can you swallow some broth? It will be nice to have your assistance rather than pouring it down your throat and making a mess of it."

She nodded, and he helped raise her head, bringing the cup to her lips. When she emptied the cup, he settled her back against the pillow, relief pouring through him. Dorie had been weak from losing so much blood, so he knew how much she needed rest and nourishment.

He'd practically taken over Cam and Mari's house,

having had their bed brought down to the front room for Dorie. No one had fought him on any of his requests. They'd even allowed the dog in the bed. Bryce would never be able to thank them enough. Not Cam or Mari, nor Rascal.

"Thank you," she whispered.

He thought he might break into tears at the sound of her raspy voice. "Think nothing of it. Go back to sleep so you can heal. As soon as you're able to be moved, I'll take you home," he promised, though he didn't think she cared much at the moment. A bed was a bed.

He kissed her hand as he'd done hundreds of times in the past days. It had been the only way to reach her. To let her know he was there with her. That he hadn't left.

"Rest now," he said.

She nodded and mumbled something. He only made out the word *whiskers*.

"I'll take care of it." He laughed and caught himself. He rarely laughed.

Occasionally one of the children would earn a chuckle from him, but laughing and smiling was not something he did freely. Except when his wife was close by, apparently.

"How is she?" Lach asked him. Kenna had stopped by to check on Dorie earlier but had been called away when Mari complained of a backache.

"She doesn't like my beard," Bryce muttered.

"How can ye tell?"

Bryce still hadn't told the others his wife could speak. It was her secret to share, and he'd wait until she was ready. He was so glad she would live to have the chance.

"I just know," he answered Lach's question.

"Aye. Kenna and I are able to speak without words. Just a look or a touch and we know what the other is thinking. It's a blessing most days." Lach smiled but rubbed his chin. "I believe we're going to be needed to help Cam soon, though."

"Help Cam?" Bryce looked down at Dorie. There was no way he'd leave her side. He'd already left one wife to waste away. He'd stay right where he was and see this one back to health. Beard and stench be damned.

"Mari has said her back pains her."

"And? It's no wonder. She's carrying around a— Ah." Bryce finally understood what Lach was saying. "Are you an expert on birthing babes, cousin?"

"We've three, and one is on the way." He froze for a moment. "I'll thank you to forget that last part until Kenna tells her sister. She's waiting until after Mari delivers."

Bryce grinned. "I swear, I'll be the most surprised."

Lach frowned, probably remembering how bad Bryce was at acting.

Looking down at his sleeping wife, he thought of her growing large with his child, the glow of motherhood on her cheeks pulled up in a constant smile. He also allowed a moment to think of her breasts, larger and filling his palms as he caressed them.

Christ. He needed to get a hold of himself. He'd sworn not to touch her again. He'd given in to his lust once. He couldn't do it ever again. It was too great a risk. He might keep his broken heart safe from his wife, but he'd never be able to shut out a child.

She'd nearly died this week, and he knew he'd already become more attached to her than he'd planned. He needed to be careful and guard what was left of his heart before it was too late.

...

Dorie woke to find a clean-shaven Bryce sleeping on a chair near the bed where she lay. His fingers were twined loosely through hers and she smiled at the warmth, remembering it had been her beacon when she'd been so cold.

It was dark, the house quiet. When she shifted to stretch, she was reminded of the wound in her chest. A bandage held her arm firmly to her side.

Unfortunately, she couldn't wait. She needed to get up now or embarrass herself. That thought made her wonder how she'd managed the last few days. It was clear by the stiffness in her muscles that she'd been in bed a long time.

Deciding not to think of what might have happened while she was unconscious, she focused on what needed to happen now. Careful not to wake her sleeping husband, she edged up the bandage enough that she could move her arm slightly. Testing it, she found it wasn't too painful…until she leaned on it.

Letting her free hand slip out of Bryce's, she waited a beat to make sure she hadn't woken him, then used it to lever herself up to a sitting position. She threw her legs over the side of the bed and gave herself a moment for her vision to clear and her breathing to catch up.

Rascal lifted his head and whined.

"Shhh," she commanded as Bryce shifted but didn't wake.

When she stood, her dog dragged himself slowly from the bed to come stand in front of her. She bent to check him over, patting his head. "Come along then if you must protect me," she whispered. "But I must go out."

She paused after opening the door. Fortunately the brand new hinges on the door were quiet. She was able to make her way down the steps and out into the trees to relieve herself. Her dog made use of the next tree over to do the same.

She didn't make it back to the house before Bryce was outside calling her name.

"What are you doing? You're not supposed to be out of bed," he scolded, coming to help her back into the house.

While she didn't really need help walking, she allowed him to assist her since it meant he had to touch her and stand close.

"Thank you," she offered when he tucked her back in bed.

"If you need anything, let me know. I'll take care of you." He ran a hand through her hair and leaned in to press a kiss to her temple.

She'd seen Lachlan and Cameron do the same with their wives. A simple touch of lips to a fairly innocuous part of the body. But the way it made her feel was something else. As if she was treasured and cared for. His green eyes held worry, but the usual irritation in them was gone.

While she hoped she'd never be shot again, she had to admit there were some advantages.

As she settled back in bed, she thought of the last time she'd been able to walk around. Before she was shot by an arrow.

"It was the McCurdys," she whispered.

"Aye. I know." Earlier he had apologized for not telling her of the danger she was in. She recalled his pained words.

"Wallace," she stated with a grimace.

Bryce nodded as if he wasn't surprised. "I'm sorry. It must be hell to know your own brother tried to kill you."

She shrugged and regretted it instantly. She hissed but relaxed a bit as the pain lessened. At least the sting in her chest did. The ache in her heart remained.

"He's not really my brother." She'd known since she was nine that Wallace was not blood. His mother had died when he was young, and they didn't truly share a father.

When she was seven and Wallace sixteen, she'd followed him around, and he hadn't minded. He'd shown her how to stand up in the cold surf and find little creatures in the rocks on the beach.

He'd been her hero…right up until she was locked away. He'd never even tried to save her.

She frowned as she recalled something they'd said after shooting her. "Desmond said they would tell their laird the MacKinlays killed me."

"Rascal took care of Desmond. He's gone," Bryce informed her as he looked down at the dog.

She patted Rascal's head. "Thank ye, friend."

"I'm glad he was there." Bryce cleared his throat and tilted his head. "From what you heard, it sounds like the laird didn't know of the arrangement Wallace had made with Lachlan regarding our marriage."

She nodded. "That's why they're trying to find a way out of it. So Wallace can keep the money Lachlan paid him."

"Then it wasn't the laird who ordered them to hurt ye. Perhaps your father doesn't want you harmed." He gave her an encouraging look.

"I'm not sure why the laird would care. I've not seen him since he left me in my chamber all those years ago. Besides, it doesn't matter. They must be stopped from coming back and hurting someone else," she whispered.

The sinister smile that pulled up on Bryce's face should have worried her. It was clear he was eager to draw blood. But since they shared a common enemy, she smiled with him as he leaned closer and kissed her forehead.

"No one harms what's mine and lives."

Her eyes widened, not because of the threat evident in his tone, but the way he'd claimed her as his.

She was his.

Chapter Fifteen

Bryce cared.

He cared about his cousins who had grown up with him and stood beside him in battle. He cared about Kenna and Mari. He cared about their children. Including little—or not so little—Aiden who had come into the world earlier that morning.

But he also cared for Dorie.

Despite his desperate attempt to keep her at a distance and not let her into his heart, he cared about her. The lass made it impossible not to, with her quick smile and warm eyes. The more he'd watched her sleep, the more she'd called to him.

He could pretend he cared about her as he would any other clansman who had been injured by an enemy, but he didn't like to lie to himself. She was his, and he protected what was his. It was as simple as that.

Except, it wasn't just that he cared. He was also attracted to her and had become more so the longer he was with her. He remembered the feeling of those long legs wrapped around him and twitched at the memory of her heat and the sounds she'd made.

The way she'd said his name in that rough, unused voice.

He wanted his wife in his bed.

When she was deemed well enough to be moved—a week after being shot—Cameron offered to drive her up to the castle in a wagon. Worried the bouncing might cause her pain, Bryce had offered to carry her instead.

Cam smiled knowingly, as if he'd known Bryce had come up with his plan as an excuse to hold her close. No doubt the man had come up with his fair share of plans to keep his wife close as well.

In the end it hadn't mattered. Dorie had wanted to walk. Rascal was also on the mend and took his place by her side as they started off, staying closer than usual.

"I was shot in the chest. My legs are perfectly fine," she'd pointed out when Bryce complained. He couldn't argue that her legs were anything less than fine. He'd still insisted on supporting her with an arm around her waist the whole way to their room in the castle.

That was nine days ago, and he was still looking for reasons to touch and kiss her. He hadn't kissed her mouth, but he'd pressed his lips other places to the point it was now second nature. Her hair, her temples, her hands, even her neck once.

He'd put off his trip to the Campbells once again, so he could stay with her. Now that she was well, he didn't want to leave. And not just because he wasn't looking forward to seeing his father again.

She had started talking with him while they were alone but remained silent around others. He guarded her secret, knowing she would speak when she was ready. For now it was something to be shared just between them, and he found he liked that more than he should.

It was a part of her that was only for him.

The best thing by far—the thing that proved his attraction—was the pleasure he felt each night when he slid into bed behind her and pulled her body against his chest. It had started as a way to ensure she didn't roll over and re-injure her wound. But now there was no worry. Other than a bit of stiffness, she was healed enough to move around. Her skin had healed into a tight pink scar.

Neither of them mentioned that fact during the nights as he continued to hold her, even though both of them knew it wasn't necessary. At least it wasn't necessary for healing purposes.

In truth, Bryce thought he might die if he had to let her go.

...

Dorie shifted uncomfortably in bed. While her wound had healed, she was still in pain each night when Bryce pulled her close. Not from the injury, but from the deep ache in her core from wanting him so much. She'd waited as long as she could stand it. She couldn't take any more.

Shifting away, she rolled onto her back and turned her head to look at his face. The moonlight spilled through the window, lighting up their small room so she could see him clearly. His eyes, though cast in shadow, were open and his gaze was on her.

"What's the matter?" he whispered.

She didn't answer right away as she gathered the courage needed to take the next step.

Words had been a stranger to her for so long, she found they eluded her now. Instead, she rested her hand on his cheek and leaned forward to press her lips to his.

Like a spark to tinder, her husband caught fire. His lips

moved against hers; his tongue invaded her mouth with a moan. She wound her leg around his hip and used her thigh to draw him closer to where she needed him most. His hand kneaded her breast as his breath quickened.

"Please," she begged when his hand moved lower across her arse to caress the heat between her legs.

"Are you sure you've healed enough?"

"I need you," was her only answer. Even if she wasn't healed enough for such activity, she didn't care. Nothing was more important than having Bryce inside her. "Please."

"God, Dorie. I want you so badly I'm not sure I'll last but a minute."

She wasn't sure she needed that long, but instead of joining with her, he continued to rub his fingers over that place where she wanted him. He pushed one of his long fingers inside her, and she moaned in pleasure. While it wasn't enough to ease the ache, she moved against him.

A second finger filled her, and when he curved them slightly to hit some divine place inside her, she cried out as her body clenched desperately around him.

He quieted her with his mouth as she calmed afterward. Her body relaxed part by part, and she could have easily fallen to sleep if not for Bryce's kisses moving down her neck to her chest.

He placed a soft kiss to the scar above her breast. "I'm so glad you're still here with me," he whispered so softly she wasn't sure he'd actually spoken.

He dipped his head to take her nipple into his mouth. Too soon, he released it, causing a shiver when the chilled air touched her damp skin.

He moved lower and lower, under the covers so she stayed in the comfort of the warm bedding. It meant she wasn't able to see him, and probably that he couldn't see. When his lips settled on the place where his fingers had just been, she thought it was by accident...until he moaned and continued with purpose.

She recalled hearing about this. She'd thought she'd never be so bold as to allow such a thing, but here she was with her fingers clenched in her husband's hair, holding him in place while she moved against his ministrations.

How strange life was. The way it changed. The way a person could learn to accept something one never thought possible. Long for it, even.

When he moved back up her body, she wiggled with excitement. She knew what would happen next and was eager for him to join his body with hers. She couldn't keep her hips still as he placed kisses up her body.

Soon he was positioned between her thighs and his lips had found hers. Instead of thrusting in quickly as she'd expected, he entered her with slow, exquisite pleasure.

"Bryce," she called out.

"I like hearing my name on your lips," he said next to her ear, his hot breath adding to the heat searing her body with every touch.

"Faster," she begged, allowing instincts to guide her in what she needed.

"Faster means it will be over too soon."

She understood, and a grin came to her face.

"Ah, I see you're embracing your powers, witch." A smile pulled at his lips.

She knew from his laughter he was teasing her, so she teased him back by nipping the skin below his ear.

She wasn't prepared for his reaction, which was a deeper thrust followed immediately by another. She'd lost count when she felt the tension build to overflowing. She screamed in pleasure at the same time fire shot into her core. A moment later Bryce fell slack next to her, panting and smiling.

Life was indeed full of changes.

...

Bryce needed to leave. Not just because he'd promised to go to the Campbells to ask for men, but because he was in danger of more than just caring for his wife. He desperately needed to put distance between them, to have time to regain control over the situation, but he couldn't make himself go.

She was well now, but he used her injury as an excuse to keep her in bed for a few more days. He wanted her touch, her body, her cries in the darkness. A trip through the Highlands in late November was less than appealing compared to the lure of Dorie's warmth.

He snuggled under their bedding, pulling her naked body next to his to share the heat between them. A fire in the hearth took the chill from the room, but their cozy fortress was too tempting to abandon, even though he'd told his men to be ready for drills this morning.

He groaned when someone pounded on the door. "Bryce? Are you well?" Liam asked, concern in his low voice.

"Aye. I'll be there shortly."

"You've missed the morning meal," the lad informed him.

Bryce groaned, both for having to leave his wife's embrace as well as missing the meal. After making love to Dorie most of the night, he was famished.

"I'll be there shortly," he repeated as Dorie muttered her objections.

"Stay," she said in a sleepy voice.

"God, woman. You cannot say such things. I can't resist you. I think maybe you truly are a witch. You've cast a spell over me. I can't get enough of you." He kissed her smiling lips and pulled away before it was too late.

After dressing as quickly as possible, he ran a finger down her cheek and kissed her forehead. "Sleep well, angel," he whispered and left while he still could. When he opened the door, the dog pushed past him and took his place in the bed next to her. "Lucky bastard."

It was a testament to his need that he found himself slightly jealous of a dog. He took a moment to flirt with the women in the kitchen until they offered him a meat pie, and then headed to the bailey to train with his men.

The constant drills combined with carrying rocks for Cam's new home had turned his men into strong, formidable warriors. While they were fierce, Bryce knew they were still outnumbered. It didn't matter how well a man could fight if there were enemies on all sides.

He would need to leave to meet with the Campbells soon, which meant leaving Dorie.

Even now he fought as hard with Liam as he fought thoughts of her naked body, her arms reaching for him.

"Ach!" He winced and drew his hand against his chest as blood welled along his arm.

"Sorry. I thought you were ready for that move," Liam said with wide eyes.

"I wasn't paying attention. My mind was elsewhere."

Liam chuckled. "I think I can guess."

Bryce was about to wipe the smile off the lad's face when the man on the gate yelled out, "Rider!"

Everyone stepped back, forming a line, but the gate didn't go up. Bryce ran up the steps to take a look for himself. By that time the single rider had come close enough that Bryce could see he was wearing McCurdy plaid.

The young McCurdy, Rory, if Bryce remembered correctly from the day of his wedding, held up a piece of paper. "I've a message for your laird," he said.

Bryce could only imagine what bad news awaited them next.

...

Dorie put the finishing stitches on a tiny shirt for baby Aiden in the solar and smiled down at her work. It was nice to sit with Kenna and Mari and do something useful again.

There were many times she felt the urge to speak to them, to share something or ask a question. But she remained silent and felt like a fraud. She'd had good reason for not speaking when she was younger. As an adult living away from the McCurdys, she knew there was no danger in thanking her friends for saving her life and taking care of her. Or for doting over the new babe who slept in his mother's arms.

The laird burst into the solar with a string of curses trailing behind.

"The children," Kenna reminded him as two sets of wide blue eyes stared at their father in surprise. Lizzy began to cry and Mari frowned at her brother-in-law before pulling her daughter up into her lap with the babe.

Dorie had not seen Lachlan lose his temper in the whole time she'd been at Dunardry. She could see from everyone's surprise it didn't happen often. Dorie tried to make herself smaller in case his anger was directed at her.

"Forgive me, I've just gotten word from the McCurdy." He held up a missive.

"What has happened?" Kenna asked.

"It has been more than two months since Dorie and Bryce wed, and we still hadn't received word on a ship available to take goods to trade. I wrote to inquire on the delay and the bastard returned this." He shook the paper again. "The blighter has gone back on his word. Nay, he says he never gave it in the first place."

Kenna gasped and took the paper from her husband's fist. Cam and Bryce stepped into the room, the three large men filling it to capacity.

"What is it that has you so angry?" Cam asked, taking Lizzy to calm her.

Kenna's eyes flashed back and forth as she read the document. She looked up. "He says the wedding was not a true alliance because Wallace did it without his knowledge, and because Dorie is not even his daughter."

All eyes turned to Dorie. Some with confusion, some with worry. Bryce's were filled with compassion, for he knew the truth.

"His word is not worth the air he uses to speak it," Cam said.

"'Tis not a lie," Bryce said quietly, his gaze capturing hers. "I think it's time you told them."

She nodded. It was time they all knew the truth. Time they realized exactly who they'd let join their clan. She was no more than a murdering bastard.

Cam scolded his cousin, smacking Bryce in the shoulder. "Are ye daft? You know she canna tell us anything."

Bryce's gaze didn't move from her. Instead he gave her an encouraging nod and came to kneel next to her. He took her hand, placing a kiss to her palm. "It's time."

She nodded.

Turning toward the group, she spoke to them aloud for the first time. "I'm sorry," she said first, as it was the most important.

Mari gasped and Lach whispered a curse—though Dorie heard it easily enough in the silence that followed her first words to them.

Taking a deep breath, she launched into her story and didn't stop until she reached the end, revealing how her words had caused her mother's death and that she'd been secluded in silence until her marriage to Bryce.

"It's true I'm not the laird's daughter. I didn't mean to deceive you. I had no idea he planned to use this knowledge to get out of his agreement. In truth, I wasn't even aware of the agreement."

"Of course you didn't mislead anyone on purpose. No one blames you." Kenna came to her side and wrapped her arm around Dorie's shoulders. "Though you could have told me you can talk," she added in a whisper.

"My sister is not one for secrets," Mari said with a laugh. "Unless she's on the side that's keeping them."

Dorie looked up at the laird. "I should have spoken sooner, but I was afraid you'd turn me out. And I didn't want to have to go back there."

"I wouldn't have allowed it," Bryce said sharply.

"Oh? *You* wouldn't have allowed it?" Lachlan tilted his head.

"No. I wouldn't have." Bryce stared at his cousin in a silent challenge.

Dorie didn't want to be a point of contention between them and quickly said, "I'm afraid I'm just the bastard daughter of a certain Captain Dorien Sutherland, for whom I was named." She hung her head and prayed they wouldn't run her out of the castle. This was the first place she'd felt at home since her mother died. If only she'd remained silent back then, perhaps her mother would still be alive. And the MacKinlays would have their alliance.

A hush followed her confession for only a few seconds. Marian was the first to speak. "My God," she said with a frown.

Dorie bit her lip. Of anyone, she had thought the kindhearted Marian would be most accepting of her situation. After all, she'd murdered a duke with her own hands.

Cam went to his wife. "It's fine, love. We'll find another way."

"No. It's not the agreement. It's— I've met Captain Dorien Sutherland." She looked at Dorie and then broke into a smile. "I know your father."

Chapter Sixteen

Bryce was glad to be standing close to Dorie, for she looked like she might fall over at Mari's announcement. "You know him?" he asked.

"I shouldn't say I *know* him, exactly. But we've met. I was introduced to him and his wife when I lived in London."

"What… What is he like?" Dorie asked timidly.

"He's no longer a captain, for one thing. He's a viscount. Viscount Rutherford. If I recall, he was a second or third son, but the elder brothers passed quite a while ago, so he's had the title for some time now."

"My father is a viscount?" Dorie's voice cracked, and she swayed.

Bryce wrapped an arm around her waist, then guided her back to her seat and settled her next to Marian.

"Yes." Mari tilted her head to the side, studying Dorie. "You look like him. Now that I know it, I see it clear as day. You have the same coloring. Same eyes."

Dorie clenched her hands together in front of her chest. "What is he like?" she repeated. "Is he kind or is he…like the

McCurdy?"

Mari's brows creased as she shook her head. "I've only met him briefly, but he seemed a nice enough man." She rested her index finger along her chin. "We could write to him if you wish."

"Oh, yes. Please."

Bryce cut in then. "I don't think that's a good idea." He crossed his arms.

All eyes in the room landed on him as they waited for him to explain himself. It took a moment for him to figure out why he was opposed to the notion. He was as surprised as everyone else when he answered. "He may not acknowledge you, no matter how much you look alike. I'll not have you reach out just to be brushed aside. It's not worth it. You've been through enough already."

She placed her hand on his and squeezed. "I haven't been accepted by the man I called father for most of my life, so if this man doesn't want to acknowledge me, I'll not be any worse off."

"I don't want to see you hurt," he said quietly, despite the other people in the room.

"But I will always wonder." She gave him a look of longing, and he knew he couldn't forbid her anything.

He understood why she would be willing to take a risk for a connection. He would want the same thing if he found himself in a similar situation. And someone like Dorie, who had spent years hoping for someone to love her, would not be stopped. Besides, he wasn't an overbearing arse who would keep a woman from finding her real father.

He gave a nod—not that she actually required his approval.

"Excellent," Mari said with a bright smile. "We'll write to him after supper."

...

Dorie could barely sit still through the evening meal. She was so excited she only managed to eat a few bites.

Bryce spared her an indulgent smile when they were finished eating and she jumped up to head to the solar that had been turned into a nursery. Would she and Bryce have a child here soon? She loved the way the sisters visited while the children played together. They were there when disputes broke out, and to rock the little ones to sleep for their naps. Since there were now more children than mothers, Dorie was happy to lend her arms where needed. But today she silently wished the children would cooperate with bedtime.

It seemed to take forever for Mari to have a moment to collect the things needed to send a letter to Dorie's father. She tried her best to be patient since her friend had given birth to a rather large baby recently, but still wished she'd hurry. Dorie had so many questions, and so much to say to her father.

"What should we write?" Mari asked, quill poised at the paper.

All the words and questions seemed to flit right out of Dorie's head as doubt crept in. What if Bryce was right and her father didn't want to know her? What could she say to make him change his mind? She must think carefully and choose the perfect words.

It took them a few hours and many attempts to complete the letter to her father. In the end, she allowed Mari to take the lead and keep the letter to the facts instead of getting into too many details.

She hugged Mari as the letter was sealed and put aside to be sent out.

As Dorie walked to her chamber, she still couldn't imagine being related to a viscount. She was still chatting about it when she and Bryce went to bed that night.

"A viscount. Do you think he'll bother to write back? What if he has other children, and I'm just an annoyance?" She gasped. "If he has other children, then I'm a sister. By blood."

"We'll have to wait and see," Bryce said vaguely, the way he'd answered the last hundred questions she'd asked. She barely noticed when he put Rascal out of the room so they were alone.

"I suppose there's no harm in trying. If he's too busy, it would be understand—" Her words were cut off when Bryce's lips came down on hers. He kissed her until she moaned and rubbed against him, her heart pounding. He nipped at her bottom lip and pulled away to smile down at her.

"Enough talking about the man. He'll either write you back or he won't. For now, I will do my best to distract you."

She laughed as he lowered his head to kiss her jaw and then her neck. He continued lower, as he pulled down her shift, exposing her breasts. He sucked in a nipple and ran his tongue over her tightened flesh while his fingers found their way to that special place just for him.

Soon she felt the familiar tension building in her core. It wouldn't take much to push her over into that place where she ceased to exist. Where there was only pleasure and light.

Before she reached that place, he stopped. When she groaned her disappointment, the wretch chuckled.

"Steady, lass, I'll see you're taken care of, but we have all night."

She relaxed at the truth of his words. Many nights one of them would wake and reach for the other. They would join in the darkness quietly. Taking and sharing when needed.

He rolled on his back, taking her with him, and she smiled down into his cocky grin. At first she thought it a great honor to be given the position of power, but when Bryce crossed his arms behind his head and settled in, she realized she'd been tricked.

"Ye lazy beast," she teased as she slid him inside her.

He sucked in a quick breath when she was seated, and then a devilish smile took over his face. "Aye. You've found me out. Should I apologize?" he asked while pressing up from the bed to fill her completely.

She didn't think an apology was necessary.

She rocked her body on top of his, sometimes moving quickly, sometimes moving so slowly he groaned in frustration and pushed up. In the end, when he'd finished with play, he grabbed hold of her hips and thrust into her, causing her to reach her pleasure and cry out.

She crumpled on top of him, her ear over his heart where it beat so fast she feared it might burst. "Am I a good lover?" she asked, curious to know.

He chuckled, the sound echoing through his chest to her ear. "You are better than good. You are the greatest of lovers."

The greatest? She didn't say anything as his body tensed under hers. Perhaps he had just realized what he'd said. For it sounded as if he was saying she was somehow a better lover than Maggie.

Surely that couldn't be true. No doubt Maggie was great as well. That must have been the case. It seemed as such to hear him speak of her. The way she haunted him still. Dorie didn't let that bother her. She held on to the compliment with joy in her heart.

"Thank you, Bryce. I think you're the greatest as well."

...

Had Bryce just told Dorie she was the greatest lover he'd had? He rubbed his temple as she lay sprawled across his chest in bliss, and thought over his words.

He hadn't said it exactly that way, but he understood what his words implied. He'd said Dorie was the greatest. What was worse, it was true. From a purely physical way, at least.

His heart would only ever belong to one woman, but his body stirred even now for Dorie.

For a moment he thought he'd spoken hastily because he'd not been thinking steadily, but that wasn't the case. He knew as he held her while his breathing came back to normal that what he'd said was true.

Dorie was an uninhibited and responsive lover. He'd not had a partner long enough to learn what pleased her since Maggie. So discovering Dorie's hidden pleasures excited him. She touched him where she pleased and cried out in desire when he touched her.

He refused to compare his wives. It wasn't fair to either of them and served no purpose. Dorie was the wife that was here with him now, so he would do her the honor of being with her and her alone while they were in bed together.

He kissed her hair and then her temple. She raised her head to smile at him and slid her leg over his, pressing her hips against his thigh.

"I have been blessed with a lustful wife," he uttered as his hand trailed over her back to grasp her buttock.

"And I am blessed with a dutiful husband." She giggled against his neck, the sound stirring him to action.

Over the following weeks, Bryce allowed himself to be happy. The pain of Maggie's loss was still there, strong and unrelenting, but he was able to see past it to the life he had before him.

Dorie was a kind woman, beautiful and funny. He would take her treats he wrangled from the kitchen or look for her in the hall, hoping to catch a glimpse of her smile. She was always smiling these days. And when he got her alone in their room, they came together as if they were made for each other.

He thought if he had met her first, he would have easily loved her. Occasionally he even thought he might now.

Thanks to poor weather, he wasn't able to travel to the Campbells yet, so it was an easy thing to stay inside with his wife as the snow piled up outside in the hills.

She only left the safety of the castle when she was with him. They'd seen no sign of a McCurdy on their lands. Yet he continued to use the excuse to go with her when she went to visit Mari and Cam and to exercise her giant hound. It seemed the mutt had finally stopped growing when his head reached Bryce's waist.

One afternoon when they'd left Cam and Mari's place it started snowing again. Their feet squeaked in the wet snow on the ground. Bryce swiped a snowflake from Dorie's top lip, making her laugh. He loved to hear her laugh, even now when it was muffled by the snow falling around them.

He bent to steal another snowflake from her skin, but she squealed and ran. He chased after her and fell on top of her when she tripped in a drift. Once she was thoroughly trapped, he kissed her relentlessly while she squirmed under him.

She held him back by his ears, a wide grin on her face when he finally gave up and stilled.

"Thank you for marrying me, Bryce," she said, the smile fading into seriousness.

The moment would have been perfect for him to respond in kind, but he said nothing. He was frozen, and not from the snow.

But from terror.

He was happy.

Which meant any day now, fate would come to take everything away.

...

Dorie put on her best gown and fixed her hair into a design Mari had shown her. Bryce was clean and in his best shirt and kilt. His blond hair was still damp and curling on the ends. Fortunately the new year had brought warmer temperatures, so he'd not have icicles.

"Are you sure my gift will do?" she asked as she fretted over the tied bundle.

"It's beautiful. They will love it."

She had worked hard on the embroidered pillow covering she'd made for Mari and Cam's new home. Bryce's words of praise put her mind at ease, and his following kiss had her wishing they could stay in their chamber rather than go to the other couple's new home for supper with the whole family.

Bryce helped her up on his horse and nuzzled her neck most of the way.

She'd come to love the trip between Dunardry and the manor house. Bryce was usually unable to keep his lips off her for the entire journey.

"Stop it, or I'll arrive flushed and they'll wonder what we were doing along the way."

"They won't wonder." He laughed. "But rest assured, I won't risk wrinkles to your pretty gown, though I make no promises on the way home in the privacy of the trees."

"Outside? But it's cold." Her voice squeaked in surprise.

"We'll find a place sheltered from the breeze where you can look up at the stars while I have my way with you. I'll keep you warm."

She wasn't certain he was serious, but she had to admit it did sound rather intriguing. By the time she was ready to suggest they offer their friends an excuse, they had arrived at Cam and Mari's home.

The manor house was still not finished. As grand as it was,

it would probably be years before it was completed. But the kitchen was in working order and the table was overflowing when they were welcomed inside.

The older boys were running about, laughing and squealing while wee Cameron and Lizzy sat and watched. Aiden was in his cradle by the fire, asleep.

Dorie hadn't felt like part of a family since she was a small child. The scents and warmth in this home made her want to cry with happiness.

She belonged here. She belonged with these people.

She still wondered now and then about her real family—her father, the viscount, who had yet to write her back. Though she'd tried not to get her hopes up, she couldn't deny the disappointment she felt each day when no return message arrived. Would it have taken so long to write a few lines and send it off?

Perhaps he never received her missive. Maybe she should write another, just in case. She let out a sigh and took a seat next to Bryce, determined not to let anything ruin the evening.

After everyone had finished eating, it became clear the evening wasn't just so everyone could share a meal, but to share some good news as well.

"Kenna's increasing," Lachlan said, looking at his wife with love clear in his eyes.

Mari laughed and turned to Cameron. "I told ye she was with child. You must put the children to bed tonight since you lost."

Cam glared playfully at Lach. "You couldn't have given me a hint?"

"And ruin the surprise?"

"It seems it was already ruined," Kenna said ruefully. "I guess I still can't keep anything a secret from you, sister."

"Nay. I'll ferret out the truth of it." Mari turned to Bryce and Dorie. "I expect we'll have more news of the like soon enough from you two."

Dorie swallowed and felt her face go red, while Bryce cleared his throat and said nothing. When she'd gained the courage to look at him, he was frowning as if the idea of them having children was a horrible thought.

She tried not to let it bother her but had a difficult time hiding it. It was made even more difficult when Lizzy teetered over to Dorie's feet and reached for her.

Dorie picked up the little girl as she often did when they worked in the solar. She kissed her plump cheeks and made her giggle.

At the same moment, the twins got into a scuffle over Lizzy's doll and Roddy pushed wee Douglas, knocking him off balance and making him fall. His head hit the hearth with a horrifying *thump*.

Dorie, being closest to them, handed Lizzy to Bryce and jumped up to get to Douglas. She wasn't sure what could be done, she just knew she had to help him.

When the boy didn't make a sound, she thought maybe she'd heard something else falling. But Douglas was merely drawing in enough air to let out a fierce and terrifying wail. Dorie picked him up and turned to hand him over to Kenna, who didn't look overly worried.

Kenna checked him over and kissed the knot that was already growing on his forehead. "'Tis a good thing you have a hard head like your da," she said to the boy as she soothed him with kisses and rocked him in her arms.

Bryce quickly handed Lizzy over to Cam, holding her out at arm's length as if afraid he would get something on his shirt. All the children were crying now, including wee Cameron and baby Aiden, as if in sympathy with Douglas. Though, Dorie thought maybe Lizzy was more upset over being thrust across the table at her father. Cam was frowning as he cuddled his daughter in his huge arms. But her clout hadn't needed changing, so that probably wasn't the reason Bryce didn't want to hold her.

Before Dorie had the chance to ask him what was wrong, Bryce left the table and walked out of the house.

"Maybe it would be better if you don't have children. You'd be the only one who can hold them," Cam complained, and tickled Lizzy until she stopped crying and was giggling again.

A few minutes later, Douglas was back to running around with his brother. Lizzy had calmed down, her long lashes spiked with tears as she cuddled close on her mother's lap beside her new brother.

Dorie wanted her own child snuggled on her lap. But it seemed Bryce didn't want the same thing, despite his obvious enjoyment of the act that produced babes.

She looked toward the door, and Lachlan shook his head. "If you go to him now, he'll say hateful things he doesn't mean. It's best to let him deal with his pain until he can beat it into submission and be civil."

Dorie understood and appreciated the warning. This man had known Bryce for a long time and had probably seen all his moods. But she couldn't ignore her husband if he was in pain. She ducked out of the door when the group was watching wee Cameron and Lizzy playing with Rascal.

Bryce wasn't far away. She found him standing in the clearing looking up at the stars. The same stars he'd mentioned her looking up at when he took her off to a place in search of privacy later.

"You dinna need to come check on me. It's not as if I could leave you. Even if I wanted to, I'm bound to you for the rest of my life." His voice was colder than the icy air.

Lachlan had warned her, but she still felt the shock of his words in the center of her chest. He was attempting to scare her away so he could be alone in his pain. She'd seen how he embraced the loneliness and let it consume him.

Instead of running off to ease her own pain, she stepped closer and wrapped her arms around his waist. His body stiffened, and for a moment she thought he might push her away or break free of her and walk off, but a few seconds later he relaxed.

"You wrap yourself in your pain rather than face living," she said quietly. "Before you know it, you truly will be alone, having run off anyone who ever attempts to care for you. I know it hurts. Trust me, I've lost someone, too. And it is my own fault they're gone." Her breath shuddered out. "But I'm here for you. I'll never be Maggie. I would never try to take her place. But I'm here."

He wrapped his arms around her and tugged her roughly against his body, squeezing her so tightly she could barely breathe.

"I'm sorry, Dorie. I'm sorry for what I said. I dinna mean it."

"I know. I understand."

He shook his head. "You canna understand. You deal with your grief in a way that doesn't hurt other people. While I act the arse."

She didn't know what to say to that. When her silence went on, he chuckled against her hair and released her enough to look down at her. "Ye were not quick to tell me I'm wrong about that."

A smile came to her lips. "I'm sorry for my delay. I assure you, you're wrong. I haven't always been kind in my grief."

"Ye clever minx." He laughed, and the sound touched her heart. He rested his forehead against hers and closed his eyes. "Can you forgive me, Dorie? It was just…holding Lizzy."

"It made you think of your Isabel."

When he nodded, her head moved with his since they

were still touching.

"It is not fair to Lizzy to be deprived of her kin's love."

"She's not deprived of it. I would lay down my life to protect her."

"But until there's a need for such a thing—and I hope there never is—she will not know."

"Are you nagging me, wife?" His eyes were soft and his mouth was pulled up on one side.

"Aye. 'Tis my duty, and I've been lax in it thus far," she teased, liking that they'd worked through their problems without him shutting her out. It was a step in the right direction.

"Perhaps ye can wait to start until after I take you home and make you scream."

She felt the heat of her skin in the cool night breeze. "We should say goodbye to our hosts and thank them."

He nodded, not looking happy about the task. She took his hand and gave it a squeeze.

"Thank you," he said as they went back to the house.

She didn't know exactly why he was thanking her, but she leaned up on her toes and kissed his chin.

She'd thought lying with Bryce in the marriage bed made her his wife, but she realized now it was moments like these.

Chapter Seventeen

Bryce was fortunate to have Dorie. Not just because she warmed his bed and gave him such pleasure he thought he might lose his mind, but for her steady patience that supported him when he thought he might crumble under the weight of his sorrow.

She stood by him when even he would rather walk away from his stupidity. And she encouraged him to be better than he'd been for years.

For all those reasons, he picked up his pace as he headed toward the castle to find her. When he didn't see her in the hall or the kitchen, he went to the solar. She was sitting with Kenna and Mari, her hound at her feet. The children sat scattered on the floor. Except wee Aiden, who was in the cradle by his mother.

It was a pleasant scene. One that had been repeated for generations before and would be again in those to come.

"Dorie, do you have a moment?" he asked.

She nodded and slipped out of the room after patting Douglas on the head.

He took her hand and led her to their chamber. When she stopped still a few feet from the door, he thought perhaps she was still worried about being trapped in a room.

But it was a different concern that bothered her today. "I told you, we canna keep running off to bed in the middle of the day. People talk."

He smiled at her rosy cheeks. It was so easy to bring a pretty blush to her lovely skin.

"Are ye saying you don't want me? Even if I do that thing you like with my tongue on your—"

"Shhh. Someone will hear your naughty talk." With that she grabbed his arm and dragged him into their room. With the door shut, she stretched up to kiss him, at the same time reaching for his belt.

This truly wasn't the reason he'd brought her here, but when she moaned as he covered her breasts with his hands, he decided to let it play out. He'd share the real reason for his visit after they were both satisfied.

He stripped her down, kissing her in strategic places to make gooseflesh rise on her creamy skin. For someone who was adamant they weren't to be sneaking off to bed, she was the first to be naked and in their bed.

He'd certainly never complain. In fact, he might keep coming up with reasons to take her to their room.

...

Dorie had yet to catch her breath when Bryce rolled out of their bed. She groaned in disappointment and let her head fall back. She didn't think she'd be able to stand, let alone dress yet. She needed a few more moments before moving.

Fortunately he came back, sitting on the edge of the bed, still naked. He leaned down to kiss her again and held out a bundle of cloth.

"As I said before you seduced me into your bed, I had another reason for bringing you to our room." His wink told her he was pleased with her misunderstanding, so she didn't bother to apologize. "This is for you. I'm sorry I'm so late."

She frowned at the bundle and looked at him in confusion. He'd gotten her a gift? She couldn't imagine why. She'd already gotten so much. She didn't need another thing.

"Go on. Open it," he encouraged.

She unfolded the linen to find the most beautiful brush and comb set she'd ever seen. Her mouth fell open and her throat went tight with emotion. She'd never had anything so beautiful to call her own.

"There's even a mirror." He pointed to a small metal mirror that reflected a wavy vision of them, heads bent to explore her treasure.

"They're so beautiful. But you didna need to go to the expense since the dowager already gave me a set."

"You deserve your own things. Pretty things. I'm sorry I've not been a better husband."

Was he jesting? He was the best husband she'd never even thought to have. Tears stung her eyes as she reached up to kiss him. She knew well enough what he wasn't saying. He was sorry he couldn't love her.

He'd told her many times his heart was too broken to love again, and yet he treated her better than anyone ever had. She wouldn't ask him for more, because what they had was enough. She'd never expected anyone to love her anyway.

They shared a life together, and a bed. He was happy to make her laugh, and he'd been thoughtful to get her such a wonderful gift. But she'd never have his heart.

And in truth, it was safer this way for both of them. Love had made her mother so sad in those days before her death. She'd wanted a man she couldn't have. If Dorie wasn't careful, she could end up the same way.

She smiled up at him as he took the brush and sat behind her to stroke it through her hair. She would be content with what he was able to give. Hoping for more would only cause pain and resentment. In the days when she'd been locked away, she'd wished for a prince to come save her and love her forever.

She should be so happy that half her wish had come true.

...

Lach had put off Bryce's trip to the Campbells until the spring. The logic being that the longer they waited, the less money the McCurdys would have for weapons and supplies. They'd already heard that some of the clan were leaving to join neighboring clans.

Bryce was happy to stay at Dunardry. Not only to avoid his father, but to spend more time with Dorie. His favorite thing to do in winter was to keep his wife warm in their bed.

His second favorite thing was to go hunting with his cousins.

They went out one crisp March morning at dawn as they used to do when they were younger men. Unlike those times, his friends were chatting loudly as they walked through the woods toward the meadow.

It wasn't just because they would scare off all the game that Bryce wished they'd shut their gobs.

"Mari told me how excited Dorie was with the gift you gave her," Cam said with a smirk.

Bryce had enjoyed Dorie's reaction to the brush and comb set so much he'd made a habit of getting her a trinket whenever the tinker visited. The last time it had been a locket. She'd not taken it off since he gave it to her. He rather liked the way the pendant dangled between her naked breasts. The thought brought a smile to his face.

"It's not a large manor house like I'm building for my wife, mind you, but it's a step in the right direction," Cam said. They all knew the funds for the manor house had come from Mari, and they chuckled at Cam's joke.

"Have you finally decided to give the marriage a chance?" Lach asked, hope clear in his voice.

The smile on Bryce's face faded as it normally did when Lach or someone else made more of the relationship than they should. He needed to be honest so Lach wouldn't expect too much from him.

"I've decided to be pleasant to my wife. She didna do anything to deserve my boorish treatment of her, and I've made amends. As for the marriage, it's still not something I wanted, but I'm making the best of it, as you bid me to do."

Lach didn't seem appeased by Bryce's answer. Bryce knew Lach felt guilty for having married him off for no good reason, since they hadn't gotten the alliance they'd planned.

The laird opened his mouth to say something when Cam interrupted. "What the bloody hell?"

Rascal growled, and Bryce silenced him and bid him to stay so he wouldn't give away their position as a dozen warriors wearing McCurdy plaid rode leisurely across the meadow.

Cam and Bryce stepped in front of Lach, protecting their laird despite being hidden in the shadows of the trees.

"Should we run them off?" Cam asked, pulling his sword.

"Nay. They outnumber us," Lach reasoned. "And we're not armed for battle."

Bryce looked down at the simple hunting bow in his hand and agreed they were not up for a fight with the McCurdys.

"They look to be scouting," Bryce said with a frown.

"Do you think they intend to take us over?" Cam's brow creased.

"We should already have moved on them and taken them

down. Now they pose a danger." Both Bryce and Cameron had wanted to take a more aggressive approach, but Lach wouldn't put his men in harm's way. Not unless he could ensure a victory.

"They'll not act yet," Lach said. "I've word from Kenna's brother that clan Fletcher raided them recently. The McCurdys are hurting for supplies. Their already dwindling coin is now in even shorter supply. My guess is they are on the search for men and just passing through."

"I need to go to the Campbells to secure allies so we can take over their clan and gain the access we were promised."

Lach let out a breath.

Bryce knew he didn't want a war. As laird, Lach didn't want to risk losing any of his clan. Their safety was his responsibility. But it was time. They couldn't continue to hide in the bushes while these blighters rode across their lands.

Lach nodded in agreement. "Go to the Campbells and see to an alliance. I'll write to the Fletchers, and we'll send for the Stewarts. I think they will aid us since Cam and Mari helped the laird's daughter last year. I want as many men as we can find on our side so it's a quick victory with the least amount of bloodshed."

"Should we watch this group or eliminate them?" Bryce asked.

Lach looked out over the field and nodded once. "See it done."

Bryce and Cam exchanged a glance, showing their surprise. This was sure to cause the McCurdys to launch a counterattack and start a war.

"Let's gather the men."

Chapter Eighteen

Something was clearly going on. Not only did Dorie notice a number of men rush past the door to the solar, but she could feel the tension building in the castle.

Kenna and Mari must have noticed it, too, for they left the children with the nurse and headed down to the hall which was filled with the sounds of orders and clanking weapons.

"Oh, no," Dorie said, realizing what was happening.

Battle.

"What is it?" Kenna asked Liam.

"McCurdy men were spotted on our lands. The laird has given the order to…uh…remove them, mistress."

Despite his reluctance to clarify, Dorie understood exactly what he meant. She also knew there was rarely a battle launched that didn't have the war chief at the lead. Which meant Bryce was here somewhere, preparing to leave. She stood on a bench to search him out and headed straight for him when she found him.

She said nothing when she stopped in front of him, but it didn't matter. Her fear must have been written on her face.

"Don't start with your worrying, Dorie. I already have the worry of twenty other wives on my shoulders. I don't need any more." He softened his order with a smile and bent to kiss her on the forehead.

How could he be smiling and teasing her when he was readying for battle and might not see the next day? Men confounded her. Even the bloody dog was excited.

Of course she knew the answer. None of these men would be able to step onto the field with a sword drawn if they thought in detail about what could happen. It was better for them to focus on this moment of readiness.

She offered a smile. Though it shook and lacked sincerity, it was the best she could summon with her heart pounding the way it was. She needed to do something so he'd not be thinking of her here worrying over him.

"I will not lay my worry at your feet, then. Instead I will offer you a promise."

"Oh?"

She stood up on her tiptoes so she could whisper in his ear. "If ye return unharmed, I shall…" She looked around to make sure no one would overhear her bargain. Her skin heated, but she went on. "I shall put my mouth on you. Down there." She used her chin to indicate where she meant, though it was clear he knew well enough.

His eyes went wide. "And how do you know of such things?"

"The women in the kitchen are quite fond of talking about it."

He chuckled and kissed her. "I will hold you to that, and it will spur me on, so as not to miss it." He winked at her and she offered a smile that was more genuine than the first. "Thank you, lass, for understanding."

She nodded as he ran another dagger through the scabbard on his chest strap and pulled it tight. "I wish you well." She kept the words light despite the strength of their meaning.

"It's time," he announced in a voice of authority. As one, all the warriors moved to the bailey where their mounts waited. The horses had already been warmed up and armored, ready to take the men into battle. "I'll see you soon. And I'll wake you if you're sleeping to claim my reward upon my return."

She laughed at his eagerness as he planted a fierce kiss on her lips before striding off. She stood back as Kenna and Lachlan said their farewells. Mari and Cam smiled at one another and he bent to place a kiss on the babe in her arms. Another kiss for their daughter, and he mounted.

All around Dorie, the married men were wrapped in the arms of worried women. The unmarried sat their horses patiently. Bryce was already mounted at the front of the group with Liam by his side.

As he moved toward the gate, she felt a rush of dread in the pit of her stomach. But when he turned and smiled at her, she made sure her anxiety didn't show on her face. She blew him a kiss, and he was gone.

When the last man was out of the bailey, the gate was let down with a *thud* that echoed in the empty courtyard. The large bar was run through, and the second gate was lowered. The remaining soldiers took their places on the battlements.

It was just a precaution. Liam had told her they knew how many men were waiting, and Bryce had taken more with him than were needed to ensure victory. Still, she knew well enough how cunning the McCurdys could be.

The children began to cry, either feeling the tension from their mothers or from seeing their fathers ride away. Dorie helped comfort one of the twins since Kenna had more children than hands, and the nurse's arms were already full with Lizzy.

"Hush, lads. You'll not be joining the battle today, thank God," Kenna said.

"Don't speak of such things. I can't imagine having to watch our husbands *and* our sons go off to battle," Mari said. "I'd not survive it."

Kenna grimaced. "We will survive it. Because it's what we do."

Dorie nodded in agreement. It wasn't easy to watch Bryce go off, knowing he might not return.

"They'll be home in no time," she said, hoping to God it was true.

...

Bryce had a smile on his face as he led his men toward the meadow where the McCurdys would be dealt with. The smile wasn't the result of heading into battle, for he had long since learned there was little joy in fighting to the death. Even if he was the victor.

Killing a man, having blood on his hands, stayed with him and gave no enjoyment.

No, the smile was stuck on his face because of Dorie's send-off—the incentive she'd provided to encourage him to come home to her unharmed. Thoughts of her mouth on him made it difficult to sit his horse. It was more than enough reason to return to her unscathed. If the obvious incentive weren't enough.

The way her innocence bloomed on her cheeks from just speaking of the act made certain he would be granted the thrill of her curiosity and exuberance.

"What are you smiling about?" Cam asked with his brows pulled down.

"Something Dorie promised me if I returned."

"Did she hear about it in the kitchen?" he asked with a

smirk.

"Aye."

Lach chuckled, coming up next to them. "Who would have thought the women who cooked our meals were such wicked imps?"

"I surely wouldn't have thought it, but I tell you true, I'd like to hug each one of them for their lessons," Cam said.

Bryce couldn't argue.

"Kenna has promised me a pleasure as well. It's a handy motivator," Lach reasoned.

Cam laughed loudly. "*Handy?* Mari's promise doesn't require I use my hands."

Bryce wondered if they'd all been promised the same thing. If so, the McCurdys waiting in the field didn't stand a chance. He and his two friends would slay them all down by themselves, just so they could return to their wives as quickly as possible.

On the edge of the woods, the men all gathered. Bryce looked down the line, still hidden in the shadow of the trees. Liam was at the farthest point to his left and gave a nod of readiness. Cam at the end of the line on his right gave the same assurance.

As was his right, Bryce let out the war cry, and with his sword in hand he led his warriors into the field to take down the intruders.

Metal clashed and men called out in pain. Horses ran past unmanned. Bryce came down from his horse, taking out two McCurdys in one wide blow. The matter was over quickly. The MacKinlays had enough men, in addition to the element of surprise. Some of the younger men were sent to track down the McCurdy horses, spoils of war to add to their stables, as well as a resource not to be used against them in the larger battle that was yet to come.

Today's victory had been nearly guaranteed when they

descended on the McCurdys, but Bryce breathed a sigh of relief when the call came back that there were no MacKinlay losses. While none of their enemies were able to escape, some were spared and sent to the dungeon until their loyalties could be swayed.

Bryce checked each of his men personally to confirm their health. It was common for men not to realize they'd been injured until well after the battle was over. The rush of fear and excitement kept a man from feeling pain.

"No MacKinlay losses," he reported to the laird after he'd confirmed.

Lach gave a nod as the prisoners were bound. "Very good. Let's go home."

Covered in blood, Cam, Lach, and Bryce rode for the loch to wash.

"We were victorious today," Lach said as they scrubbed themselves clean. Though the blood might be gone, the deaths they'd caused that day would stain their souls the rest of their lives. It was the way of things.

"And our rewards await our arrival home," Cam said with a crooked smile.

"What reward?" Liam asked.

The men shook their heads, not wanting the lad to know what he was missing by being unmarried. With a sigh, he left to head for the castle and give word of their success.

The thought of what awaited them at home, along with the chill of the water, had Bryce and his cousins hurrying and heading back toward Dunardry in no time.

...

Dorie paced the hall with the other women. Each of them held a sleeping child who was startled awake when the men poured into the hall talking loudly and covered in blood. She watched for a tall blond head over the rest and felt her heart pick up when she didn't see her husband.

Liam came to stand in front of them. "Your men are well. They stopped at the loch to clean up a bit before returning home. Three guards remained with them, just in case, but we made a clean victory and expect no retaliation."

"Thank ye, Liam. Go and have some food. You've done us proud today," Kenna said, making the lad's ears turn pink in embarrassment. When he was away, Kenna turned to them. "I believe I shall put the children down and wait in our chamber for Lachlan's return."

"Yes, I think I shall do the same. It's late, after all. There's no sense in leaving for the house now. We'll stay the night here," Mari agreed.

Could it be these women were as anxious to get their heroes alone in bed as Dorie was?

In the corridor upstairs, Kenna left her boys with the nurse while Mari carried her sleeping children into their chamber. Dorie felt the faint clench of jealousy that she had no children of her own to settle into bed.

The feeling was quickly brushed aside with the knowledge that she might even now be with child. And if not, tonight there would be another chance.

She didn't think Bryce wanted children, but she knew if they were blessed with a babe, he would treat it well. Perhaps even find a way to love their child. If he couldn't, would their son or daughter notice Bryce wasn't giving everything?

With a sigh and a bunch of unanswered questions, she went to their room to wait for her husband to return to her. She was seated on the bed in just her shift when Bryce entered their chamber. She stood immediately to help him remove his weapons and clothing as he told her of their victory.

He twitched when her warm hands touched his cool skin, still damp from his dip in the icy waters of the loch. When he was naked, he lifted her gown from her body and pressed against her, making her squeal and squirm from the chill.

"I believe you promised me a wicked pleasure, wife."

Of course he wouldn't have forgotten. He'd probably slayed every McCurdy singlehandedly so he could return as quickly as possible.

"Aye." She licked her bottom lip and enjoyed the way his green eyes turned dark with hunger. She hoped she wouldn't disappoint and told him so.

"No worries, lass. I'll be patient while you master the skill." His sly smile told her it was no hardship for him to be used for practice.

It wasn't until she knelt before him and stared down his impressive size that she realized she should have considered how this would work. Perhaps Bryce was larger than the men the other women spoke of.

He shuddered when she reached out and placed her hand on him. And she smiled when she remembered that part of their story. Eager to get underway, she leaned in and stroked her tongue across him.

The sound that rumbled from his chest encouraged her to continue. She managed to put her lips partly around him, gaining another moan of approval. In her excitement she picked up the pace, enjoying the control she had in making him lose his breath and groan with pleasure.

But soon he pulled her away and lifted her to the bed so he could pounce on her.

"Was I not doing it fast enough?" she asked at his impatience.

"Nay. It was perfect, but I want to make sure you get your release before me. I canna guarantee I'll be good for anything afterward."

He smiled down at her as he slid inside. She lifted up to meet him, still wanting to enjoy that feeling of control.

"Lusty," he muttered by her ear as he nipped her lobe with his teeth. "You are too much for me, wife, but I canna get enough."

His words propelled her over the edge and her body throbbed around his. He cried out her name, spilling inside her in a fiery thrust.

He pulled her into his arms, his quick breath moving her hair.

"That was worth going to battle. Mayhap I should hunt down the McCurdys daily so I can claim my reward."

"If you promise to stay with me always, I shall reward you as you wish."

When he didn't answer, she sat up to look down on her sleeping husband, worn out from battle.

He had told her he would never be able to love her. He'd even been sorry for it. She'd told herself what she had was enough, but as she watched him, she began to wonder how she might heal him enough that he could one day love her.

. . .

Bryce had heard the promise Dorie attempted to extract from him the night before but hadn't answered. She'd asked him to stay with her always. She may have meant in the physical sense, but Bryce thought something might have shifted between them.

He'd made it clear over and over that he'd not be able to be a real husband in a love match. He could offer protection, friendship, and pleasure, but love was not available.

Fortunately sleep had come over him like a crashing wave, so he wasn't forced to break a promise the very next morning.

He had plans to leave for the Campbells to secure an alliance and a promise of men to aid in their takeover of

Baehaven so everyone in the Highlands could be free of the McCurdy threat, once and for all.

Rather than sneak out while she slept so as not to see the disappointment in her blue eyes, he waited for her to rise so he could tell her of his plans like a respectable husband.

She said nothing until they were in the bailey and he was ready to leave.

"I could come with you," she offered, holding on to his arm tightly.

"Nay, you're not a seasoned rider, and it's a few days' ride from here."

The frown on her full lips—lips that had been wrapped around him the night before—nearly forced him to change his mind. But he knew the pace of his trip would be uncomfortable for her.

"I'll be home as soon—"

Just then the guard on the gate called down, "Riders approach the castle!"

At that, the gate was opened and a single boy rode in, nearly out of breath.

"What do you have to report?"

The lad gulped in air and swallowed. "Soldiers. Heavily armed, riding for the castle."

He turned to Liam who was also preparing to leave for the Stewarts. "Gather the men," Bryce ordered.

Mere minutes later they were galloping across the field to intercept their visitors. Everyone was surprised when it was English outriders who were spread out across the field, armed and fierce. They remained in place surrounding a fancy carriage until it came to a halt at the line of MacKinlay warriors.

"You are on MacKinlay lands," Lach bellowed to the intruders. "Please state your purpose."

The door opened and a tall man stepped out. Elegantly

dressed, his hair graying at the temples, he offered an easy smile. As he stepped closer, Bryce noted the man's posture, thinking he moved with the fluidity of a soldier. Then Bryce noticed the color of the man's eyes and the way they tipped up in the same way Dorie's did.

"Good day. Allow me to introduce myself. I am Dorien Sutherland, Viscount Rutherford, and I believe my daughter is here."

Chapter Nineteen

Both Lach and Cam turned to Bryce as if expecting him to say something. Bryce considered asking the blighter if he didn't know how to return a goddammed letter but decided that was rude and thus remained silent.

While Dorie had stopped talking about her real father daily, Bryce saw the sadness in her eyes each day when she got no word from him. Bryce might have ridden to London and forced the man's hand if it weren't so far away. He didn't want his wife to be disappointed, so it was important that this man be cleared by him and his cousins first.

Lach slid down from his horse and took the few steps to shake hands with the man. "Lachlan MacKinlay, Laird of Clan MacKinlay. This is Bryce MacKinlay Campbell, war chief and your son-in-law."

Bryce had already dismounted and stepped forward to shake Dorien's hand as well. "Dorie's been beside herself waiting for a response from ye. She thought you dinna want anything to do with her." If his tone sounded accusing, so be it.

The man frowned. "I started many letters and didn't know where to begin. The thought of waiting to hear back had me packing to come here instead, though the weather hindered my progress until the thaw. I just couldn't leave it to letters. I needed to see her in the flesh."

Bryce and Dorien took each other's measure for a full minute before Bryce finally let out a breath and nodded. "I'll not send you away. Not when I know she'll want to meet you. But tread carefully. She's been mistreated her whole life; I'll not have you treat her ill."

"Of course not. I appreciate how fiercely you protect her."

"We'll escort you to the castle. Bryce, mayhap you should go prepare Dorie for the viscount's arrival."

"Aye." Bryce nodded and mounted his horse. He tore off for the castle to get there before her father. The man seemed pleasant enough. Bryce could only hope he wasn't setting Dorie up for more pain. She didn't need another man to let her down. He knew he was more than enough of a disappointment.

...

Dorie sat on the floor playing with Lizzy when Bryce rushed into the solar. For a moment she worried there was another battle. While it would mean he would have to delay his trip to the Campbells again, she didn't like this alternative.

"We've a visitor," Bryce relayed, looking only at her.

Normally the duty of delivering messages to the laird's wife fell to one of the younger boys in the clan. Dorie didn't understand why Bryce would do such when he was planning to leave.

"Who has come to visit?" Kenna asked excitedly. The woman had no patience for surprises.

Rather than answer, his gaze scanned the room and

returned to her. He stepped closer and took the little girl from her arms and passed her to Kenna, whose arms were empty. He reached for Dorie and helped her to her feet.

Something prickled down her spine. The way he hadn't answered Kenna's question. The way he was focused only on her.

"You'll want to come to the bailey," he said finally. "Your father is on his way."

Dorie gasped and placed her hand on her chest. "Is he attacking? Are there enough warriors in the castle to defend against a McCurdy assault?" She moved for the door, not knowing what she might do to thwart his plans, but she'd do her best to reason with the man or die trying. This was her home; she would do her part to protect the people she loved.

Bryce shook his head and took her elbow to hold her in place. "We're not under attack, Dorie. It's not the McCurdy who rides on the castle. It's your real father. Dorien Sutherland, Viscount Rutherford. He's come to see you."

Dorie blinked as the words surged around her, not making any sense. Finally she pieced them together and nearly fell over. Bryce righted her by wrapping a sturdy arm around her waist.

"He's here?" she whispered.

"Nearly. I rode ahead to tell you so you could be ready to greet him when he arrives. He's not far behind me."

"Do I look all right? Perhaps I should change." She was wearing her best gown already, though there was dust along the hem where she'd been sitting on the floor with the children.

"You look beautiful. I doubt he will notice what you're wearing. He's very excited to meet you." Bryce offered a tight smile.

"He is? He came all this way, for me?"

"Aye. You have his eyes and they crinkle at the corners

when he's excited just like yours do."

"My father?" Tears pooled in her eyes and she tried to brush them away. She didn't want to meet the man with red, puffy eyes. "What should I do? What if he doesn't like me, Bryce?"

Bryce gave her an indulgent smile. "How could he not like you? Let's go down to the bailey to meet him. I'll be standing right beside you, holding your hand. Don't worry about a thing." Bryce cleared his throat. "If he says anything unkind, I'll have him on his back with my blade against his throat before his next breath."

"Please don't kill my father," she said, patting his shoulder. He gave a nod and offered her his arm. She slipped hers through it and he led her down through the hall and out to the bailey just as an elaborate carriage pulled up.

There must have been twenty riders with him in addition to Lach, Cam, and the other warriors from Dunardry. The driver hopped down and reached for the door, but it had already opened and a tall man stepped out, offering a wide smile.

Her feet moved a step, but she held on to Bryce's arm to help keep her in place. It wouldn't do to run down the steps and hug him. He was a viscount. He wouldn't like a strange woman attacking him.

A viscount. She recalled hearing that women were to curtsey to nobility, but she worried she would fall over if she tried such a thing.

Bryce led her closer. "Dorie, this is your father, Dorien Sutherland, Viscount Rutherford. My lord, your daughter, Dorie MacKinlay."

He'd barely got out the introductions before her father reached for her and drew her into a powerful embrace. Of course she failed to keep from crying. At least she felt better when he finally pulled away and she saw his cheeks were wet with his own tears.

"My child. It's beyond a pleasure to meet you. Please forgive my showing up unannounced. I didn't know how to reply to your letter. I just knew I had to come see you for myself."

"You are forgiven, of course. I'm so glad you're here. I have so many questions I'd like to ask ye."

"And you'll have time to ask every one," Bryce said. "But let's get him settled inside first. He's been traveling and will probably need refreshment."

"Aye. I'm sorry. I get overly excited about things," she admitted. Her dog was running in circles in excitement as well. "This is Rascal."

To her relief her father patted the large dog without fear. "He's a formidable beast."

"He doesn't seem to realize he's not a small puppy anymore and often tries to climb upon vacant laps."

"I'll be sure to keep something on my lap at all times," he joked.

Her father was teasing her. He was pleasant and smiling. So different from the man who had been called her father. She worried this was all a dream. She'd envisioned her father many ways, but she'd not thought he would be funny. What a wonderful surprise.

Kenna was waiting to greet Dorien inside the hall. She'd sent off the maids to ready a room for him and allowed Dorie to escort him to his chamber.

"The solar is free of children for the moment. I'll have refreshments sent there so you can visit in private. And we ask for your company at our table for the evening meal."

"Thank you for your hospitality, my lady. I am grateful for the invitation and look forward to spending time getting to know all of you. After I've had time to get to know my daughter, of course." He smiled again.

"Of course." Kenna returned the pleasantries. "I can assure you, your daughter looks forward to making your acquaintance."

"He's wonderful," Dorie whispered to Bryce before letting go of his arm to take her father's.

...

Bryce watched father and daughter leave through the arch at the stairs. He couldn't help the feeling of unease that pricked along his spine. The man was pleasant enough, and he didn't think he would hurt Dorie, but something bothered him about the man's presence.

"She's so happy," Kenna said by his side.

"Aye." It was clear that Dorie was elated to meet her father.

"It looks like you might be visiting London regularly," Mari added.

"London? I'm not going to London." Bryce snorted at the very thought.

"Her family is there. If she wants to see them…"

"I'm her family and I am here." Once he'd made himself clear he bowed and left them to their snickering.

Dorie wouldn't want to travel all the way to London. She only wanted to know the man. Now that he was here, she'd ask her questions and get her answers, and that would be it.

Even as Bryce thought it, he realized that probably wouldn't be enough for Dorie. Her only remaining blood relative had been found. A caring, kind father who would want to keep in touch.

"Blast and damn," he said as he headed for the solar. He found them deep in conversation regarding her father's long trip to Dunardry. Bryce sat silently in the corner, in case he was needed. But it was clear no one had even noticed him enter.

Once the man finished his ale and meat pie, he went to the window. It was another thing he had in common with his daughter. Dorie didn't like being trapped in a room, either.

"I'd forgotten how beautiful Scotland is. When I was here last, I had other distractions."

Meaning he'd been busy having an affair with a married woman and getting her with child. Bryce didn't mention it. Everyone knew.

"Would you like to go for a walk? I can show you my new home," Dorie offered, still beaming with happiness.

"That would be lovely. It's a mild day."

Dorie startled when she finally noticed Bryce. "We're going for a walk."

"I'll have to come along to guard you."

"No need," Dorien said. "My guards will be with us. They'll protect Dorie as well as myself."

"I'm safe with my father," Dorie said with a wide smile and left Bryce alone as she strode off.

It was true enough she was safe with the man, but Bryce still felt as if something bad was going to happen with the arrival of their new guest.

He could only hope he was wrong.

Chapter Twenty

"How did you meet my mother?" Dorie asked her father as soon as they sat down on a fallen log. Despite the cool breeze, she was happy to be outside, having spent so much of her life indoors.

Rascal ran off to explore as her father smiled and threw a stick for him to chase. The dog wasn't so great about bringing it back.

It was a good minute before her father answered, but the silence wasn't awkward. "It was fate, I'm sure. I stopped to get water while she happened to be sitting by the creek crying."

"Crying? What was wrong?"

"She was newly married and unhappy. She didn't tell me that day, but later I found out that she'd gotten her courses and the McCurdy wasn't pleased about it."

"He wasn't pleased about many things," Dorie agreed with a frown as she remembered the man she'd thought was her father. In the early years, he'd offered a smile here and there to her. Occasionally he'd pull her onto his lap and chat with her as if she had great things to share. But most of the time he was too busy for a daughter. Instead, he gave all his attention to Wallace.

"I planned to see her safely back to her home, but she looked at me with eyes the color of moss in the spring, and I was struck. I'd always thought myself honorable. But I fell in love with a married woman. I didn't care about the consequences. All that mattered was her."

"And you saw her again?"

His cheeks turned pink and the blush moved up to the tips of his ears. "Every chance I could."

Dorie thought she understood what he wasn't saying. She and Bryce had been seeing a lot of each other over the last few months. And they weren't even in love.

"Eventually my regiment was called away and I was forced to leave her. But not before I made her promise to write me. We'd talked of running away together. We exchanged letters through her sister so the laird wouldn't find out. For a decade we went on with nothing between us but words on a page. The letters were all the same. Me begging her to meet me, and her telling me she couldn't yet. She wanted to come to me as a free woman so we could be wed, so she was waiting for the laird to die."

Dorie wished it had been the laird who had died. Not that Wallace would have been much better, but at least she and her mother could have left to live with her real father. They might have been happy.

"I was willing to wait for her, only because she never told me about you. I would have come immediately if I'd known we shared a child. When I found myself strapped with a title, our plans changed. I needed to marry for duty. I thought perhaps that was why she'd stopped writing. I didn't blame her."

He let out a breath and frowned at the stick Rascal had returned to him.

"Eventually your aunt wrote to tell me she had died."

"She didn't die," Dorie said, taking a breath. She could only hope her father wouldn't hate her for what she needed to tell him next, but she had to confess. "She was killed, and it was all my fault."

She spilled the entire story and waited for her father's anger. If it hadn't been for Dorie, her mother might have, one day, been able to leave and join him.

Dorie knew the reason her mother had never left in all the years Dorien had begged her to run away with him. The laird would have hunted her down if she'd taken Dorie. At least as long as he believed her to be his child. Dorie's mother never would have left her. Not even to spend her life with her true love.

The familiar guilt washed over Dorie, nearly drowning her.

"I'm so sorry. I'm the reason you weren't able to be together."

"Shhh. It's not your fault. Sometimes things don't work out the way one thinks they should. I got married to a wonderful woman. We have four children that have brought joy to my life."

"But it's not the same as having someone you love, as you did my mother."

He frowned and shook his head. "I will not lie to you. I still think of your mother every day. I miss her as I would miss a limb or a part of my heart. Having you in my life eases some of that pain. It's like having a part of her. A part of us."

"But your wife? Isn't she upset that you have a child with another woman?" Dorie couldn't bring herself to say the word bastard, though that was what she was.

His smile seemed strained. "It wasn't a love match, at least not for me. We respect one another and I care for her deeply. She actually encouraged me to come here when I told her of you."

"She loves you?" Dorie guessed.

"I think so, yes." He frowned, and Dorie assumed he felt guilty that he wasn't able to love her back.

She felt a wave of sympathy for the woman. Dorie had been trying so hard not to expect anything from Bryce. She'd done her best to protect her heart, knowing he couldn't offer her anything in return but a warm bed. But she loved him. And it hurt to know he didn't love her back.

"I understand," she said. "Not what you're feeling, but what your wife is. I'm in love with a man who canna love me the way you loved my mother. He gave his heart to his first wife and their child. When they died, they took his heart with them. There's nothing left for me."

"I hate that I cannot feel for Harriet the way I felt for your mother. It's just the way of things, I guess. I don't want that for you. I don't want you to have to settle for the fragments of someone's broken heart."

"At times I think perhaps it's not important, that maybe I could love him enough for both of us. But I do wonder what it would be like to have more." She shook her head. "He treats me well enough. Being here at Dunardry is better than I ever expected. Much better than my life with the McCurdys."

"Well enough is not what I want for my daughter," he said, his brows pulling together as he threw the stick for her dog. "I wish you to be happy."

She understood his displeasure but didn't think there was anything to be done. She was married to Bryce. It didn't matter if her father liked it or not, it was legal and consummated.

"Tell me about my sisters and brothers," she said to change the topic.

A proud smile pulled up on his face and he told her about all of them. The oldest, Philip, was nine. Nadia was seven.

The twins, Geneva and George, only five.

"Geneva looks like you. Like me." He smiled. His eyes went wide. "Perhaps you could return to England to meet them. We're staying at my estate right now."

"I couldn't. They would hate me."

He chuckled. "They wouldn't hate you. They'd be surprised, yes, but they would give you a chance. I'm sure you would become great friends with all of them."

"But I would disgrace you. I'm illegitimate. And Scottish." She added the last part when he didn't seem deterred by the first.

Again he chuckled. "I'm not sure there's a member of the peerage who doesn't have illegitimate issue. As far as being Scottish, it's not a crime."

It might not be, but Marian had told her stories of how the English treated Scots. Mari even sounded English, and they'd still teased her about her accent.

"I'm married," she reminded him. "I belong here."

He nodded and let it drop. They returned to the keep for supper and the laird kept her father's attention for most of the meal.

Bryce didn't say much as they ate. Now that she knew how she felt about him, it was difficult to look him in the eye. She feared he might see her affection when he looked at her.

He'd warned her he couldn't give her more, and she'd foolishly fallen for him anyway. She couldn't let him find out.

...

That night when Bryce came to bed, Dorie was in bed staring at the ceiling. She'd hardly said a word at dinner. And now he noticed she wasn't able to look at him.

There was a time when he would wonder what she was thinking, but time had cured him of patience so he sat on the bed and took off his boots before turning to her and asking directly, "What's the matter?"

Her eyes darted toward him quickly and away again. "I'm just trying to grasp the fact that I have family again. A father. It's wonderful."

"Aye. But it doesn't explain why you refuse to look me in the eye. Or why you're so quiet."

She let out a breath and bit her bottom lip for a moment. If she didn't look so serious, he might have considered leaning over to take a nibble for himself, but he refrained, waiting for her to gather her courage to tell him what was bothering her.

"My father was in love with my mother. Gave his heart to her. He's married now, but it's clear he doesn't feel anything but respect and friendship for my stepmother, even though she loves him."

"I see." Bryce didn't say anything for a moment. He wasn't sure what to say. She was obviously making comparisons between him and her father. Did that mean she and her stepmother had something in common as well? Was Dorie telling him she was in love with a man who didn't love her back?

Part of him wanted to yell and remind her of all the times he'd warned her of such action. But he knew how love worked. It didn't always do what one wished. If it did, he would have forced himself to stop feeling for Maggie so it wouldn't hurt so much.

"What are you saying?" he asked, hoping he'd misunderstood.

"I'm not saying anything. Good night." She turned away from him.

Rather than force her to tell him something he didn't think he'd bear hearing, he blew out the light and tossed and turned the whole night.

He shouldn't feel guilty. He'd told her it wasn't possible

for him to be a real husband to her. Not in that way. But he should have known she might form an attachment if he slept with her.

"I'm sorry," he whispered before giving up on sleep and going to pace the battlements.

He wasn't the only one having difficulty sleeping. Cam was also there trying to calm a screaming Aiden.

"What seems to be the problem?" Bryce asked as he tapped the baby's chin, who paused in his crying for a moment before letting out a loud wail.

"His belly hurts him and he wants all the world to know about it."

"Poor lad."

"Did he wake you?"

"Nay. I have my own pains to fuss about." Bryce leaned over the wall to look down into the bailey. A few months ago he'd wished himself able to take the next step. Odd that now he had no desire to leave this life. The pain was still there, but it was not as sharp as it once had been. His life was not as grim. Not with Dorie in it to bring him pleasure and laughter.

"I can offer you a pat on the back. However it doesn't appear to be working for this little one, so you might find any comfort lacking on my part," Cam said.

Bryce nodded and let out a breath.

"If you're not interested in a pat, I could listen to your fussing. I've already heard everything this lad has to share."

Bryce didn't want to talk. He'd come up to the battlements for a bit of quiet and to be alone, so it was a surprise when he opened his mouth and told Cam what was on his mind.

"I fear Dorie has come to expect more from this marriage than I can give."

"You mean love?"

"Aye. I warned her from the first day not to get attached, for it could only lead to disappointment."

"Ah. So it's the lass's fault she feels something for you. Despite you treating her like a real wife in every way. Laughing with her. Running off to your chamber at any time of day. Worrying over her all the times she was injured by the McCurdys. Buying her gifts as a husband ought to do. It's *her* fault she thought she stood a chance to win your heart when it appeared to all of us that she already had."

"I suppose you want me to argue that it isn't her fault?"

"Yes, I do. If you wanted to make it clear you'd not be a husband to her, you should have kept your distance."

"I tried. But the bloody McCurdys burned down her cottage!" he defended.

"When you moved her to your room, there wasn't any other place you might have slept?" His brows went up and Bryce was thankful for the darkness so not to see the full expression of challenge.

Bryce preferred to stay wrapped up in his denial. It was easier to claim he wasn't at fault that way. "What do I do?"

"Let yourself love her back, and be happy."

"I can't do that."

"Can't or won't?" Cam pushed. Aiden quieted as if he wanted to hear the answer as well.

"I can't remember the sound of Maggie's voice or her smell. Sometimes I can't even recall her face. It's even worse for Isabel. I had so little time with her. The memory was almost too short to grasp. Dorie is taking up the space where those memories had been, and I hate her for it as much as I'm relieved not to have to feel the pain so intensely. It's not right."

"It's the way of things. I remember when I first moved to the castle after my mother died, and how I didn't want to let Lach's parents care for me because it felt like I was betraying my own parents if I cared for them. But I realized it wasn't true. Sometimes we imagine things because of the pain we're dealing with at the time. You've been in yours for so long it might take you longer to realize it's not a betrayal to Maggie and Isabel for you to be happy with Dorie."

Bryce was quick to shake his head. He even squeezed his eyes shut as if to block out Cam's words.

"You're allowed to be happy, Bryce. You're even allowed to love again. It doesn't mean you loved Maggie and Isabel any less while they were alive."

Fortunately, Aiden picked that time to let loose with another scream of displeasure, so they were able to focus their attentions on the baby instead of the impossibility of Bryce ever opening himself up to that kind of pain again.

He needed to keep his walls of protection firmly in place.

Chapter Twenty-One

Dorie woke alone and hurried to meet her father in the hall. Part of her worried that the day before had been a dream and he wasn't really there. She let out a breath of relief when she entered the hall and saw him sitting with the laird at the front table.

He was already smiling at something Lach had said, but when he noticed her, his smile grew and he stood to greet her.

"I hope you slept well," she said as he brushed a kiss on her cheek.

"Very well, thank you."

"Bryce is already with his men?" she asked Lachlan as she took her seat next to Kenna.

"Aye. He was in a rush to get to it this morning. He wants to get things settled before he leaves for the Campbells."

"Is he leaving today?" she asked.

"No. He has put it off since we have a visitor."

Another delay because of her. At this rate they would never gather the men needed to win the battle with the McCurdys. She'd not been able to help her new clan with an alliance, and now she was stalling their plans to move forward and take over Baehaven.

She felt she should apologize, but remained silent.

After the morning meal, she and her father went to visit Mari and Cam at their manor house. The couple was happy to give her father a tour.

"We stay here some nights. But lately we've been staying the night at the castle so the nurse can help with Aiden."

"Ah, yes. I remember having a babe in the house," her father said with a nod. "My youngest two are five now. Do you mind?"

Mari held Aiden out to Dorien and he took the baby as if he'd held hundreds of infants in his life.

"I can't wait to have a grandchild," he hinted with a smile toward Dorie.

Her face went hot and she looked away. She'd found herself hoping each month, only to be disappointed when her courses came. She didn't think Bryce minded since he'd said he didn't want children. But still, she felt that she had failed in some way.

Her father and Cam talked of other things, and Dorie was happy to change the subject. But on the way back to the castle it became clear the topic had only been delayed.

"Do you want children?" he asked.

"Yes. I find I want them more each day. But so far it hasn't happened."

"Has Bryce put any pressure on you about it?"

She let out a laugh that held no humor. "Definitely not. I don't think he wants children. It would be yet another person he doesn't want to have to care for." Her father looked upset on her account, so she felt the need to explain. "He lost a child. I wish I could help to heal his pain."

"It's not your job to heal him. Your love should heal him."

"Did Harriet's love heal you?"

"Eventually."

Dorie didn't think she wanted to know how long it took, so she refrained from asking.

"Are you unhappy?" he asked as they turned to stroll through the village.

"No." She shook her head quickly.

"Are you happy?"

"Isn't that the same question?" She laughed.

"It isn't at all the same question."

She thought it over and realized the difference.

She wasn't unhappy. Especially when she compared her life at Baehaven to her life now. She'd been terribly unhappy before, so it was easy to know the answer to that question. The other question—whether or not she was happy—was more difficult to answer.

"I'm not sure," she said honestly. "I want to be." She frowned, hating how ungrateful she sounded. "When I was locked in my room at Baehaven, I spent a lot of time hoping for something different. Sometimes I would wish for someone to come save me. Sometimes I wished someone would care about me. Occasionally I dreamed of sprouting wings so I might fly out the window. I fear I may spend the rest of my life hoping for something I'll never have."

Dorien stopped walking and turned to her. "Come to England with me. I can have an annulment drawn up. You'll be free of this marriage to a man who can't love you as you deserve. You'll be able to find someone suitable who can see how wonderful you are and treasure you."

She blinked in surprise. She'd never thought of such a thing. She stood there staring at him while she thought. Her legs wobbled with the shock over her father's suggestion. Why was she even considering such a thing? She loved Bryce. *He can't love me back.* She was content. *But is that enough?*

Bryce hadn't wanted to marry her. He'd only done so

to secure an alliance for his clan. An alliance that was now invalid.

There were dozens of reasons to agree to her father's suggestion, and only one selfish reason not to. She loved Bryce and would miss him.

But that wasn't enough to sentence him to a lifetime of unhappiness.

...

Having accepted the viscount's invitation to join him for a hunt, Bryce slipped from his bed before dawn to meet the man in the stables. He knew better than to think this was about gathering food or sport.

This was their first time alone since his arrival, and Bryce knew he was being measured as a match for Dorie. He could save the man some time and tell him he did not measure up, but pride kept him from admitting such. Bryce held no titles. He held power in the clan as war chief, but that did nothing but ensure he had a greater chance of leaving his wife a widow than any real status.

Being a viscount, and an army captain, meant Dorien Sutherland spent his days around powerful, honorable men. He was bound to be disappointed by his time with Bryce.

Rascal followed along despite Bryce's order for him to stay with his mistress. Apparently the beast thought Bryce was more in need of his support than Dorie. Animals were able to sense things men could not, so he took the dog's companionship as an omen.

"Faithful dog," Dorien said, nodding to the mutt. "It is a dog, correct?"

They both laughed at the joke, the tension lessening slightly.

"Aye. I think he's mostly dog. Mayhap his father was a

horse."

"I wouldn't doubt it."

"When Dorie found him, he was only knee-high and I thought he was fully grown. I may not have suggested she keep him if I'd known what a monstrosity he would turn into. Especially when a storm moves in and he seeks comfort on our bed."

"You permit him in your room?"

"Permit is not quite the word. It makes my wife happy, and 'tis an easy thing to allow if it puts a smile on her face."

The man seemed confused by this, if his creased brow was any indication. "I was under the impression you were forced into the match with my daughter."

"Aye. And I fought it for some time. But once I was done pouting like a lad, I realized it wasn't her fault, and I've tried to make it up to her." A few silly trinkets were little recompense for the way he'd treated her when they'd first wed.

"But you do not love her." The man was looking right at him. Even so, Bryce wouldn't lie. He'd expected the man would ask. It was something a father would want to know about the man married to his daughter.

"I've heard a bit of your story from Dorie," Bryce started. "She told me ye truly loved her mother. It's clear by the fact you came here instead of sending a letter, and by the smile on your face when you saw your daughter, that you must have loved her mother more than anything. You've traveled all this way for the piece of her that remains in Dorie."

Bryce watched the man. Dorien glanced away but nodded. "True enough."

"I understand such things because I was married before to the love of my life. I'd known her since we were babes. When I was sent here as a young lad, I thought only of her. And when she was old enough, I asked the Campbell to marry her. We were happy and blessed with a child. My life was complete. When she and my daughter died from fever, I lost my ability to love anyone else."

Another nod of understanding from the man beside him. "I see."

"While I canna love Dorie the way I wish I could, I take care of her, protect her, and make her happy in the ways I'm able." He nodded to the dog. "Even waking up to this monster's smelly breath on occasion."

The dog had paused to lick himself in a scandalous fashion. The viscount laughed and gave a look of distaste. "Perhaps you're more capable of love than you think."

Bryce knew the man was joking, but he felt a tug of longing in his chest. The truth was, he wished he could heal enough to love again. Dorie was a good woman. Beautiful, kind, and funny. And her passion left him unable to make it through the day without searching her out and carrying her off for a bit of wickedness.

But there was distance between them. A place within him she was not allowed. Whether for her protection or his, it didn't matter. He could not allow her to breach his walls.

Just then Rascal tensed and growled. He had hunted enough with the deerhound to know this wasn't an alert of game but danger.

"This way, my lord. Quickly." Bryce led them into a grove of trees and dismounted as four McCurdy warriors entered the far end of the meadow. Rascal growled again when they headed toward them.

"Quiet," Bryce commanded. The dog obeyed, coming to sit in front of him at his feet. Earlier he'd thought the beast was there to protect him from an angry father. Apparently not.

The viscount's horse whinnied, calling the attention of the group. It was clear they would not be able to escape without bloodshed today.

"Tell me, my lord, are you a good shot with your pistols?"

The man's lips pulled up in a grin sure to make any son-in-law cringe. "Oh, yes."

...

Dorie paced the bailey, waiting for her men to return. All of them, father, husband, and dog, had gone out on a hunting trip in the wee hours of the morning. It was now late afternoon, and she worried what could be keeping them.

Her first concern was that someone might have said something to cause an argument. Both her father and husband wouldn't be above baiting the other if it amused them. But she knew neither would take it so far as to cause actual harm.

As the maids in the hall began preparing for the evening meal, Dorie became even more anxious and went to find Lachlan.

While he didn't seem worried, he indulged her request to go look for them.

He was mounting up to go search for Bryce and her father when the guard on the gate yelled down.

"Riders!"

The sound of the gate opening meant the guard knew who it was. Her heart lifted when Bryce and her father rode through the gate, but it quickly fell when she looked closer.

Both men were covered in blood. Her father had a piece of linen tied tightly around his thigh. When they stopped in front of her, she noticed a moaning man lashed to the back of her husband's horse.

"Get the healer," he called to a maid.

"What's happened?" Lach was the one to put a voice to her question.

"McCurdys. Four of them. The viscount was able to take out one with his pistol and injure this one. Rascal got one, leaving only one for me." Bryce patted the dog whose fur was matted with blood.

The way he wagged his tail when he came to her made it clear none of the blood was his. She swallowed and patted the dog on the head, not wanting to think of any of her men in danger.

"Father?" she said as he dismounted gingerly and nearly crumbled when he put weight on his injured leg. Bryce was quick to his side to support him and help him into the hall.

He called to two men seated, ordering them to bring the injured McCurdy inside.

Abagail, Kenna, and Mari all rushed to her father to look at his injury. Abagail barked out commands to the maids and they rushed toward the kitchen.

"It's nothing but a cut," her father said, brushing it off. Dorie wasn't so certain by the amount of blood staining his breeches.

"'Tis true. Though it is a deep cut and will require stitching," Abagail said as Kenna nodded her agreement.

Lachlan brought out the whisky and supplied generous amounts to her father with a sympathetic look. She held her father's hand when Abagail began stitching. To her surprise, her father barely registered the pain. He surely didn't squeeze her hand fiercely, as she'd expected. A wince here and there was his only sign of displeasure. Most of the time he smiled at her and asked her questions to distract himself.

"Have you suffered great pain before?" she asked when the stitching was done and he'd not even broken out in a sweat.

He offered a grim smile and nodded. "Yes, love. When I found out your mother had died. This cut is nothing compared to that pain."

Dorie glanced over at Bryce, who was dealing with their prisoner, and considered what he'd lived through. His great love and the child from their union lost. It was no wonder he was dulled to any other pain.

She understood then there was nothing she could do to spare him, except perhaps leave him to his grief.

She thought of her father's offer of an annulment. While there was a certain excitement at the chance to fall in love with someone who could truly love her back, she knew the real reason she would go through with it was to give Bryce his peace.

And just like that, she made up her mind. It was better for both of them that way.

She wondered if he would even remember her after she was gone.

Chapter Twenty-Two

Bryce stared down into the eyes of the wounded McCurdy and repeated his question. "Why are you on MacKinlay lands?"

"I'll not tell you anything. If I'm going to die, I'll not do so as a traitor to my clan." He spit at Bryce's feet as Lach stepped up.

"It looks as if our guest has no manners. Allow me to welcome you to Dunardry. I'm the laird. And I don't appreciate people sullying my hall."

The man winced in pain but said nothing, as had been his way the last half hour.

Abagail pushed through the small crowd with all the authority of a person of power. "Let me take a look."

She pulled away the soaked linen and tilted her head back and forth before turning to Bryce to whisper loudly, "I can save him if you wish me to." Her expression, however, did not match her words. Bryce didn't need to be a healer to know this man was far gone and would not live the rest of the day. Still, she'd given them leverage if he wished it.

After constant invasions by their enemies, he chose to take the advantage. "Nay, he wishes to die," Bryce said.

Lach waved a hand. "Then let's leave him to it."

Abagail gave a nod and turned away. Bryce stepped behind her to follow.

"Wait!" the man called. "If you save me, I'll tell you why we're here."

Bryce shook his head. "If we heal you first, you'd have no reason to tell us the truth. Nay. You tell us why you're here and *then* we'll do our best to heal you."

Lachlan nodded. "I think even ye can agree, a MacKinlay's word is more trustworthy than yours."

The man made no attempt to dispute his claim, which was telling. All of Bryce's life he'd heard tales of the lowly McCurdys and how their word wasn't worth shite. How horrible to not have pride in your word.

"We lost a group of scouts a few weeks ago. We were sent to find them."

Bryce knew well enough what had happened to their scouts, but he was willing to play along to get the information he needed. "Why would you be looking for your scouts on MacKinlay lands unless it was the MacKinlays you were spying on?"

The man looked away, jaw set.

"Come along, Bryce. We'll leave him to his fate."

"Hold. I'll tell you."

Bryce waited.

"Wallace sent us to see if you've brought in other clans to aid you in your plans to take over Baehaven."

"And why would ye think we plan to try such a thing?" Lachlan asked while eyeing Bryce.

"Wallace wants you to attack, but not to win. He's tired of waiting for his sire to die and wants to speed it along. But the war chief worries he's gotten the clan into a battle we might not win."

"You're aiding Wallace to overthrow your laird?" Lach sneered in disgust at the man who had only a few moments ago planned to die rather than be a traitor to his clan.

"Aye, but not because I chose to. Most of the castle is shifting sides because they fear what Wallace will do to them when he takes over."

"There's no hope for the laird to remain in his seat?"

"It doesna appear so. Either Wallace takes him or you do."

Lach raised a brow in Bryce's direction but said nothing in front of the McCurdy. He didn't need to. Bryce understood. It was a good sign that the McCurdy clan was fracturing. It would be easier to convert their loyalty when the time came. If the clan was already warring with itself, they might reduce their own numbers enough that the MacKinlays would be positioned for an easy takeover.

"The scouts and the men today were there under direction of Wallace, but the laird dinna know?"

"Aye."

"How many of your men do you think are loyal to the heir?"

"All but a few. But if you think they will follow you, you're wrong. Wallace McCurdy will be the next laird of Baehaven." The man coughed and moaned, sweat beading on his forehead from the pain.

"Bring this man whisky," Lach ordered, and one of the maids brought it immediately.

"Do what you can to make him comfortable," Bryce whispered to Abagail. To the man he said, "I wish you well, and if you don't live, my men and I will say a prayer for your soul."

The man only nodded and took a big swig of whisky, along with whatever Abagail had sneaked into the liquid, and the man drifted quickly off to sleep.

"Can you save him?" he asked the healer, knowing the answer already.

She shook her head. "Nay. But it doesna mean I won't give it my best effort."

"Make certain he's not in any pain." When the time came, that was all any of them could ever ask for.

...

During the next week, while the viscount's leg healed, he and Dorie didn't speak again of the annulment. Her father didn't bring it up once during all the hours they spent together in the solar during those days, though she could tell he'd wanted to ask.

She often caught him staring at her with his lips pressed together, but still he said nothing. She almost wanted him to bring it up…as much as she never wanted to hear the word again.

This morning he'd told her he needed to leave for his estate in a few days, now that his leg had healed enough for travel. Her time was running out. She had to decide what to do to ensure a happy life. Would that be with the man she loved, who couldn't love her back, or in a new country with a new family and a chance at love for herself?

She stepped into their chamber to find Bryce getting ready for the evening meal. All day she'd been planning what she might say, and now that the time had come, she wasn't any more prepared. She hovered by the door a moment, taking in her shirtless husband.

When he turned to her with a sly smile, she shut the door and moved closer.

"I have news," she said.

He kissed her neck and her mind skittered away for

a second. While he might not love her, he seemed happy enough to touch her whenever she was close. Most nights they made love and fell asleep in each other's arms.

Each time she thought she might be closer to accepting this life.

She thought it would be good enough. The physical pleasure and the friendship were more than she'd ever hoped for all those years she'd been locked up in a room alone. But she'd come to realize it wasn't enough now. She wanted a man to look at her the way Lachlan and Cameron looked at their wives.

"Will you share your news?" he prompted as he moved to her ear.

"Aye. Mayhap you can put on your shirt." She needed to keep her wits about her. She wanted to do the right thing for both of them, but she was teetering.

With his shirt in place, she patted the edge of the bed and took his hand when he sat next to her.

"My father has offered to take me back to England with him. To his estate and his family."

Bryce's brows pulled together. "England?" The word came out as a sneer. As if the country were the most vile place on earth.

"Yes. To live with him."

"You live here. With me." He looked confused, and she could understand why.

Swallowing down her nervousness, she went on. "That's the part I thought you'd be pleased about. He's offered to provide an annulment."

Bryce didn't seem pleased. His brows stayed locked in place, pulled together in irritation.

"An annulment?" he repeated.

"You'll be free of me. Just as you have always wanted." Her throat burned, but she continued. This was better for both of them. They each had lives they wanted to live in their own way.

He shook his head. "We've consummated the marriage, lass. There can be no annulment."

She frowned that consummation was his reason not to consider it, rather than that he wanted her to stay because he cared for her. She blinked to keep the tears from forming and cleared her throat.

"My father says money pays for anything ye could want from the church."

Please ask me to stay. Tell me you want me.

"Nay. You're my wife. Your place is here." That was not a good enough answer. Not now.

"*My place?*" She laughed. "I have no *place*, husband. I exist wherever people will have me."

"Aye. And I'll *have* you here at Dunardry."

She stepped back from him, tilting her head and watching as he reached for his boots. As if the discussion were over.

She was now even more determined to find a man who would consider her feelings fully before making a decision that affected her. That man might not exist, but she had to think there was someone closer to the mark than this stubborn Highlander she was currently married to.

"I wish to be more than tolerated. Since my mother died, no one has truly wanted me. Not the McCurdy, not my brother, not *you*." The last word came out like a curse. "I finally have a chance to be with family who *wants* me. *My* family." She snatched his other boot to make sure she had his attention. "Do you understand what that means to me? To actually *belong* somewhere?"

He frowned but said nothing.

"My father is a viscount. He has great influence. He said I would have the chance to meet people, and perhaps a man might fall in love with me." She couldn't hold back the smile. "I never thought I'd have a chance for such a thing. For someone to love me the way you loved your Maggie. The way I love—" She swallowed rather than finish her thought. It didn't matter how she felt about Bryce. He could never return her feelings.

He shook his head. "No. You're not going. You're my wife."

"I am your wife," she agreed. "But don't I deserve a chance at love?" she asked. "Haven't I lived as a prisoner for long enough?"

"A *prisoner*?" he snapped. "You may come and go whenever you wish."

"Then I wish to go with my father. I wish to live the life I should have had if he'd been able to marry my mother and give us both a home in England. A life with suitors who would offer for me, not because of what advantages our marriage brings with it, but because they want me. *Me*." She swallowed down the acute longing the words had burned into her heart.

When he opened his mouth, she expected him to say a final no. So she sealed her lips over his to stop his words. He kissed her roughly, his hands pulling her closer. She wanted to believe he loved her. Wanted her to stay because he couldn't live without her, but she knew better than to give in to silly, girlish dreams.

He'd told her his heart was broken beyond repair. He'd warned her against trying. He'd tried his best to protect her from disappointment and pain, but it hadn't mattered in the end. She'd still fallen in love with him.

When the kiss faded, she spoke against his lips. "Please think about it. Don't say no until you've thought it over. Please?"

He nodded and brushed past her without a word.

She packed her few things. No matter what he decided, she'd already made her choice. She was leaving Dunardry.

And the man she loved.

Chapter Twenty-Three

Bryce was furious when he stepped into the hall. He searched the crowd, finding his quarry. Glaring at the viscount, he stormed up to him, barely refraining from grabbing him and dragging him outside.

"A word alone, my lord." He didn't even bother to make it sound like a request. He'd interrupted the man's conversation with the dowager duchess of Endsmere, but he couldn't care about that. The woman already knew Bryce was a barbarian.

"Very well," the viscount agreed. Not that he had much choice. Bryce would have gladly carried him from the hall if he'd refused. The viscount was a large man, but Bryce was seething with anger and could have easily dragged him off.

"What seems to be the matter?" Dorien asked when they'd crossed the bailey to stand near the kitchen.

"*What's the matter?*" Bryce had made a new habit of repeating everyone. "My wife told me of your plans to take her back to England and have our marriage annulled."

Bryce detected a moment of surprise before the man nodded. "Yes. She said you would be quite pleased to be free of her. I daresay, you don't seem to be pleased at all." Did the man's lips curve up on one side? Bryce studied him, but it was gone too quickly, if it had been there at all.

"Nay. I'm not *pleased*. Far from it. She's *my wife*. In every sense, if you take my meaning."

"Yes. She told me she'd lain with you." The man swallowed and looked away.

Bryce wanted to laugh. Dorie hadn't lain with him as much as they'd coupled like rabbits on any flat surface available, and some walls and doors as well. But this man was her father, so Bryce skipped the details.

The viscount cleared his throat. "While it's not favorable circumstances, it doesn't prohibit an annulment. There are ways to procure your freedom."

Bryce didn't know why the man was making it sound like he was doing Bryce a big favor taking his wife off his hands.

"Just like that, you ride in here and take her away with you? And I'm supposed to just sign a document as if we'd never been wed?"

The viscount leveled a gaze at him. "I was under the impression you did not want to wed in the first place. You told me yourself you had no feelings for my daughter, save protection and providing for her. For those reasons alone I am forever indebted to you, as they were far more than what she'd been given by the McCurdys. And for that reason I'm willing to procure an annulment at considerable expense, to free you both from the bonds neither of you wanted. My daughter will be free to start over. A new name, a new country. She can walk away from the Highlands as my daughter. She'll be loved and well cared for. With a chance for real happiness."

Bryce stepped away, running a hand through his hair. He needed to find a way to stop this. "She's my wife," he repeated, as if this time it might make a difference to someone.

"She's my child," Dorien countered.

"And your child could be with child. *My* child," Bryce pointed out.

He hadn't wanted children. Hadn't wanted to risk losing something precious ever again. But he hoped now she was carrying his babe, if only so he could keep her with him.

Of course the man had thought of everything.

"We'll wait to make sure she's not increasing before we proceed in procuring the annulment. If she is, you need not worry. I can still take her with me and help her raise the child. We can simply say she's widowed."

"The hell you will. You'll not take my family from me." He'd already lost one family. He'd damn well not lose another.

The other man stepped back, surprise clear on his face. "Perhaps Dorie misunderstood. Could it be that you care for her more than she knows?" His voice, mostly curious, had a tinge of hope mixed in.

Did Bryce care for his wife? Of course he did. But could he be a loving husband? No, he didn't want that. Too many things could happen as people aged. Nothing was guaranteed or promised. He could end up in more pain than he was able to carry. How would he bear to lose someone else he loved?

Which meant he should be eager to let her go.

Why was he resistant to the idea? He should be thanking the man for taking her off his hands. With his marriage annulled, he could go back to his life the way it had been before Lach forced him to marry her.

He didn't want to be married.

He frowned.

Was he only unwilling to consider the offer of annulment because he didn't want anyone else to have her? He didn't think himself such a selfish brute, but the idea of another man touching her had his stomach tied in knots.

She was *his*.

Needing to get a handle on his feelings before he made

a bigger mess of things, he left the viscount standing in the bailey and made his way to the loch.

It had always been his place for thinking. Or his place to stop thinking when he'd been doing too much of it.

He didn't want to feel. Didn't want to care. He just wanted things to go back to the way they were before he'd met Dorie, when he'd been content to live in the shadow of his grief, surrounded by memories with no chance to be hurt again.

Instead, he thought about Dorie…and what it would be like to never see her again.

...

Dorie found Bryce sitting on a large rock by the loch. It seemed to be his place. She'd found him there before. They'd even made use of that boulder, twice.

But this time she was there to ask again for her freedom.

When she'd told him of her father's offer, she'd expected him to be quick to sign away their marriage, having never wanted it in the first place. She hadn't anticipated his disapproval. She hated the hope she felt because he was reluctant to let her go.

Could it be that he cared enough for her not to want her to leave? She needed to push him so he would either admit to his feelings or allow her to go. Living like this forever was not an option.

She almost wished her father hadn't come. For if he hadn't, she might never have noticed the lack in her life. But when he spoke of her mother and then of Harriet, his wife and the mother of his children, Dorie could plainly see how differently he felt for the two women.

Perhaps Dorie was being selfish and unrealistic, but she didn't want to settle for friendship and respect when she might also have love.

"My father told me you're not pleased about his proposal," she said.

He glanced over at her then looked away with a shrug. He tossed a small stone into the loch and stared down at the water as if it held all the answers. "You're my wife. I suppose I got used to the idea and had settled into it."

She nodded and tossed a stick for Rascal before she took a seat next to Bryce. She picked up her own pile of stones and tossed one into the water next to his. The rings overlapped one another and then faded off into nothing.

Just like them. Their lives had overlapped for a time, but it was time for the ripples to fade and come to peace.

"I have the chance to meet a man who doesn't need to settle. There might be someone out there who actually wants me and could truly love me."

"Dorie, if you came out here to talk about you being with another man, I'll tell you that it's just going to make me angrier."

"Is that it, then? Possession? You don't want me for yourself, but you don't want anyone else to have me, either?" She had truly thought he'd want her to be happy.

He winced and shook his head. "I hope I'm not that selfish. You deserve happiness. I just thought you were happy here. With me."

"I was. I am. But you've told me it can never be more than physical between us. And while I enjoy the pleasure of your touch, I know there's something missing. Something I want for myself very badly."

He nodded but didn't look any happier.

"You can find any lass to give you pleasure, Bryce. I would never think I'm special in that way, or in any way, really."

But *that* was what she wanted more than anything. After years of being shut away in her room, forgotten, she wanted someone to see *her*. To want *her*.

"And if you're carrying our child, you would consider keeping the bairn from me?" He glared down at the water and threw in a stone with more effort, causing a splash.

"I would do whatever you wished. Whatever was better for our child." She realized then they weren't necessarily the same thing. Would it make sense to raise a child with a man who couldn't love them the way they deserved? To sentence someone else, her child, to her lot in life? It wasn't fair.

He nodded and threw another stone, not looking at her. "I'm not one to give up on things."

"If you think it's a failure to give up on this marriage, you're wrong. You didn't fail me. You were kind. You gave me a home and made me feel things I never imagined. I've never been happier in my life." She sighed. "But I know there's more to being married. I see it with Lach and Kenna, and Cam and Mari. The way they look at each other... I want that for myself."

Bryce swallowed and finally looked at her. He kept looking. She met his gaze and waited. Eventually he let out a breath and nodded. "Then you should not settle for someone who canna give ye what you want. I hope you find what you're looking for in England."

"I have your blessing to go with my father?"

"Aye. But if you are carrying my babe, I ask that you come back. That we continue on as we were. I can't stand the thought that I'd have a child out in the world I didn't know."

Dorie thought of her own father unknowingly going about his life without being aware Dorie existed. "Of course. I will write to you when I know for sure."

When he said nothing else, she took his hand and squeezed it. "Thank you for everything, Bryce."

He cleared his throat and squeezed her hand back. "Thank you for making me laugh again."

She took pleasure in knowing she'd made his life better in some small way. With a smile on her face, she left him to his boulder to go share the news with her father.

On the trail, Rascal caught up with her and whined. She stopped, in case he was warning her of danger, but his ears were still down as he tilted his head and looked back toward Bryce.

"Come now. We must get ready for a long trip. We're going to England."

Another whine as he turned in a circle toward the loch. With a sharp pain in her chest, she realized her dog belonged here. While she was at her father's country estate, Rascal would have rabbits to hunt and a place to run. But when they went to London he would not be able to come with her.

"You should stay here with him. He needs someone in his life to look after him when I'm no longer here to do it."

As she continued on her trek to the castle alone, a few tears fell. She was glad to have a chance for a happy future, but she also realized how much she'd been hoping Bryce would say he couldn't live without her and wanted her to stay here with him.

She took a deep breath and moved on.

...

It took a few days for the viscount to prepare for the trip back to London. Bryce thought the delay might have been to give him enough time to change his mind, or for Dorie to change hers, but that didn't happen.

Bryce had come to terms with the idea. The selfish part of him eased and he was able to see how this plan was best for Dorie. How she deserved to be happy, and since he couldn't be the man to make her dreams come true, he needed to release her and let her go.

It still angered him to think of another man touching her the way he had. To envision another man causing her to squeal and gasp in delight. But he managed to push those parts of the plan aside to focus on Dorie and her needs.

The entire process would have been easier if everyone would just leave him alone, but of course that didn't happen.

Her father found him out in the stables preparing his horse for a ride. Bryce was planning to check the borders, and when Dorien began hinting of going for a ride before his long journey in the cramped carriage, Bryce relented and invited the man to go with him.

He and Dorien left through the gates alone other than the hound that lumbered along next to them. Bryce expected the viscount to have outriders with him, especially after the last time when he'd been injured, but no one came along. Dorien Sutherland was a fancy lord and, from the number of men he'd brought with him to Scotland, all of England would fall to ruin if he weren't to return. But Bryce was glad for the privacy as they crossed the field in silence. Though he still hadn't figured out how to approach what he needed to say.

They rode quietly for most of the morning. Spring was coming upon the Highlands, and the singing birds had returned. The trees remained bare, but the ends of the branches held tight buds, promising an explosion of color in the next month. And Dorie would miss it.

Damn if he couldn't stop thinking of all the things she wouldn't be able to experience with him.

Eventually they stopped to fill their flasks at a stream.

"This is beautiful country. I almost hate to leave," the viscount said.

Bryce nodded but said nothing.

Dorien lifted a brow. "That was your opportunity to suggest I tarry so you would have more time to convince Dorie to stay."

"I can't ask her to stay." Bryce sniffed and shook his head. "I've given my blessing for you to take her to England, and I've agreed to an annulment after she's certain she's not increasing. I'll not go back on my word."

"Truly?" The other man looked genuinely surprised. "I didn't think you would give her up so easily."

Had his offer been something as drastic as a father's test? If so, it hadn't worked the way he'd planned. He hadn't forced Bryce to acknowledge feelings he'd ignored, but rather it had made clear that Bryce had gotten too close and needed to back off.

"I was taken aback by your offer initially. But after I had some time to think it over, I think it's for the best." That may have been an overstatement. In truth, Bryce's stomach was tied in knots to know he'd never see her again.

"I see." The man frowned. "I have to admit, I didn't think you'd agree."

"You thought me a selfish bastard?" Bryce couldn't blame him.

"I thought perhaps you would realize you want her."

Ah. So it had been a test. Or at least an enlightening.

"I know you're probably used to having people do what you want them to do. I'm sorry I wasn't easier to manipulate into doing your bidding."

The other man chuckled. "It's not what I expected, but I'm not disappointed. If you truly don't want her, it's better that we go. She deserves a full life."

Bryce didn't tell the viscount how much he did want her to stay. Especially since his reasons were selfish and of the carnal variety. He enjoyed having Dorie in his bed. She was lovely, and even after they'd taken their pleasure, he liked holding her and laughing with her. He'd missed the closeness of a lover. But he couldn't love her the way she needed and deserved to be loved. So he would let her go.

"This is the best thing for both of us," he said firmly, more to convince himself than her father.

"Very well. We'll leave for England tomorrow. Once we're certain she's not carrying your child, I'll have the annulment papers drawn up and sent to you for your signature."

"Thank you for giving her what I can't," Bryce managed to say, though his chest grew tight.

Dorien shook his head. "In truth, I fear I may be making a mess of things. It's obvious she loves you. It may be too late for her heart to heal from that. We both know too well what that's like."

"I've given her no reason to love me," Bryce said.

"You know it doesn't work that way."

Indeed, he knew.

• • •

Bryce wasn't coming.

Dorie stood in the bailey outside her father's fancy carriage looking for her husband, but he wasn't there to see her off.

He hadn't come to their bed the night before, either, and she'd wanted to touch him one last time. Wanted to feel his warmth and sleep next to him.

Strange how she'd come to take those things for granted. Had she known the last time was truly the last, she would have savored every moment and burned them into her memory.

Kenna stepped closer and drew her into a tight embrace. "I'm so glad things worked out with your father. I just wish he wouldn't be taking you away from us. I'll miss you."

"I'll miss you all as well. I'll write often," Dorie promised.

Mari hugged her next. "Remember what I told you."

"If anyone makes fun of my accent I'm supposed to thump them in the nose?"

"Good girl." Mari gave a nod and backed away. For such a dainty thing, she sure was a bloodthirsty wench. And Dorie would miss her so much.

"We're ready," her father announced, and waited to help her into the carriage.

"Where is he?" she asked Cam.

The large man frowned and patted her shoulder. "It's nothing to do with you. He was broken before ye arrived."

She didn't have to bend over far to hug her dog. "Thank you for being my first friend here. Thank you for keeping me safe. Look after Bryce. Keep him safe and make him play with you." She kissed Rascal's bristly fur and gave him a scratch behind the ears.

"I'll hold him so he doesn't follow after you," Cam said with pity in his eyes.

She gave a nod and paused a few seconds longer before allowing her father to hand her up to her seat. With another wave to everyone, they were moving through the gates and off to England.

Fear and panic clogged her throat. What if this was a mistake? What if her life would never be better than this and she was throwing it all away? She had people here who cared for her. Friends. Her loyal hound. A husband who was kind.

It isn't enough. The admonition filled her mind.

She tried her best to hide her tears, but they got the best of her.

"Shhh, child," her father said, pulling her close to offer comfort. It was a nice gesture, but it did little to alleviate the pain she experienced as her heart shattered.

How had Bryce survived this kind of agony for so long?

"It will be better soon. Time has a way of easing the pain."

She knew from Bryce that the pain didn't ease. The memories faded, but that wasn't the same thing at all. And even when she stopped thinking of him as much, when she did it would still hurt.

"It's never completely gone," she said. She'd seen the way Bryce and her father wore that pain, had carried it for years.

"No. I suppose not. I'm sorry. But you do learn to live around it. We'll find someone who will love you so you won't notice as much."

She couldn't imagine trying to find someone else at the moment. Even if it were possible to ride into her father's estate in Durham and find the perfect gentleman waiting for her when she stepped down from the carriage, she didn't think her heart would risk it. Nothing could be worth suffering like this again.

"If it makes you feel any better, I would guess Bryce isn't dealing with your departure very well. If he were, he would have been able to be there to say goodbye."

"Ye think he was too distraught with my leaving to come to the bailey and wish me off?" She laughed through her tears at the thought. "I'm sorry, Father, but I'm sure you have it wrong. My guess is he didn't come because he forgot I was leaving. It will probably be a week before he notices I'm gone."

Maybe it wouldn't take a week. He might actually miss her at night when his bed was empty. Unless it didn't remain empty for long. He was free to do whatever he wanted now. She'd released him from his obligation.

The tears came again, and this time they flowed for a long time.

Chapter Twenty-Four

Bryce didn't think he could hurt any more than he did already. He hadn't expected the tiny fragments of his heart to throb in pain as he watched the carriage roll away. From his view on the battlements, he could watch the carriage until it turned into nothing but a dot that disappeared behind the trees.

Dorie was gone.

She was going to England to find a new husband. Someone worthy of her. Someone who could love her the way she deserved. A man better than him.

He stayed where he was until the sun set and the last of the glow had disappeared over the horizon. He sat even when his stomach protested his neglect. He merely stacked that pain onto the pile with the other pains.

When he was certain everyone had gone to bed, he went to his own. He lay there in the dark, breathing in the scent of his wife and remembering the times they'd shared in the short time they'd had together. He spent a restless night thinking and second-guessing his decision to let her go. The honorable man he wished to be warred with the selfish bastard he was.

Eventually honor won out, but dawn had broken by then.

Bad-tempered and miserable, he went to the hall to seek a distraction. After filling his belly, he called his men to the bailey to begin drills and spent the entire morning barking orders at them.

If he could not do anything about missing Dorie, he could focus on the task of taking down the McCurdys. How many times had he planned to go to the Campbells only to have to stay behind to care for his wife because she'd fallen victim to another McCurdy attack?

He no longer needed to worry of such things. He was free to do whatever he wished.

Alone.

Except for the hound that followed him everywhere, looking even more grim than was his normal countenance. Even now Rascal lay at the edge of the bailey with his head on his paws, looking morose.

Bryce wasn't sure which one of them missed her more. The only difference was Rascal wasn't even trying to hide it, while Bryce used his misery to fuel his orders.

The drills continued until the sun was low in the sky, and the grunts of his men were overpowered by the sound of their bellies grumbling.

"You must move faster," Bryce snapped at Liam. "Do you want the McCurdys to take you down? Do you never wish to see a ship bearing the MacKinlay crest sailing home to our own shores?" He raised his sword again and felt his muscles lag with fatigue.

Lach came up behind him. "That's enough for today. See yourselves fed," the laird ordered.

Bryce glared at Lach, happy to have a place to vent his anger. His cousin shouldn't have stepped in and countered his orders. Bryce was the war chief.

"Let's walk," Lach said, nodding toward the gates.

Bryce gladly followed. The fewer people who saw his outrage the better.

They strode in silence until they came to a stop in front of the place where his burned-out cabin had been. The first one. This spot was cursed and held nothing but bad memories for him.

It figured Lach would bring him here. No doubt the man had some plan brewing. He'd had enough of Lachlan MacKinlay's damned plans. He was still reeling from the last one. The one that had brought Dorie into his life.

He looked away from the darkened spot where his life had been ripped to shreds the first time, wanting to block out all the memories, and cursed Lachlan for forcing him to come here.

"I'm your laird," Lach finally said.

"I'm aware." Bryce crossed his arms over his chest in defiance. If Lach was going to try to force him into something else, he'd picked the wrong time to do so. Bryce was spoiling for a fight. He and his cousin often disagreed on things. But Lach was the laird and always had the final say.

Maybe it was time for Bryce to move on. Maybe he'd be able to make peace when he visited his father and find a place with the Campbells.

"I'm also your blood," Lach went on. "And, I hope, a friend."

Bryce frowned and dropped his stance. He let out a shaky breath before giving a short nod of agreement. The fight went out of him. "You are that."

It would have been easier if Lach had criticized his orders to the men. Bryce might have had an outlet for his anger. He didn't want understanding and pity. Never pity.

"You say we're friends," Lach said quietly, "yet you continue to wrap yourself in pain and misery, instead of letting me help you."

"You know well enough there is no help for me. You've been trying for years."

"Dorie healed you. I saw it."

"You carry battle scars. You ken well enough how those scarred bits are numb. You canna feel them anymore. They're never the same as they were before. Nothing can make you feel those places the same way again."

Didn't the man understand how Bryce *wanted* the numbness? It didn't hurt as much that way.

"I didn't know your Maggie well, but I know Kenna. I know how much I care for her and our children. And I know if she were gone, I would want to crawl into a hole and die rather than live without her. But I also know I'd have to face her some day in the place after this one, and I would bloody well make sure she wouldn't be waiting there to blister me for not living the best life I could."

"It's easy to say the words. It's another to live it."

Lach crossed his arms. "I'm sure that's true, but if we're speaking of truths, tell me this. Why are you here?" Clearly, he wasn't going to give up on this conversation. Perhaps Bryce still had a chance to turn this into a good physical fight.

"What do you mean?" Bryce held his hands out. "I followed you here."

"Nay. I mean why are you still here, breathing, eating, talking? If you're committed to only living a sliver of a real life, why not just get it over with? End it and be done with it already. What keeps ye here? Why not take that final step off the battlements?"

Bryce pulled his brows together in confusion and irritation. Didn't the man just tell him he was a friend? What kind of friend suggested such a thing?

"It would have been easy enough to let yourself be taken in battle, yet you fight hard to survive each time I stand next to ye on the battlefield. Why not let go? Just let it happen?"

Bryce continued to stand there staring at his laird as the last of the day's sun faded away.

The second day gone since Dorie had left him.

Nay, that wasn't right. She hadn't left him. He'd let her go. She would have stayed if he'd but asked. If he'd begged her to remain his wife. If he'd only tried.

Lach raised his hand, palm out. "Before you think me cruel, know that I'm asking this with your best interests in mind. For years I've seen you—a shadow of who you once were—haunting our lives like a wraith, but not really living. Sure, you're there next to us in the flesh. Through marriages and children born. As well as battles won and lost. But you've not truly been a part of our lives since Maggie died. You keep to the edges of our lives. You never hold my boys, or Lizzy or Aiden."

Bryce tried to swallow the lump that had grown in his throat, but it wouldn't budge. "I would lay down my life in protection of any of your wee hellions."

"I don't doubt it for a minute. But what sacrifice is that from a man with no life to forfeit?"

Bryce choked and swiped at his eyes. "You ask too much."

"I don't think so. You're stronger than you think."

"I'm not." Bryce shook his head, turned abruptly, and left.

The damn dog followed on his heels, but he wanted to be alone.

"Go away!" he yelled when he'd regained his voice.

The dog ducked his head but continued to walk behind him as he stomped through the forest at the edge of the village.

"Leave! Get!" He waved his hands, which caused Rascal to retreat only a few feet.

When Bryce sat on a log by a stream, the dog stayed back and sat down to wait.

"I don't need you following me about, making me feel worse." He turned to see if his words had done any good, but naturally the dog remained. "Christ. I should never have let her make you into a pet. You were supposed to keep *her* company, not pester me to death."

Good God. Was he so in need for a place to put his rage that he was yelling at a poor dog?

He let out a breath and let his head hang in his hands. "It's too late," he muttered. "She's gone."

He felt the hot burn of tears a moment before the wetness dripped off his jaw. He wiped them away with the heel of his palm, but more took their place. Squeezing his eyes shut, he gave up and let them come.

Until he felt moist breath on his face and grimaced at the foul odor. Opening his eyes, he found himself face to face with large brown eyes framed in gray fur. The dog nuzzled under his arm and sat as close as physically possible. Bryce chuckled through his tears and wiped them away once more. He scratched Rascal behind the ears and patted the dog's sturdy shoulder.

After he'd collected himself, he stood and swatted his thigh. "Come. We've things to do. What's done is done. Best we both move on."

. . .

After days of bumping along in the carriage, Dorie actually found herself wishing she could curl into a corner of a room alone with a book—something she'd never thought to want ever again after her isolation as a child.

She enjoyed her father's company. She loved hearing his stories and seeing the way his lips pulled into a smile when he spoke of her mother. But she was always grateful when they stopped for the night at an inn where she could be quiet and still for a little while. And alone.

Sleep had been elusive during their journey. She'd always spent the nights tossing and turning, wondering if she'd made the right choice.

It was midday when they arrived at her father's country estate in Durham, England. As she stepped out of the carriage with her father's assistance, a group of people hurried out of the house to greet them. A handful of them were children who came running and screaming in excitement for her father.

"Papa!" they all called and crowded around him. He was smiling as he bent to hug and kiss them all.

He had spoken often of the children on the journey, so she could guess their names by their ages.

"I missed you," the littlest girl said in an accusatory tone. She must be Geneva.

"I've missed you as well, button. Have you been a good girl?" he asked.

"Of course not," the little boy beside her said as if the idea was preposterous. No doubt this was George.

"And what of you?"

"No!" the boy admitted, causing them all to laugh.

The older girl was watching Dorie, her eyes squinting. Nadia, if she wasn't mistaken.

"Papa, who is that?" It was the oldest boy who finally asked. He was tall, but his face still held the soft curves of youth. This was Philip, then.

"Right. I guess we should just get on with it then." Her father seemed nervous.

Just then a blond woman hurried down the steps with a warm smile. At first Dorie thought it was another child, for she was small. But as she came closer, it was clear from the resemblance to the oldest daughter that this was Harriet, their mother.

The woman her father had married even though he still

loved Dorie's mother.

Something made Dorie want to reach for the woman and pull her into an embrace. Some bond of kindred spirits, she supposed. But she suppressed it and remained in place as her half brothers and sisters stared at her expectantly.

"Children, this is your sister," her father announced.

Four sets of eyes narrowed on her in disbelief.

Little Geneva gasped as her eyes went bright. "You look like me," she said happily.

"Yes. I see the resemblance." Dorie smiled down at the little girl, happy to be accepted. "I guess we both look like our father."

"Why does she talk funny?" her little brother George asked.

Rather than pop him in the nose as Mari had suggested, Dorie laughed. "Because I'm Scottish."

"I don't have a Scottish sister," Philip, the oldest, said in shock.

"It turns out you do. This is Dorie. She's come to live with us."

"For how long?" Nadia asked, her eyes still narrowed.

"For as long as she wishes. And I expect you all to welcome her and treat her like a sister."

Dorie's smile faltered as she watched George contemplate the request and then smile in the most devious way for someone so young. She made a note to check her bed for frogs—or worse—before sliding beneath the covers.

"Welcome, Dorie. It's so nice to meet you," the blond woman offered as she came closer and pulled Dorie into a hug. "Dorien wrote to me of you. He's so happy to have found you."

"Are you upset to have me here?" Dorie whispered. She knew the children would come around eventually, but this woman was not blood and had no reason to accept her. In fact, she might hate Dorie for being an intruder, the bastard daughter of her husband.

But Harriet kept smiling. "I'm not upset at all. You're part of our family now."

"Thank you." Dorie squeezed the woman's hands.

"Come, we have your room ready. You would probably like to rest on something that stays still before dinner."

"Aye."

"Aye," George imitated with a giggle, earning a frown from Philip and Nadia.

Geneva came closer and took Dorie's hand. The resemblance between them was uncanny. The same shiny black hair and blue eyes that seemed almost too big for the elfin face gazing up at her. Geneva stayed with Dorie until she was settled in her room and Harriet shooed her away.

"Welcome home, Dorie. Let us know if there's anything you need."

She gave her stepmother a warm smile. "Thank you."

Harriet closed the door, leaving Dorie alone in the room. The bed was extravagant and soft. She kicked off her shoes and slipped out of her gown to rest in her shift. But as she lay there, all she could think of was the empty space in the bed next to her. The space that would have been filled with her husband if she were still at Dunardry.

She wondered what he was doing right now.

Did he ever think of her at all?

Chapter Twenty-Five

Bryce rolled out of his bed before dawn, having slept horribly the night before. The bed was much too empty without Dorie in it. Her scent had faded from the room when the maids had changed out the bedding, and he hated the absence of her from his life.

To keep his mind busy, he focused every waking minute on how to take Baehaven. He manned a small party that rode out and kidnapped a McCurdy guard. Lachlan was able to get vital information from the man regarding the state of the infighting within their clan.

As expected, the other clan was splitting apart. Father against son. While a more even split might have worked in their favor, it was still an advantage to have the McCurdy men distracted with their own problems.

"We've plenty enough men to take the McCurdys in their current state. Our warriors are well trained and strong," Bryce reported to Cam and Lach.

"They are trained and strong, but not so much so that they can take on three McCurdy soldiers each if the enemy remains banded together," Lach said. "I'll not risk my men unless victory is clear. Which means we need you to go to the Campbells. I'll send Liam to the Stewarts."

"We don't need them."

"Are you saying this because you do not want help, or because you're not as bright as I gave you credit for?" Lach paused. "Or perhaps you have a death wish? I tell you, cousin, I have many great things to live for and I'll not let ye drag me into a fight we're not sure to win," Lach said with his arms crossed over his formidable chest.

Bryce wasn't able to refute any of the given choices. Mayhap because the answer lay somewhere between all three. And he didn't want to think about how much the last option appealed. To be cut down in battle had been his wish for years after he lost Maggie. He'd been reckless on the battlefield and even picked fights with traveling soldiers in hopes of putting an end to the pain without having to do the deed himself.

But he'd never been able to stand there and allow a blade to fall on him without reacting. Some small part of his soul didn't want to die and always raised his arm in defense each time.

Lach, indeed, had many reasons to stay alive. Three boys and another child on the way. A healthy, happy wife. The respect of his clan.

Including Bryce.

"It certainly won't hurt to have more men," he reluctantly agreed, though he hated the idea of a delay.

"I've sent word to the Fletchers, so we have their assistance when we're ready. Once everything is in order and we have three times the men the McCurdys do, *then* we attack, and not before." Lach spoke with the authority of a laird, but also with reason that had eluded Bryce since Dorie's carriage rolled away.

He didn't want to put his men or family in danger, even if he didn't much care about what happened to himself. He wanted to leave that afternoon for Baehaven and be done with it. But he would wait.

The end would come soon enough.

Either for the McCurdys, or for him.

...

Dorie had settled in at Sutherland House, but she couldn't say that she felt at home. She'd never seen such lovely things, and the house was filled with beautiful furnishings, paintings, and objects. Her siblings treated her kindly, but as they would a stranger rather than family. Either because she wasn't a full sibling or because of the age difference between them, she had not been brought into the circle of their secret jokes and knowing looks.

Harriet was wonderful, though. A pleasant mix of friend and mother, offering advice and comfort when needed.

Her father spent time with her each day, checking to make sure she was happy and didn't need anything. She couldn't imagine she would ever need anything more. She had been given more dresses in the few weeks she'd been there than she'd ever owned in her whole life combined.

Her father had even gotten her a dog. Though he wasn't a great beast like Rascal, he was happy and obedient. She'd let the other children name him, so she was the proud owner of a white pup named Brownie.

But even Brownie felt like a character in the books she read while in seclusion rather than part of her real life. Day after day she waited to settle into the feeling that this was all real. She was happy at Sutherland House, but not like she'd been at Dunardry.

A week later, she felt no closer to being at home.

Especially on the morning it was confirmed that she was not carrying Bryce's child. Dorie cried for hours, realizing only then that she'd been holding out hope to have a reason to go back to Dunardry and Bryce.

But she no longer had a reason, so it was time for her to move on. This was her life now, and she would have to make the best of it.

That evening she put on a fancy dress and a strained smile and went down to dinner.

Everyone was quiet at first, as if they knew how fragile she felt, like she might break at any moment if someone said something comforting.

Thankfully, dinner with the children proved to be distracting.

"Stop, ye wee beast," George scolded his twin, Geneva, who sat next to him at the table. He'd taken to Dorie's brogue quickly, despite his parents' dismay.

"George. You'll stop calling your sister names or you'll be sent from the table." Her father gave him a stern look to go with the reprimand.

"Aye," he answered glumly and sank lower in his chair. His success was short lived. A moment later he sat up and looked at Dorie. "Are you a bastard?"

Everyone at the table gasped in surprise and shock.

"George! To your room right this moment," Harriet snapped, her face red with embarrassment.

"Why must I go?" he whined. "Philip said she was. I was just asking."

Dorie felt sympathy for her youngest brother.

"Room. *Now*. I'll deal with you later," her father said, and turned to his oldest son who had flushed red with anger at his brother. "Why would you say such a thing? Especially in front of the little ones? I'm ashamed of you."

"Ashamed of *m-me*?" Philip stammered in affront. "I'm

not the one who was born out of wedlock," the boy declared.

Harriet muttered and looked up at the ceiling as if praying for patience. "You can go to your room as well, young man."

At this point in the horrible ordeal, Geneva began to cry and ran from her seat to fling herself into Dorie's lap, begging her not to leave because George was bad and Philip was mean.

"It's okay. I'm not going anywhere, love," Dorie promised her little sister.

Nadia glared at her and left without a word. Dorie thought perhaps the other girl was upset that Geneva liked Dorie more than her. Or maybe Nadia blamed Dorie for the trouble Philip had landed in. Dorie hadn't yet won the older children over, that was obvious.

"I'm sorry to have caused so much trouble," Dorie said while patting Geneva.

"It's not your fault, dear. It's me who is sorry for the way my children have behaved," Harriet said, frowning toward the door where three of the children had gone.

"It's a big change for them. For all of us, really," her father explained. "Everyone will settle in soon enough. It will be fine."

Dorie nodded, but she wasn't sure if her father was trying to convince her or himself.

Each day she waited for something to change. For the pain to lessen. For her to be happy here in England. But each night she went to bed having failed.

She missed her friends. Her dog. She wanted her old bed. And most of all she craved her husband.

Surely things would have to get better soon.

• • •

Lach's brows were drawn in that way that meant he was about

to bestow bad news. Bryce didn't need bad news. He was miserable enough as it was.

"What is it now?" he asked. Better to head off trouble.

"Before Dorien left, he offered to send men to aid in the takeover of Baehaven. As you can imagine, he has his own reasons to make sure the laird falls."

Bryce's eyes went wide at this news. He knew the viscount would be happy to put an end to the McCurdy who'd killed the woman he'd loved. Not that he needed a good reason. If he was willing to give help, they'd surely take it. Before Bryce could say anything, Lach put up his hand to halt any questions.

"I didn't tell you and Cam because I wasn't certain if he would come through, and it didn't change our plans. I still want the Fletchers, Campbells, and Stewarts next to us when we overtake the McCurdys. It will show the rest of the clans we have the support of others, and ensure no one challenges us after we take Baehaven."

"How many men does Sutherland offer?" Cam asked.

Bryce only wanted to know if there was news of Dorie and if she was well.

"Enough to make the difference between facing a battle and facing their surrender."

Surrender meant no risk of spilling MacKinlay blood, something Lachlan had fretted over all this time. This was the answer to moving on and finishing this once and for all.

But it was clear something was the matter. Lach still looked anxious. Sutherland had proven himself a friend, so Bryce wasn't sure why Lach would delay.

"What is it you're not telling us?" Bryce asked.

"I've gotten word from Dorien. His men can leave England within the month."

"That's good news," Cam said. "Why do you look so angry about it?"

"There's a condition."

"Of course there is." Bryce tossed up his arms. "The bloody English have conditions for everything."

"So do the Scots," Cam reminded him with a shrug. "What is his condition?"

"He sent a copy of the annulment. Bryce must sign it, send it back, and promise never to see Dorie again."

"That doesna seem like much of a condition." Cam looked at Bryce. "You haven't seen the lass since she left, and you haven't seemed worried over it. You'll be free. Back to the way you were before she arrived and you had to marry her. It's just what you'd hoped for."

Aye. It was what he'd hoped for. So why wasn't he ripping the papers out of Lach's hand and signing them? He spared himself a moment of sadness. Receiving the annulment meant Dorie wasn't with child. That should be good news as well…so why did he wish he could hold her?

Because she had always been sad each time her courses came. She'd not said anything, but he had known she was disappointed while he'd only been relieved.

But this time he wasn't relieved. For it meant she wasn't coming back.

"We're sure there's no way he can double-cross us?" Bryce asked Lach.

"I've read through his agreement and it's quite clear. The only condition is for you to stay out of England."

Bryce nodded and reached for the documents, but Lach pulled them out of his reach. "You'll not sign them today. Think it over and we can discuss it tomorrow."

"What's there to discuss? Cam's right, I never wanted the marriage in the first place. I have no reason to go to England, so why not sign it and have it done with? It will take care of all our problems."

"I understand it will take care of our problems with the

McCurdy, but I want to make sure I'm not creating other problems."

"What other problems?" Bryce didn't want to talk about this. He just wanted to sign the bloody papers and go on with his miserable life.

"Like ruining my war chief's chance to find happiness again."

Bryce snorted and left the hall. There would be no changing Lachlan's mind. Bryce would have to wait until the next day to be done with it. In the bailey, he sat on the steps and ran his hands through his hair. He didn't need time to think. He'd been a husband to Maggie and he hadn't wanted to marry another. How many times did he need to say it?

This annulment was exactly what he needed to put an end to his thoughts of what could happen if Dorie returned. It would ensure he never saw her again. He could be done with all of this unwanted situation with the scratch of a quill across parchment.

Rascal came up and nudged his hand. "Go away."

Surprisingly enough, the dog listened and lumbered away, leaving Bryce to his unsettled thoughts. It figured the dog would obey when he hadn't really wanted him to go.

"Razz, come." The dog stopped and looked back at him as if asking if Bryce actually knew what he wanted. The answer was no. "Here, boy," he said with more excitement. The big ox ran to him, tongue out and tail wagging. "How are you holding up, lad? Do you still remember her? Do you miss her?"

As if in answer, the dog barked and ran toward the gate. When he saw Bryce wasn't following, he ran back to sit in front of him, lifted his paw, and scratched it against Bryce's thigh. He barked again and took off for the gate once more.

"I'm sorry, boy. She's not coming back. Duty forced me to marry her, and now duty will keep me from ever getting her back."

It was easy to blame his lack of action on duty to his clan, but he knew the real reason he wasn't willing to rip up the annulment and head for England. Because if he did, he'd have to admit to the world—and worse, himself—that he missed her and needed her. He'd have to face the fact that he wanted Dorie.

After tossing and turning all night, he was in a poor mood when he entered the hall for the morning meal.

"Where are the bloody papers? I'll sign them now and be done with it," he snapped without even bothering to wish anyone a good morning. Kenna frowned when Lach shrugged.

"Very well. They're in my study. We'll take care of it after we eat."

"I'd rather do it now. I don't want this ruining my appetite."

"Fine." Lach kissed his glaring wife and stepped down from the main table.

They crossed paths with Cam and Mari as they were heading upstairs. Cam kissed his wife and their children and turned to follow behind Lach and Bryce.

In the study, Lach went to his desk and pulled out the papers. Without a word, Bryce stepped up and dipped a quill to sign.

Lach held out his hand to stop him. "Before you do that, I want to be clear that I'm not forcing you to do this. If you want to keep Dorie as your wife and bring her back to Dunardry, I would support you fully, even if it meant we didn't have the aid of Sutherland's men."

Bryce blinked at him. "Is Kenna making you say such things?"

"Nay. Well, in a roundabout way. When I first met Kenna, I didn't want a wife, either. And even if I could have brought myself to want one, I surely hadn't wanted a wife like her."

"We recall," Bryce said as Cam nodded with a scowl.

"And then I gave her a chance, and she gave me a second chance, and I've since realized I wouldn't want to live without her. She's made my life happier than I ever imagined."

"I'm glad for ye, truly. As you may remember, I felt the same way when I married Maggie. And I dinna want to live my life without her, either. But then she died, and I was forced to do just that. I managed to piece together enough bloody parts of my soul to barely be called a man. And then you lashed me to another woman. One who—"

He stepped away to compose himself for a moment, then continued.

"One who also left me. Fortunately, this time I was smart enough to protect myself from falling into the same trap as before. So step aside and let me end this farce of a marriage once and for all."

But Lach didn't step aside. In fact, Cam came to stand next to him. There was no way Bryce could get past the giant, let alone both his cousins. Even the dog who had stayed by his side since Dorie left seemed to side with the other men.

"Please, I beg you, let this be done," Bryce said in defeat.

Cam reached out and placed a heavy hand on his shoulder. "Maggie was taken from you. You had no say in the matter. If you lose Dorie, it will be because you made it so. I know you were happy with the lass. She made you smile. You deserve to be happy again. You have a choice. Make sure you make the right decision."

Bryce laughed harshly at his words. Nay, he didn't deserve to be happy, and he had no choice in anything. His life was far out of his own control. He was nothing but a fluff of a feather caught in a storm. He had no choice but to ride it out.

"What happened with Maggie was a tragedy," Lach said. "You canna blame yourself. You were called to duty and ye went. Just as any of us would go right now if asked. If they'd fallen ill while you were still at home, it wouldn't have mattered. They would still be gone."

"It would have mattered to me. It would have been the difference between saying goodbye, telling them how much I loved them, and living with the fact they died alone thinking I'd abandoned them."

Cam threw his hands in the air as if giving up on convincing him, then stepped away. Bryce looked Lach in the eyes for a good minute before the other man finally conceded and stepped aside.

With them out of his way, he was able to sign his name.

And with that, he ended his marriage.

Chapter Twenty-Six

After the handful of dinner parties Dorie had attended with her father and stepmother in Durham, she'd thought she was prepared for London.

How wrong she was.

Not only was it intimidating because of the sheer number of people, but the sheer daunting splendor of the city made her feel all the more out of her element. Her father's house in London was filled with furniture that looked more like art. Her wardrobe was filled to bursting with the latest fashions, and her maids—now there were two—busied themselves for hours with her hair and clothing.

The thing she hated most about being in the city was that her family had only come after making certain she was not carrying Bryce's child. It had been determined the first month, and the second. But her father wanted to be absolutely certain there were no mishaps before presenting her in London.

And present her he did. From the frequent visitors to their home for dinner or cards, to the endless trips to the theater where inquisitive people came up to be introduced, she was surrounded by people who looked at her as something amusing. They tittered and laughed at her speech to the point she rarely spoke.

It reminded her of the years she'd spent alone in her room unwilling to talk for fear she would say the wrong thing. Her silence now was brought on by a similar apprehension.

She didn't want to embarrass her father, but she wasn't sure how to be entertaining. Once she spoke of something funny one of the twins had done earlier in the day, only to receive stares in return. Perhaps she had told the story poorly, for she found their antics hilarious.

Even so, men flocked to her—though she had to think it was more because of the property her father offered as part of a marriage settlement rather than any interest in her as a person.

Her father was very careful in his wording when the subject of her "late" husband came up. Rather than say she was a widow, he merely said she'd lost her husband.

She couldn't argue with the statement. She had in fact lost Bryce. Not that she'd ever really had him in the first place. But the fact remained, she felt his loss immensely.

Especially when she was introduced to some English nobleman who was clearly not Bryce.

She'd written her husband a dozen letters, though they all sat in her room. She'd not had the courage to send them. She'd promised him freedom and promised herself happiness when she left Dunardry. And she was going to see that at least one of them got what was promised.

It was with this thought that she allowed herself to be primped and polished for a dance where she would spend time with Lord Reginald Truman...who had mentioned an interest in asking her father for her hand.

"Perhaps we should wait a little while longer," Dorie

suggested while smoothing her dress.

"What would we be waiting on, dear?" her stepmother asked as though truly confused.

Had she not been with Dorie every day when she'd asked if there'd been word from Bryce?

"My husband might still change his mind and come for me. I don't think he'd like to find out I spent the evening at a dance, interacting with a stranger."

"He is not a stranger. You have been properly introduced. Now, do you remember the steps?"

Her father had spent lord knows how much money for a baroque dance instructor in the hopes of making her seem graceful. Perhaps he thought if he could keep her dancing, the men would look past her Scottishness.

"There." Her stepmother stepped back to look at her. "You look lovely."

"Thank ye—you," she corrected, though she knew she still sounded like a lass from the Highlands. "Might I have a moment alone?"

"Of course. I'll see you downstairs." Harriet squeezed her shoulder as she passed, as mothers did naturally. "Everything will work out. You'll see."

When Dorie was alone, she sat on her bed and tried to gather her courage to move on. She'd been hoping for months that Bryce would come to get her and take her home.

But he wasn't coming. She had to accept that.

And she wouldn't meet a man to love her sitting in her room and giving in to her fears. Perhaps Reginald was the answer to her prayers and all she needed to do was give him a chance to win her heart. With a deep breath she brushed a hand over her gown again and left her room.

As she neared the bottom of the stairs she caught her father and stepmother in a quiet argument. Their words sounded like hissing as Harriet informed him of her displeasure. It wasn't until Dorie heard her name a moment before they turned to look at her that she realized their disagreement was about her.

Her father frowned and turned back to his wife, who nodded encouragingly.

With a deep breath—much like the one she'd taken in her room for courage—her father pasted a strained smile on his face.

"Before we leave, might you have a moment to speak in my study?"

"Aye—I mean, yes, of course."

The frown deepened. She wasn't sure if she was making a hack of her attempt to sound more British or if something else was bothering him. She hated to disappoint her father. He'd gone to so much trouble in order to secure her happiness. She hated for him to think he'd failed. Especially because he'd never actually had a fair chance of accomplishing his goal.

"You don't need to try to change your accent, sweetheart. You're Scottish, and anyone who is interested in you will have to accept and appreciate that."

"Yes, Father."

"And don't be so accommodating. If you're upset with me, you should just tell me so. If you don't care for Reginald, you don't have to accept his suit, understood?"

"Yes, Father."

Her acquiescence didn't seem to please him. The frown remained.

"Please sit," he said, his words abrupt.

"Have I done something wrong?" she asked immediately, hoping she'd not upset him. She knew him well enough to know he'd not lock her in her room for years, but still, she didn't want to risk his anger.

"Of course not. I don't know how you could think such a thing. You've been the perfect guest. Not a complaint. Even when your brothers and sisters pester you for hours."

"They are lovely," she said, wanting him to know how much she loved her siblings...terrors that they were at times.

"You've not hounded me for a single thing. No trinkets or dresses."

"I don't need anything, Papa. You've already given me so much. I couldn't ask for more." She truly didn't know what was left to ask for. If he'd tell her, she'd demand it that moment if it took the sad look from his face.

"You didn't even resist when I hired a dancing instructor, though the fellow seemed a snobbish wretch."

The man had been unpleasant. He'd looked down his nose at her as if she were a clump of horse dung. But she'd been treated far worse by Wallace, so it was an easy thing to grit her teeth and bear it so she could please her father.

"I don't understand, Papa. It seems that you wish I were more trouble, when I've striven to be the opposite. Why would you want me to complain and fuss?"

"Because," he practically shouted as he paced and ran his hand through his hair. "If you were just a bit less perfect maybe I wouldn't feel so horrible for what I've done."

"But what have you done?" she asked as she watched him, his body tense. Whatever it was, she knew it was bad. No one would be this upset over nothing. Had he already accepted Reginald's proposal before she'd had the chance to consider it? It seemed drastic for a man who had encouraged her to hold out for love.

After a few more laps of the room, her father came to sit next to her.

"I made sure Bryce would never come to London." He rubbed his temples. "There, I've confessed. Why don't I feel any better?"

Dorie gasped and nearly fell out of her chair. The dizziness only became worse as he told her what he'd done, sending an offer to Lachlan to provide men to take down the McCurdy in exchange for a promise from Bryce never to approach her again. And…requiring the annulment signed and returned.

"Why would you do this?" she asked, her voice not much louder than a whisper.

"I thought it would make it easier for you to heal. To move on with your life. I wanted to be certain he didn't show up out of selfishness. Loneliness is not the same as love, and I'll not have him keep you as his wife because he didn't want to be alone. You deserve love, Dorie. You deserve to live your life with someone the way your mother and I should have lived ours."

Dorie nodded and looked down at her hands, her fingers twisted. She took a few deep breaths and relaxed. She appreciated her father's honesty, and no harm had really been done.

She cleared her throat and looked up at the man who obviously cared about her enough to go to so much trouble and expense to see her happy. What a difference from the horrible man she'd thought was her father.

"It's fine, Papa. I know he wouldn't have come even if you'd not forced him to stay away. It's foolish of me to waste time hoping he will come when I know in my heart he won't. Let's go to the ball. I'll give Lord Reginald a chance. As you've said, it's time for me to press on."

"I'm so sorry. If you'd rather, I can send a letter stating I'll not support their cause *unless* he comes to London to see you."

She laughed at his change of heart. He was willing to do anything for her, and that brought tears to her eyes. She was loved. She wasn't loved by her husband. But she was loved by her family.

"Nay." She leaned up to kiss her father on the cheek.

"But thank you. I wouldn't want him to come because he was forced to do so. I do have some pride." She smiled.

"You are an amazing woman. The men will be lining up to ask me for your hand. I shall sharpen a stick and keep it at hand to fend them all off."

She laughed and smacked his arm. "I'm afraid the dancing instructor was far too full of himself to teach me anything of value. You'll be lucky if we make it through the night without having to replace someone's shoes."

They were still laughing when they entered the hall to find Harriet watching them. Dorie knew the worry on the woman's face was for her. Even though this woman wasn't related by blood, it was clear she cared.

She hugged the woman tightly. "All is well," Dorie assured her.

"I've confessed my sins and my eldest has forgiven me," her father said. "Let's go tread on some shoes, shall we?" He held out his elbow and gave Harriet a smile. He offered his other elbow to Dorie and she took it, eager to get on with it.

Dorie stepped out of the house determined to find someone who could help mend her broken heart. Or at the very least survive a dance with her.

Chapter Twenty-Seven

"You asked for me?" Bryce said when he entered the laird's study. Lach was playing with his boys and there was happiness in his eyes when he looked up.

"Aye." He stood and placed a hand on each of the bairns' heads before coming closer. "It's time for you to go to the Campbell and ask for men."

Bryce understood and agreed. He had put it off long enough. It was time to face his father, as well as the memories of another woman he'd lost far too soon. His mother was buried on the Campbell lands. While his father might not still mourn her, Bryce did.

Lach held out a letter. "Take this to the laird."

"Ah, so I'm a messenger now?" Bryce knew better than to snap at Lach. He wasn't angry with the laird. And he didn't mind taking the letter with him. His cousin was simply an easy target.

"I'm hoping you'll be able to sway your father to help talk the laird into helping us. Lairds listen to their chiefs."

Bryce snorted. "Ye don't listen to a bloody thing I say."

"Not true. I listen. I just don't always *agree* with what you say. Thus the reason for the letter." He gave Bryce a swat on the shoulder.

The truth was, Bryce and Lach rarely agreed on how to handle things. But it wasn't Bryce's clan to run.

"You'll see this done?" Lach lifted a brow in question.

Bryce felt a pinch of insult. The laird knew better than to question his loyalty or obedience. Bryce might not always agree or appreciate his orders, but he always—*always*—carried them through. Even if it had him married when he didn't want it.

A familiar pain tightened in his chest at the thought of Dorie. He swallowed and shook it off, grateful he'd managed to keep enough distance from her that the pain hadn't grown into what he'd felt after Maggie's death. He was right to sign the annulment. It was the best thing for Dorie. For both of them.

"You know I'll do what you ask." Bryce allowed his irritation to color his tone.

"Just not without a comment about it." Lach smirked and Bryce had to admit he was right about that.

Bryce smiled. "It's my way. You'd wonder what was wrong with me if I didn't push you on such matters."

Lach was younger, after all. Growing up, Bryce had always been the one in charge of their adventures. And the one responsible for the punishment when those adventures didn't work out so well.

Lach nodded. "Godspeed, and know I'll stand by whatever decision you make."

Bryce's eyes narrowed on his cousin. What did he mean by that? There was no decision Bryce needed to make. He would go to the Campbells and ask for men. He'd either manage an agreement or he wouldn't.

The choice wasn't up to him.

Not many choices were.

...

Since the choice was up to her, Dorie decided Lord Reginald Truman was never going to be her new husband. He was nice enough, and even handsome, but he didn't make her heart flutter, and she was rather relieved when he walked off to speak to someone else.

She was grateful that until the annulment arrived from Scotland, she wasn't free to marry anyway.

She tried her best to seem impressed by all the sights in London, but in truth, she felt suffocated in the city. The number of people was overwhelming, and she just wanted to take a walk and toss stones into a loch. Not that she could do that in Durham, either, but the country estate was closer to the Highlands than the city.

"We're going back to Durham," her father announced one evening as they were waiting to leave for the theater. Dorie had just reached the door and paused outside in the hall to prepare herself. It wouldn't do to be overly excited. He might think she didn't appreciate his efforts.

It didn't change the fact that she was overcome with relief at this news. A wide smile pulled up on her lips.

"So soon?" Harriet asked in surprise from inside the parlor.

"Yes. In truth, we shouldn't have come at all. It was premature to bring her here for a match. Not when we haven't received the signed annulment from Scotland."

Harriet pushed out a breath. "Do you really think he'll sign it? Dorie is such a wonderful young woman. I can't imagine anyone letting her get away."

"I have no doubt that when the man gets his head out of his arse he will regret his decision. But he is likely too bloody stubborn to do anything about it."

"I don't think Dorie is going to get over him. She hasn't shown the slightest interest in anyone she's met so far."

"Then we'll just have to try harder. The Duke of Sheffield will be in residence when we return. Perhaps his son."

"He's just eighteen, Dorien. Your daughter won't want a boy after she's been married to a man."

Her father let out a groan. "I hope you're not talking of physical pleasure, Harriet. I don't want to think of such things."

Dorie heard Harriet chuckle. And to her surprise she heard the sound of a kiss. In the months she'd lived with her father and his wife, she'd never seen any physical contact between the two of them.

It was clear there had been. Four children didn't come from the fairies. But listening to Dorien and Harriet now, knowing they'd shared a kiss, made her think there was more between them than she'd originally thought. Perhaps there was even a chance they were in love but didn't realize it. Could it be that her father only had the one love with her mother to compare? Maybe there were different kinds of love. Such as familial love, and the love she felt for Rascal. Perhaps there were different levels of romantic love as well. A first love might be stronger or more passionate than a more mature love.

She stepped into the parlor to find them in an embrace with smiles on their faces. It was clear to her that her father loved this woman in some way. It might not be the fiery emotion he'd felt for her mother, but there was love.

For a moment Dorie thought there might be hope for her to find the same thing with Bryce. But then she remembered he'd not come for her, nor had he written. Chances were he was glad to be alone again.

She appreciated her father trying to make her happy, but

she was beginning to realize that might be an impossible task.

...

"The laird's not available. He might be able to see you in a few days."

"Bloody hell," Bryce complained. He just wanted to get the task done and go back home. He didn't like being here. It churned up too many memories.

Good and bad.

"What do you mean, *unavailable*? Is he here or no?"

The man smiled. "Oh, he's here, all right. But he just got married and he and his bride are tucked away in their chamber, if ye ken."

Bryce understood perfectly, but in case he didn't, the man pumped his hips to make it disgustingly clear.

Disrupting the laird's activities with his new wife was a sure way to be sent away with no men to aid their fight. "Who's in charge while he's away?" he tried.

"His son." The man nodded toward the hall. "Might as well get something to eat until he wakes."

"*Wakes?* It's near noon."

"Aye. The lad likes his drink along with tiring himself with the lasses."

"Christ," Bryce cursed and wiped a hand over his face. "Where's Thomas Campbell? He's the war chief now, I understand."

"Aye. He'd be in the hall as well."

Bryce stepped into the crowded hall and looked toward the main table. He saw his father right away.

His father saw him, too, and jumped up in surprise. "Bryce, my son!" he yelled, bringing everyone seated to abrupt silence and stares.

Bryce frowned and made his way to the front table.

"Father. How do you fare?"

"Well, well. And you?"

"Good."

"What brings you here? Are you planning to join us?" The hope in his eyes made Bryce uneasy.

"Nay." His father had sent him away when he was fifteen. He was no longer a Campbell, even though he claimed the name. His loyalty belonged to the MacKinlays. "I came to speak to your laird and ask if you would join us."

His father looked at the other men around the table in confusion.

"The MacKinlays plan to take over the McCurdy clan, and we'd like to have the Campbells by our side when we do," Bryce explained.

Thomas smiled. "We've been waiting for the bastards to grow weaker from lack of coin, but so far they aren't yielding. They put all the money they have to keeping their warriors fitted out and ready for defense."

"Do you think our two armies could take them if we joined forces?"

His father turned toward him. "Perhaps, but I'm not sure the young Campbell will side with you over the McCurdy. Best to wait to speak to the laird. Jathen is unreliable."

"I wanted to have the task done so I could return home. But I suppose I will have to wait until the laird grows tired." Bryce let out a sigh.

"You should think of remaining. The laird's youngest daughter is of age. You could marry her."

"Aren't you wed to the laird's daughter?" Bryce may have missed news of yet another marriage.

"Aye. But from a different mother. Our marriage assured my position as war chief. The match has brought a lot of power."

"I am already war chief of Clan MacKinlay."

"But you and I—together—could sway decisions with the Campbells."

"Besides, I'm already married," Bryce said without thinking. It wasn't exactly true anymore. He'd signed the annulment. He was free to marry again. Not that he would. Especially not to the Campbell lass. And not just because he was having difficulty figuring out their relationship. Would his stepmother also be his sister-in-law?

It didn't matter. He moved on.

His father's eyes went wide. "That surprises me. I didna think you planned to wed again after your dear Maggie."

"I didn't want to. But it was my duty."

His father nodded and rubbed the back of his neck. "I understand. You know how bad off I was after your ma died. But I had to remarry to have someone to take care of you."

"Except your new wife didna want to take care of me, so I got shipped off to my mother's clan instead."

"Och." He waved the comment away. "It was for the best. You just said you're their war chief. Now tell me of your lass. Was it a good match?"

And just like that, his abandonment was brushed aside. Bryce didn't press it. There was no use. Instead, he allowed his father to change the subject.

"She's a McCurdy," he said. That wasn't exactly true, either, but it was much easier than explaining the confusing truth of it.

The other man's lip curled in disgust. He leaned closer and whispered, "I'll not tell a soul you're already wed. You can come here and marry again. No one will have to know. Leave the MacKinlays with their own trouble."

Bryce snorted at the suggestion. It was just like his father to turn his back on a vow of honor for the sake of convenience. The man lived only for himself and what others could give him. Those who had nothing to offer were discarded and shipped off so as not to cause him any bother.

Even if they were his son.

"I'll wait to talk to the laird. Then I must return." Even if no one would be there waiting for him.

"Bah!" Thomas shook his head. "You're loyal like your ma."

"Aye," Bryce said proudly. A man was only as good as his word. Lach's father—the old laird—had taught him that. He'd taken up the void left by Bryce's da, and Bryce felt a better man because of it.

Bryce was served his meal, and he listened to the men as he ate. They were much like the warriors at Dunardry, speaking of battles and lasses. No doubt, each time they told their tales they sounded better and better, their foes and their women's breasts both growing larger with each telling.

Bryce chuckled, thinking he might have been happy here if he'd stayed. Perhaps if he had, Maggie and Isabel wouldn't have gotten ill and died.

It wasn't the first time he'd thought such a thing, but it was the first time he'd thought it and realized he could have made it work. If he'd only tried.

He swallowed down the guilt and left the castle to go see his mother's grave. It was too early for flowers so he visited her empty-handed. Sitting on the ground he told her all the things he'd been worrying over.

"I let her go before she could cause me the type of pain Maggie caused. Or *you* caused." That last part came out in a sneer, and it wasn't until he'd heard the words spoken aloud that he realized he was angry with his mother.

She'd been the first to leave him.

"I'm a bitter mess," he told her. "I don't want to be like this, but I don't know how else to be." He shook his head and smiled. "I hope you're with Maggie and wee Isabel. Give them a kiss for me. I love you all." He kissed his fingertips and touched them to her stone before heading back to the castle.

He needed to stop by the village before he left. There was someone else he must visit. But perhaps not today. He'd dredged up enough ghosts for now.

He hadn't seen Walter since he'd been here after Maggie's death to tell the man his daughter and granddaughter had died. Bryce barely remembered the trip. Cam had come with him. Had guided him when he was so drunk he nearly fell off his horse. At the time, it was the only way he'd been able to function—by numbing the pain with drink.

Eventually Cam and Lach had forced him to deal with it another way. They'd allowed him to rage at them, even fighting with swords, until he was so exhausted he could no longer get up. When he'd awoken, he'd felt a change. The pain had lessened enough that he could breathe. But a dull anger had taken its place. The sun hadn't shone as bright, the sky had no longer been as blue.

Or at least it hadn't been until Dorie came into his life.

But now she was gone, too.

Chapter Twenty-Eight

It was raining again, which did nothing to bolster Dorie's mood. Her younger siblings had entertained her after the family's return to Durham, but now they'd been called away for lessons, leaving Dorie to sit and think.

Thinking led to wishing, which led to hoping and dreaming. All things she'd spent too much time doing in her past. After her mother's death she'd sat in her prison and wished for someone to come for her. Hoped for someone to care and dreamed of having a husband and family.

Her time with Bryce had been a mockery of those dreams. She'd thought he might at least miss her enough to send a note. Perhaps see how she fared in her new life. But nothing.

When someone knocked on her door, she nearly didn't answer. She wanted to be left alone in her misery. Which was a testament to how much she'd changed. Months ago she would have wanted a visitor more than anything and wouldn't have wanted to spend another minute alone in her room.

"Yes," she answered.

Her father opened the door and entered. "Are you well?"

"Yes. I'm fine. I'm just…" She looked out the window as if the end of the sentence lived out there on the lane she'd been watching for days.

"He's not coming," her father said, his voice low and flat.

"I know," she agreed. "I thought mayhap he would send a letter, at least. Simply scratch a few words and send them off. Would that be so difficult?"

He swallowed and took her hand. "I'm waiting for a letter from Scotland as well."

"You are?" She turned to face her father.

"I hate to see you so unhappy. I thought it best to carry out our plan so perhaps you could find someone else. Someone who can give you his heart."

"Bryce hasn't signed the annulment?" she said, hating the way the words squeaked when she spoke. She tried not to hope. Was there a reason for the delay? Had he changed his mind?

"I expect it any day," her father said assuredly.

"Unless he changed his mind." She mentally calculated the time she'd been in England at the estate and then in town and now back in Durham. Surely it should have arrived by now.

"It may have been delayed when we left London."

She nodded and felt her shoulders slump as the hope left her once again.

He let out a breath and pulled her to him. "I'm sorry you're hurting. I tell you, if he were here right now I'd run him through for breaking your heart. You deserve happiness, and I'll spend the rest of my days seeing that you find someone who's good enough for you."

She smiled. "Thank you, Papa."

While she loved her father and knew he wanted the best for her, the thought of him hurting Bryce caused a flare of mutiny. She didn't blame Bryce for her pain. He'd been honest from the beginning about not wanting their marriage. She'd seen the struggle in his eyes between duty and emotion. And later, between longing and loyalty.

She thought he'd wanted to love her in the end, but neither of them were in charge of their hearts. No one could help loving someone, and no one could force another to love them when there wasn't anything to give.

"I know it may not seem like it at the moment, but you will feel better, in time," her father said. "Hearts do have a way of healing so we're able to go on living."

She knew it was possible. She'd seen the way Bryce managed to go on living with half a heart. Even her father had a sadness in his eyes she knew was from missing her mother.

She had no doubt her heart would continue to beat. That she would go on living, just as her father said. But finding happiness was another matter.

And at the moment that felt impossible.

...

Bryce frowned at his father as the man slurred a sloppy invitation to one of the serving maids. It was clear from her frown the lass was used to dodging the man's advances.

"Leave her be, you sot," Bryce ordered. "I can't imagine how you would forget you're married, having done it so many times."

Thomas snorted and shook his head before taking another swallow of ale. "I keep trying to get it back," he said.

"Get what back?"

"The way I felt with your mother. She was the one. The others were simply ways to forget how much I love and miss her."

Bryce swallowed, hating that he and his father had

anything in common. "Do you remember Ma's smile or her laugh?"

The man's eyes grew watery as he shook his head. "Nay. It's lost to the years." He slammed his hand on the table. Drink was known to make men more emotional, but it was clear his father still hurt for Bryce's mother. They'd come up with two complete opposite ways to cope with their grief.

Except Bryce's form of grief didn't hurt anyone. Except Dorie. And himself. Still... "It doesn't seem fair to your other wives." While he spoke of his father's situation, he knew he was referring to his own relationship with Dorie. It wasn't fair to want her when he couldn't love her fully. She deserved more, and he hoped she'd found it in England.

The ale tasted bitter when he swallowed. Or perhaps it was that he wasn't truly happy for Dorie. He just needed a little more time.

He'd done the right thing to let her go. To sign the annulment so she would be free to find a man who could love her the way she ought to be loved.

"It wasn't fair to you, either." His father's head fell closer to his chest. It wouldn't be long before he would be asleep until late the next morning.

Bryce might get an honest answer from him, if he only dared to ask. "What wasn't fair to me?"

"I sent you away so I wouldn't have to look at you. Seeing you reminded me too much of her. You have her coloring and her heart. I couldn't stand it. So I sent you away so you wouldn't be a constant reminder."

The man was right about the coloring. Bryce had his mother's fair hair and green eyes. But he didn't have her heart. Maybe at one time he did, but not anymore.

He didn't have a heart at all.

And he'd sent Dorie away because she'd made him feel again when he hadn't thought it possible. She'd made him laugh and smile. She'd made him want and need.

And then she'd left him.

No. She hadn't left.

He'd sent her away.

Maybe he was his father's son, after all.

...

Bryce managed a visit with Walter the next morning. The man was well and spoke of his daughter with a fond smile rather than heart-crushing pain. Bryce wondered how he managed it, but didn't ask.

While he was with Walter, he'd received word the laird was attending to clan business today, so Bryce headed up to the castle. He hoped to be on his way home directly after delivering his message and securing an alliance with the laird. He wanted to get home. He had a battle to prepare for. His men were ready, but they would run through drills until the day before they left.

An older woman carrying a basket out of a cottage stumbled and dropped her load as he made his way up the path. He stopped to help her gather her things. She looked up to thank him, but the smile fell from her face, and she gasped in surprise.

Bryce recognized her but couldn't place where he knew her from. Had she been one of his mother's friends? "Do I know you?" he asked politely.

After looking over her shoulder as if for a place to flee, she frowned and nodded. "I'm Rebecca MacKinlay."

Her name brought back the memory in a rush. The reason he hadn't recognized her immediately was because he was trying to place her here with the Campbells where she didn't belong. "You lived next door to…" He swallowed and forced the name out. "Maggie and me."

"Aye."

He hadn't known what happened to the woman. Hadn't known what happened to anyone in those months and years after his wife and child had died. He'd folded into his grief and hadn't come out for a long time. Hadn't wanted to come out. Not until a shy, lanky lass dragged him out.

"How did ye find yourself here with the Campbells?" he asked.

"I came here... You see, I lost my family, too. My husband and my boys. I tried to care for them all, your lasses and my men." She sighed heavily.

"You took care of my family when they were ill?" he asked.

She shrugged. "I wasn't able to do anything for any of them in the end. But I was there with Maggie and wee Isabel when they passed. I was no healer, but I tried my best to make them comfortable. There were so many sick. I'd lost Edgar and the boys the day before, and hoped I'd have better luck helping Maggie and Isabel. But I knew when I entered the house, they were too far gone."

Tears filled the woman's eyes as he stared at her dry-eyed, waiting to hear the rest of her story. How many times had he wanted to know the details? If his wife had hated him when she died? If his daughter had cried for her mother. For him. He'd found them in their beds and hadn't known who had succumbed first.

This woman could tell him, if he was brave enough to ask.

He finally spoke, but his voice didn't sound like his own. "How did they go?"

"Isabel went first. The morning before Maggie. I—I lied to your wife. She was so worried about your daughter, I told her Isabel was doing better. That she was eating." The woman crossed herself. "I told her I only kept her away because I didn't want the child to catch the sickness again. Maggie was able to relax then. She worried about you as well. She told me I must keep you away. That you were to return soon and she didn't want you to be exposed. That night she grew weaker and she told me to tell you that she was so sorry to leave you. That she loved you. I told her you loved her as well, and she smiled and said she knew. It was easy to see the way the two of you felt about each other."

She smiled at that, but her smile faded. "I wish I'd left a missive to pass on her words, but I don't know my letters." She hung her head.

"I understand."

"I was so lost in my grief. My sister lost her husband as well. We were both Campbells before we wed MacKinlay men, so we decided to come back home together. I should have gone back to give you her message, but there were too many memories there I wasna willing to face. I hope you're not angry."

Bryce put his hand on hers and offered a brittle smile. "It comforts me to know they were not alone at the end. There was nothing you could have done to save them," he said. The ague that had ravaged the village took many lives while leaving others unaffected. Some would call it God's will, but what god would will the death of innocents?

"Aye," she agreed. "There is nothing anyone could have done." It was a simple phrase. One he'd been told many times by his friends and family over the years. But at that moment, the reality of those words hit with the force of their truth.

"I wouldn't have been able to save them," he said quietly as the meaning settled in.

The old woman's hands gripped his tightly, holding him in place as he swayed from the impact of a decade of guilt suddenly pulling free from his shoulders.

"Nay. The only thing we can do for them now is to live

the best life we can to honor their memories."

Tears streamed down his cheeks. More came as fast as he could wipe them away. The old woman held him as they both wept. They must have looked a sight, standing there crying in the middle of the village, but he didn't care.

He pulled in a breath, breathing deeply without pain for the first time in so long.

He was alive.

It was time he started acting like it.

Chapter Twenty-Nine

"I'm so happy to have the chance to introduce you to our neighbors," Harriet said as Dorie's father handed them into the carriage. "How convenient for the duke to invite us to his home for a dinner party. There will be a number of wealthy landowners from the area. I know you like the country better than town."

Her father gave his wife an indulgent smile and Dorie wondered if Harriet knew what she was missing. Dorie was certain no one but her own mother had ever seen the full force of the viscount's emotions.

Dorie's own smile slipped when she remembered Bryce's smile and how guarded it was. How it was also always missing something.

He hadn't loved her. And she hadn't been able to love him enough to bridge the gap between them. Swallowing back the pain, she forced her lips up and straightened her shoulders.

Harriet had encouraged Dorie's maid to take special measures with her hair and dress this evening.

Dorie felt excitement rise in her chest. Perhaps tonight

would be the night she would meet the man who would love her. A man who could heal her wounded heart and allow her happiness.

These men would be from the country. Surely one of them would be a good match for her.

She only needed to give them a chance and certainly one of them would touch her heart.

Or so she'd hoped.

But it didn't take Dorie long to concede defeat. If one more man bowed over her hand, expounding on her beauty, she might scream. Or collapse. Not that she was the fainting type. She'd been through much worse and remained on her feet. But she'd rather feign swooning than have to participate in such tedious conversations.

The color of her eyes had been compared to bluebells, the sky, and sapphires. Her hair was likened to raven's wings, midnight, and ebony. She even waited while two men debated if her skin closer resembled fresh milk or cream.

So many times when she'd been captive at Baehaven she'd wished for someone to keep her company. But this was not the companionship she'd craved. Not fancy words said only for the sake of wooing her. Did other women actually fall for this sort of vapid nonsense?

As the men smothered her with compliments, she thought of Bryce and wished he were here to run them off with a few gruff words.

He wouldn't waste time with fancy words. He would simply look at her in that hungry way she loved and show her with his body how much she pleased him. He'd lie next to her, kissing her until she couldn't catch her breath and she was moaning with need before he came over her, his weight pressing her down into the bed, giving her a feeling of protection and possession.

And when she thought she wouldn't survive one more

second, he'd push inside her, with a sound of surrender. Her body would stretch to accommodate him, welcoming his—

"Are you well?" Harriet interrupted the best part of her evening so far. "You seem flushed." Being the mother she was, Harriet reached out and placed a cool hand on Dorie's temple. "Perhaps we should leave."

"Nay. I'm fine. I'm just a bit overwhelmed with all the attention." She offered a strained smile to the still-arguing men in front of her.

Her father gave a stern look and the men flitted away.

Did she really want a man who cowered away from her father? She preferred brave men who stood strong and fought for what they wanted.

Again her thoughts went to Bryce.

He hadn't fought for her, and she knew the reason why. She hadn't been something he'd wanted. "I'm afraid I'm not very good at this," she admitted to her stepmother.

Harriet waved a hand. "I don't blame you, dear. I'd forgotten how tedious this was. It's all rather ridiculous really."

"Did my father talk to you like this?"

That brought out a laugh. "No. Of course not."

Dorie laughed, too. "I was having a difficult time picturing it."

"No, your father did not offer any romantic words. He was much too practical for such things. He simply said he needed a wife, and would I be up for the task."

Dorie's smile faded. "You knew he wasn't in love with you."

"Not many marriages start out that way."

"What about now?" Dorie waited as Harriet waved to someone and then looked back to her.

"I love your father, and in many ways your father loves me, too. I think he loves me more than he even knows. He doesn't express it in words, but in his actions. He gets in on my side of the bed to warm it before I get there. He kisses me on the top of the head when he leaves the room. And he looks at me when one of the children do something that should be shared with a smile."

"And that's enough?"

"Dorien had a grand love affair with your mother. He was young and on a wild adventure when he met her and fell in love. Her death suspended those feelings for him, but—with no disrespect to your mother—we have no idea if their love would have remained as passionate as it seemed. The truth is, a marriage is not always passionate. It's sometimes simple and comfortable."

Dorie nodded, remembering Kenna and Mari and their relationships with their husbands. There was love in their eyes, but their days were filled talking about mundane things like which of the twins stuck a pebble up their nose or how Lizzy got the bump on her head.

"Do you think I made a mistake to leave Bryce?" Dorie asked. This woman knew better than anyone what Dorie felt.

"I can't say. I never had the opportunity to see the two of you together. I'm certain it wouldn't have mattered if he was perfect for you; your father would have found fault in the man and offered you the same escape regardless. I doubt he would find anyone worthy of you. It's the way of fathers."

"I thought it would be easier to find someone to love me than to make the man I love feel something for me. But I think maybe he did love me. In his own way. He never said it, and in fact told me he never would, so I believed that was the truth. But what if he didn't even realize? What if I gave up my only chance for happiness in my quest for…happiness?"

"Be calm. There's still time."

"But that's just it. Right this moment the signed annulment could be on its way from Scotland. My marriage could already be over."

Harriet's lips pulled up in a devious smile, and for a moment Dorie worried she'd been tricked by the woman into believing she cared. "The annulment would dissolve your marriage, but there's nothing to stop you from marrying him again."

Dorie blinked at the clever woman.

"But what if he rejects me?"

"He would have to be a fool to reject you. What with your raven-wing hair and eyes the color of—"

"Bluebells in the sky surrounded by sapphires." Dorie rolled her eyes.

"Yes, quite."

They laughed together and went to find the viscount so they could leave. Dorie was never going to find the man she loved here. For he was back in Scotland, and she was going back to spend her life with him.

An hour later they left for home. Dorie wished for silence as she thought over her options. She'd wait until morning to ask her father to take her back to Dunardry.

Her wish for silence went unfulfilled because her father asked about the men Dorie had met and if any were a candidate for a potential new husband.

"I'm afraid not, Papa."

He frowned. "I thought as much. I'm sorry."

"It's all right. In truth, they might have been lovely. I truly think it's me." Her plans for waiting until morning fell away. "I don't think I belong here."

"Of course you do. It's only been a few months. We'll cast a larger net. I know—"

"Dorien," Harriet said with the authority of a noblewoman. "Listen to your daughter. She's telling you what *she* wants."

"She is?" He looked at her. "I'm sorry, sweetheart. What

did you say? I must have missed it."

"I want to go home." The words came out in a gush.

"I'm sure I would have noticed if you'd said that." He frowned and shook his head.

Dorie patted his hand. "I'm sorry. I know you had plans for me. But in truth, I want the life I had. I was happy there."

"He told you he couldn't love you as you deserved," her father reminded her.

Not that she had forgotten.

"But he did love me in the way that he could. He might not ever say the words, but I know there's something there in his heart. And I let it go because I thought love must be some big glorious thing. But sometimes it's not. Sometimes it's simple, yet just as wonderful."

Tears started down her cheeks. All these months she'd cried because she hadn't been wanted. This time it was for the loss of something she'd willingly given up.

"You're exhausted from talking to all those ninnies. We'll speak in the morning and decide what to do. Rest tonight."

She nodded, not just to appease him, but because it was good advice and she was tired.

It was nearly midnight when they arrived home. Her father helped her down as a shadow moved closer to the carriage. In the light from the lantern she saw a large man approach and gasped in surprise.

"What are you doing here?" her father asked.

Bryce bowed in front of them and stood there, towering over all of them. "I've come to ask ye for your daughter's hand in marriage."

Chapter Thirty

Bryce knew it was much too late in the evening for such discussions. He'd planned to stay in the stables until the morning. But when the carriage had returned home, he couldn't dismiss his need to see Dorie.

Rather than spend the rest of the night tossing and turning in a mound of hay, he'd given in to his urge. They'd spent too much time apart already. Time he'd never get back.

It wasn't until Dorien had asked why he was there that he knew the answer.

When he'd left the Campbell laird with only a reluctant agreement to aid in the takeover of the McCurdys, he knew he couldn't risk losing Dorien's promise of men. But as he headed toward Dunardry, thinking of his future, he realized it looked rather bleak and lonely.

He'd embraced the loneliness before, encouraged it even, as a penance. But now that he knew the truth—felt it in his soul—he realized he'd paid enough. Maggie had loved him, even as she lay dying. She wouldn't want him to spend the rest of his life in this misery with nothing but rage in his heart.

She would have thought him a coward for keeping himself safely hidden away from any chance of further pain.

Before he knew what he was doing, he'd changed course to end up in Durham, England. And was now standing here before the woman he had given up. The woman who had made him feel something good for the first time in years.

He was most likely too late to stop the annulment from going through. But as long as she wasn't promised to another, there was a chance she might marry him again. This time in a pretty dress like the one she was wearing now. With shoes, and her own strong voice declaring she would love him until death parted them. He closed his eyes, sending up a silent prayer that death wouldn't part them for a very long time.

"I believe we should speak on the matter alone," her father said. "In the morning. It's too late to discuss such things tonight. You may stay in one of the guest rooms." Dorien's eyes flared as if waiting for Bryce to make a complaint regarding the sleeping arrangements.

As much as he wanted to hold Dorie and even pull her under him so he could make love to her, he would respect the man's home, in the hope Dorien would take Bryce's suit seriously.

Dorie said nothing, and it reminded him of when he'd first met her and the way they'd communicated on another level. As then, he could almost hear her thoughts as she watched him with wide eyes. He frowned when he noticed the dark circles under them. His wife wasn't sleeping well, and he hated to think it was his doing. Was she unhappy here? He couldn't imagine her not wanting to live here, from the look of the house and her new clothes.

He was shown to his room immediately and after removing his kilt and boots, he lay in the most elaborate bed he'd ever seen. He couldn't sleep. What was he thinking? He'd come all this way to try to get her back when he had nothing to offer her. Bloody hell. He should have brought the dog. At least then he might have had a chance.

He didn't even have a way to take Dorie home. He'd not be able to afford a luxurious carriage like the one she'd ridden in when she'd left Dunardry. He'd need to buy a horse for her.

He cast that idea aside. She wouldn't be able to bring all her nice things with her on a horse. She was a viscount's daughter. She had things now. Nice things. Like a fancy brush and comb set.

The reminder made his stomach flip with unease. What if she was glad to be rid of him? What if she didn't want him? He'd state his case. Beg for her forgiveness and hope she could see past his stupidity. And if that didn't work, he'd leave her to her life here and not bother her again.

Och. Why did he come? Surely she didn't want him after the way he'd treated her. He would rest a while and sneak off before morning so as not to embarrass himself.

He turned again and heard the door open. With the moonlight coming in through the window, he watched as Dorie stepped inside, her hair glowing blue in the dim light.

"Are you awake?" she whispered.

Rather than speak, he got up and went to her. He wanted to reach for her, but she stepped back, crossing her arms over her chest, blocking the view of her breasts through the thin gown. He had no right to touch her. She was no longer his.

He stayed a short distance away, watching and waiting to hear why she'd come to him in the middle of the night.

When she said nothing, he grew restless. "Do ye love someone else, Dorie? I wouldn't blame you. Have you found another?" If she had given her heart to someone, he could be on his way immediately.

"Why are you here?" she asked, ignoring his questions. Hers were more important, and yet he didn't know how to answer. Or rather, where to start.

He took a breath and told her everything, ending with the words she needed to hear. "I left the Campbell lands planning to go back to Dunardry, but I could only think of you and how much I miss you and want you. That's how I ended up on your doorstep this evening with nothing save my horse and a few pieces of clothing."

"You signed the annulment?" she whispered when he was done.

He winced, knowing how she must feel about it. "I did. At the time, all I could think was how much I wanted all the pain to go away. I just wanted to be alone in my sorrow. But I ken now it was a mistake. I need you, Dorie. I want you with me."

She hadn't moved closer, and he worried it was too late. He'd let her go, so of course someone would have snatched her up. She was beautiful and loving and all the things a man would want in a wife.

"I'll never be able to replace Maggie," she said. "I'm not her, and I canna live my life in her shadow. I love you, Bryce, as much as I'd tried not to. But I canna heal you. Not when ye don't want to be healed. Not when you canna let me into your heart."

He clenched his fists at his side to keep from reaching for her, pulling her to him. If he ever held her again, it would have to be because he deserved her. Which meant he had to make her see how he felt now. He had to be honest. With her. With himself.

"I've been a bastard to you all this time. I took the parts I could manage and rejected the ones I couldn't, and it wasn't fair to you. I didn't mean for you to feel less than Maggie, but I see now I left you no choice but to feel that way. I'm sorry, Dorie. So sorry. I'd like to have a life with you. A family."

She took one step closer. That small move made his chest tighten with hope.

"You loved her. And I never expected you to love me the same way. People are different, I understand that. Since I've been here in Durham, I've witnessed it by seeing my father with Harriet. Love exists in different forms. I know that you love me, Bryce. Not the way you loved Maggie, but the way you're meant to love *me*."

He nodded, happy she'd found a way to explain the way he felt better than he ever could. "Aye. I do love you. Do ye think you could want a man who took too long figuring things out? If he only wants to spend the rest of his life loving you and making you happy?"

She laughed and her hand came up to rest on his chest. The same place where he felt his heart thumping with anticipation.

He rested his forehead against hers and looked her in the eye. "If you could give me another chance, I promise you won't regret it. I'll see to it you know how special you are every day, for as long as we live."

...

Dorie had wanted to hear these words from Bryce since the first time they'd kissed, but she hadn't ever thought it could be possible. She was terrified she would wake up and find herself still in the carriage on the way home from the duke's dinner.

But the warmth of Bryce's body under her palms assured her he was really there, just as the smile on his lips and the love in his eyes told her how much he wanted her to be with him.

"There is no one true love," he whispered. "I see that now. As long as you open your heart to the possibility, you can love someone else as deeply. I know because I feel it with you. Maggie was a wonderful woman, and I did love her very much. But loving you doesn't betray what I had with her. I need to live my life. I know now how much I love you. More than I thought I could."

Looking in his eyes as he spoke, she didn't see anything but sincerity.

She placed a hand on his cheek. She loved this man. It didn't matter how many men she met at dinners and events, or how elaborate their compliments became; they wouldn't stir her heart like Bryce did. She'd been planning to leave for Scotland to beg him to take her back and love her however he was able. But now she could have all of him. It was almost too much happiness to manage.

Rather than speak, she leaned up and kissed him.

He pulled her close and kissed her like he never had before. She could feel the desperation and need in his touch, though he drew back. She wanted nothing of that and reached for him, but he put up his hand.

"I want you, Dorie. In my bed. Well, this bed, tonight. But we're no longer married, so before I lie with you, I'd like to secure your promise." He swallowed, looking rather nervous and entirely too handsome. "Would you marry me again, Dorie? Now that you have a choice in the matter?"

"Yes. Yes, I'll marry you again." This time he allowed her onslaught of kisses and wrapped his warm arms around her.

"Thank you, Dorie. You won't regret this."

"I know I won't. I was planning to leave in the morning to come to you and ask you to take me back. I didn't want to live without you anymore."

"A new beginning, the way we should have been all along."

"Aye. Now take off your shirt."

He laughed and kissed her again while tugging his shirt over his head, pulling away from her lips only to free the garment. He was naked and she wanted to be naked with him.

She reached for her shift, but his hands were already sliding up her thighs, taking her gown with them. When she was naked, he stood back and gazed at her.

"What's wrong?" she asked.

Slowly, he shook his head. "Nothing is wrong. I am just enjoying being with you without the guilt I felt before. I feel so different. So free."

She couldn't help the grin that took over her face when he wrapped his arms around her and carried her to the bed. After dropping her atop his tangled linens, he crawled into bed next to her. Propped on his elbow, he smiled down at her while his fingers traced over her skin, making her shift with impatience.

"I've missed this," she said.

"You thought of me in your bed?"

She nodded.

"What did you think of? What favorite fantasy of yours should I make reality?"

Her face heated, but she told him the things she'd longed for when she was alone in her cold bed.

He laughed and kissed her. "You shall have your every wish. I'm just glad we have the rest of the night. I think I might need it."

With that, he began fulfilling every fantasy she'd shared, as well as a few that must have been on his own list.

• • •

Bryce kissed Dorie's hair while she slept and smiled at how lucky he was she hadn't found someone else. He could have lost her forever and had no one to blame but himself. He was glad he'd gotten his head out of his arse before it was too late.

In a few hours he would talk to her father about marrying

her again so he could take her home to Dunardry. As he thought of how wonderful it would be to have someone to share his life with, he looked around the room being lit by the approaching sun.

He'd never seen such fine things before. Doubt trickled in, ruining the moment and chilling him despite the warmth their naked bodies created under the exquisite bedding.

Was she used to this life? Would she want these things, the beautiful gowns and the jewels he'd seen her wearing when she'd returned home the night before?

His soldier's pay wouldn't provide many of these luxuries. Perhaps once they took over the McCurdys and gained access to a port Bryce could learn a trade that would allow him to offer her the things she deserved.

The sun had risen and he still hadn't come up with any skills he had, save fighting. Being a warrior and protecting his clan was all he'd ever known. Still, he'd find a way. He'd promised to make her happy and he would make sure he never let her down ever again.

Dorie opened her eyes and sat up, looking around. When her gaze landed on him, she smiled. "Oh, good. I'd hoped it wasn't a dream." She snuggled up against him then jumped out of bed. "It's morning! I must go back to my room."

"I hope this is the last time we have to worry about such things. I plan to speak with your father this morning about marrying you." He frowned. "You haven't changed your mind, have you?"

"Of course not." She looked at him as if he were mad as she yanked her shift over her head, covering up his favorite parts. Her hair was ravished, and she looked radiantly rumpled and a bit tired. Male pride brought a smile to his lips, but he pressed forward with his concern.

He'd been waiting all this time to tell her, and now words didn't come easily. "This place is very nice."

"Aye. It's beautiful. I don't think I've even been in all the rooms." She laughed and he took a breath.

"I'll not be able to give you a home like this."

She blinked at him and paused by the door, ready to make her escape. "Of course we won't have a home like this. You're not a viscount, and we already have a home at Dunardry."

"What about the dresses and the jewels? I'll not be able to buy you such things, either."

She tilted her head and came back to stand before him where he sat on the edge of the bed.

"The fancy clothing and jewels were just my father's way of attracting attention to me. I believe he wanted the potential suitors to see his wealth so they would be more enticed into offering for me. In truth, I'm not one for such elaborate things. Don't take me wrong, I do enjoy having shoes, which as you recall, is more than I had when we met. But beyond that, I do not wish for more than what I had when I lived with you. I don't need baubles when I have the love of a fine man." With that, she kissed him and rushed off to slip out the door as if she'd never been there in the first place.

He fell back onto the bed and pressed his face to her pillow to breathe in the scent of her. Keeping her with him a little longer.

Soon they'd never have to be apart again.

Chapter Thirty-One

Bryce ran a hand over his shirt to smooth it—as if that would help. As soon as the viscount saw Bryce's smile he'd know immediately what they'd done. And he couldn't stop smiling.

He coughed and walked into the room where Dorie's father waited to speak with him. It was better to get it over with. Surely this village had a clergyman who could marry them so they could be on their way by noon. Bryce only had to survive this conversation.

Dorie was already seated in the room and he couldn't help but notice she was smiling as well. When she spotted him, that smile grew and a lovely blush bloomed on her cheeks. No doubt she was remembering the night before. He couldn't wait to have this morning over so they could be together as a married couple once more.

He took the seat as far from Dorie as possible so as not to touch her and offend her father. But even the distance didn't keep them from stealing glances and sharing knowing smiles.

"Bloody hell. What have you done?" the viscount snapped while looking between them.

Even the threat of death couldn't force Bryce to look away from the woman he loved. "I'm in love with your daughter, sir. I want to marry her. Today, preferably."

"Did your laird discuss my offer and the stipulations?" he asked, sitting back in his chair and steepling his long fingers.

If the man thought to intimidate him, it wouldn't work. Bryce was leaving with his wife. No matter what.

"Aye. He told me the only way you'd fund the men we asked for was if I signed the annulment and stayed away from Dorie. I may have signed it, but that was before I realized I didn't want to live without her." Bryce swallowed and his smile dimmed slightly. "My clan would like to have your assistance, but Lach told me I needed to do what was right for me. He said we'd figure out the rest later. I have his support. Will you give Dorie and me your blessing to be wed?"

The man stared at Bryce for a long time before turning to Dorie. "I'm afraid I cannot."

Bryce reached for his sword, forgetting he'd left it in his room for this very reason. It wouldn't do to slay the man and take Dorie away. She would want to have her father in her life, so Bryce needed to remain calm and not act the beast he felt.

"Papa, please!" Dorie cried, standing to come to his side. "I appreciate everything you did for me to try to find someone to love me, but it turns out I had him all along."

"This is what you want? To be second best to a ghost?"

"She's not second best," Bryce cut in. His earlier smile was long gone now. He'd not allow anyone to belittle his feelings for Dorie. Not when he'd dragged himself through hell to finally allow those feelings. "She's the most important person in my life."

"Please, Papa," Dorie said. "He's the man I want."

"Well, it's a good thing since you're still married to him. I cannot give you my blessing to be wed because you're already married."

"Excuse me?" Bryce asked in confusion.

"You say you signed the annulment, but I never received it."

He'd signed the document and— "Lachlan." This had to have been his cousin's doing. He hadn't wanted Bryce to go through with it. He must have anticipated Bryce would change his mind. Damn it. The man's head wouldn't fit through the bloody gates when he found out he'd been right.

Dorien frowned, not in anger but with sadness. "I imagine you plan to take her back to Scotland."

Bryce understood that he didn't want to lose his daughter after she'd just entered his life a few months ago. "Aye. It's our home. It's where we'll raise our children." He smiled at the man. "Your grandchildren." Dorie came close and Bryce took her hand, giving it an encouraging squeeze. "You are welcome to visit as often as you like," Bryce added, hoping to appease his father-in-law.

"This is really what you want, Dorie?" the viscount asked.

Dorie went to her father with tears in her eyes. She hugged him tightly then stepped away. "Yes, Father. I hate to lose you, now I finally got to know you. I'll miss my brothers and sisters. And Harriet. She's a wonderful woman and so accepting of me, considering the circumstances. But I must follow my heart. And my heart wants to be with Bryce."

"And if he hurts you again…?"

"I trust him, Papa." She wiped a tear away. "I just wish I didn't have to lose you to have him." A new sob overtook her, and her father pulled her close.

"Shhh. Why do you think you have to lose me?" he asked.

She backed away and blinked up at him. "Because I've displeased you."

He gave her a soft smile. "You are my daughter. I love you. You will never lose me. Never."

"Truly?"

"Truly."

She clung to him as he held her tightly.

"As long as you're happy, I'll not be displeased." The man's words sounded warm. The glare he shot Bryce over Dorie's shoulder, however, spoke of all the harm that would come to Bryce if he hurt her in any way. Bryce did not doubt he'd one day look at a man the same way when he claimed Bryce's daughter, if they were blessed in that way.

"Thank you, Papa." She turned to Bryce and smiled. "I shall go pack so we can go home."

Home. He couldn't wait.

...

Dorie expected her brothers and sisters would be happy to see her go. She'd grown attached to them but felt they'd never quite accepted her. So it was a surprise to find three crying children clinging to her as she tried to pack her things.

Philip was, of course, too old for such dramatics, but even he seemed unhappy that she was leaving.

"I'll write to you all the time," she assured them.

"But I canna write back," George said, using the Scottish word.

"Then all the more reason for you to pay attention during your lessons so you can. In the meantime, I would be happy for you to draw me a picture. I know you can do that." Though her younger brother seemed only able to draw unfathomably large horses that took up the entire page and were larger than the manor house in the background.

Harriet took Geneva and soothed her tears. "I wish you happiness," she told Dorie. "I know I'm not old enough to be your mother, but I care for you as one would."

"And I have come to rely on your advice. Thank you so

much for making me see what was right in front of me."

Harriet and Dorie both brushed tears from their cheeks as a servant came to carry her things downstairs.

Dorie heard the two men talking in the parlor and paused to see if they'd made amends or if her father was still trying to intimidate her husband. She recalled something Harriet had said about her father never finding any man to be good enough for his daughter, and guessed this tension was normal for the situation. Though as she drew closer she realized it went beyond that.

"You realize this changes the terms of the agreement I made with your laird regarding the offer of men to aid in your takeover of the McCurdys? You'll be on your own."

"Aye. My laird supports my decision," Bryce said. "It would have been good to have your added support, but we'll move forward without it." Bryce sounded confident, but Dorie worried what would happen when Bryce came home with a wife instead of an army to conquer their enemy. "Our clan has gone decades without access to the sea, but I can't go another day without my wife," Bryce added.

Dorie's heart soared at his words. Whatever they faced when they got home, they would face together. She entered the room with a smile for both the men she cared for deeply.

Her father nodded as she joined them. He hugged her and tucked a lock of her hair behind her ear like a doting father. His gaze shot to Bryce and he sighed. "I put her in your care. Don't make me regret it."

The men shook hands. "I'll make sure you don't. The rest of my life will be spent making her happy and comforting her in those times in life when happiness is not possible."

The man nodded. "I'm glad you finally realized what you were missing."

With more teary goodbyes on the lane by the waiting carriage, Bryce tied his horse behind the vehicle and helped her inside. While Dorie wasn't exactly looking forward to a long ride in the carriage, she did want to be alone with Bryce.

He only waited until they could no longer see the manor house before he leaned over to kiss her. When she kissed him back, he took advantage and kept kissing her.

A sound of interest escaped her throat and his lips pulled up in a smile against hers. Surely he wasn't planning on…in the carriage?

"It's a long ride home and I need to make up for lost time," he said, making his intentions clear.

Her blood rushed with excitement, and she moaned when he touched her breast.

"I love the sounds you make. It makes me want to keep giving you reasons to make them."

"I canna help it," she said, then gasped when his teeth nipped the sensitive skin where her neck met her shoulder.

He'd already unbuttoned her dress enough to pull it down and expose her breasts to his mouth. She would never tire of this man. Her husband in every way.

…

"Do you still plan to take over the McCurdys?" Dorie asked when they were almost home. It had been a long trip, but Bryce hadn't minded since he'd taken up much of the time satisfying his wife in all the ways allowed in the small space of the carriage.

"It will depend on whether Liam is able to get the Stewarts to agree to join us. The Campbells have already promised their support. And the Fletchers."

"But even with the Stewarts, it would have been easier if you'd had my father's men as well."

He wouldn't lie to her, but he shrugged it off. "We will find a way. I wouldn't have wanted to go off to war with your father's men at my back if it meant I had no one to come home to when it was over."

"Perhaps if you'd asked—"

"Nay. He made it clear to me that I'd breached the agreement when he didn't receive the signed annulment and I showed up at his home instead. I can't say that I understand why he wouldn't change his mind. He has every reason to hate the McCurdys as much as we do. But his offer was made with conditions I couldn't live with, so we'll manage somehow. It's nothing for you to worry about."

Unfortunately, telling someone not to worry and them doing that were two very different things. Bryce knew his wife worried that she had ruined their chances for earning surrender from the McCurdys. But he also knew that Lach and Cam would have done the same thing in his situation. Because when it came to having Dorie in his life, he'd rather fight all the McCurdys single-handed than live without her.

There wasn't any other choice to be made.

Chapter Thirty-Two

Bryce had never been so happy to see the battlements of Dunardry as he was when they crested the final ridge and the castle came into sight. The last of the day's sun lit up the stone in welcome.

Everyone was outside waiting for them when the carriage drove into the bailey. Bryce hopped down and helped Dorie out. She'd no sooner stepped down than a large, gray mass set upon her. Whining and wiggling in excitement, Rascal welcomed her with drool and muddy paws.

"Get down, beast." Bryce brushed mud off as the dog ran in circles, clearly happy to have her home. Bryce didn't blame him. He'd barely set her to rights when Kenna and Mari nearly toppled her in excited embraces.

Bryce moved away from the squealing to speak to his cousins.

"I see you have your wife back," Lach said with a smug smile.

"Aye. You were right. I surely hope this is what you were blathering on about when you told me you supported whatever decision I made, for the viscount is not going to send his men."

Lach nodded, though the smile had faded. "I expected as much." He looked over at the women. "It's worth it to have you happy."

"She's worried you will be upset with her. Make sure you put her straight on that," Bryce said.

Cam laughed. "I must say, being a protective husband suits you well."

Lach stepped forward and held out his arms to welcome Dorie home. "I'm so glad to have you back in our fold."

She frowned. "You might not think so when you find out my father is not sending his men."

Lach waved it off. "You're more valuable to my clan than a handful of British soldiers. Women are vital to the growth of our clan. After all, none of my warriors would be here if not for the women." He winked when she blushed and Bryce squeezed his shoulder in thanks for his words.

After their meal, they went up to their room which had been filled with the trunks Dorie brought home with her.

"I'll add some pegs to the walls to hang some of these things. We'll make it all fit," he said as he pushed one of the trunks away from the bed so they could get in to sleep. The large dog didn't help make the room seem bigger.

"I shouldn't have brought everything, but Harriet was insistent that this was all mine and I should have it." She frowned when she looked at the overcrowded room. "Why would I ever need so many fancy gowns?"

Why, indeed? She certainly wouldn't have use of them here in the Highlands with a war chief as her husband.

"Dorie…" He let out a breath and took her hand. "I'm sorry I can't offer you a home like the one your father has."

Her eyes went wide. "Why ever would the two of us need a house of that size? Even with all my brothers and sisters,

Sutherland House was far too big."

He loved her practicality, but she was missing his point. "I can't even give you a home like Cam and Mari's," he explained.

"Ah. I see. Do you think I'll regret coming home with you? I knew the size of our room when I left England. And I still couldn't wait to get back here to be with you." She looked around and let her arms drop by her sides. "I will say it seems much smaller now with these trunks filling the space, but we'll figure it out another time. Come to bed, husband."

That was a request he was happy to oblige. His earlier exhaustion faded slightly as excitement took its place. He pounced on the bed, toppling her over with him.

She laughed but made no attempt to escape his clutches. "I don't really care if the room is big enough to hold my trunks, so long as the bed is big enough for the two of us to romp around in," she said, warming his heart once again.

"I shall love you from one side of the bed to the other to make sure there's plenty of room."

They spent each night over the next week testing the bed to make sure it would do.

He woke up before her one morning, Rascal taking his place as Bryce slipped out of bed. He had a bite to eat and went out to run his men through their drills. The Campbells hadn't arrived yet, and Bryce began to worry they'd changed their minds.

There was no way the MacKinlays could ensure victory over the McCurdys without the help of another clan. Liam hadn't arrived home yet from the Stewarts, either, so there was still a chance both clans might join them. Or neither.

It was almost time to stop for the noon meal when the guard on the gate yelled out, "Riders. A lot of them. Armed."

Bryce smiled and called up, "What banner do they fly?" He could wait the few minutes for them to arrive, but it was better to know if it was the Campbells or Stewarts who rode on the castle.

"No banner flying."

Bryce's smile faded and his brows creased as he looked to Lachlan. They both knew a clan approaching in peace had no reason not to fly a banner.

"Bloody hell," Lach muttered. "Bryce and I will ride out. Have the men at the wall. Prepare for battle."

...

With the help of some sturdy lads, Dorie had the trunks stacked out of the way. Kenna made room in the solar for the ones that wouldn't fit.

She offered Kenna and Mari many of the gowns. Since Dorie was so tall, it would be easy to cut them down a bit to fit Kenna, or a lot to fit tiny Marian. The women were excited for the fine dresses. Especially since they didn't have to make them themselves.

"It will sadden me to have to put them aside when I grow too big to wear them," Kenna said while rubbing her bump.

"Do you hope for a girl this time?" Dorie wondered, since Kenna and Lachlan already had three boys.

"I hope for the same thing I always hope for—that whichever it is, the babe is healthy and happy." Kenna smiled and Dorie felt a yearning for that same type of joy. She felt almost greedy to wish for more than she'd already been given. Her husband loved her, which was a miracle unto itself. She was happy.

But the truth of it was, despite her blessings, she wanted a child with Bryce. Guilt washed over her as the door burst open, letting in one of the maids.

"An army is approaching the castle. The men are leaving to head them off."

Dorie jumped up and ran down the stairs into the hall, but there were only a few scattered soldiers remaining. Rascal ran out of the hall and she followed after him. In the bailey the men were mounting and preparing to leave. She searched the men closest to the gate, knowing the war chief would have the place of honor in front of his men.

"Bryce!" she called and caught his attention. Despite the seriousness of the moment he offered a smile and slid down from his horse to pull her into his arms.

"I'm sure it's just the Campbells or maybe the Stewarts."

"The maid said there was no flag."

"Aye. And that's why we're going out to greet them."

Dorie knew well enough that a welcome party didn't call for every soldier to join them. Especially not fully armed. They were preparing for what might happen if their visitor was not friendly.

"Come home to me."

"I'll do my best." He kissed her and she knew that was all the promise she would get from him. His kiss was fierce and full of intention. "That will have to do until I return. But when I do, ye might want to be ready." He gave her a wink and patted Rascal. "Guard her well, lad," he instructed, then mounted his horse.

She stepped out of the way as only a few warriors followed her husband through the gate. The rest remained in place, in case things turned bad.

・・・

Bryce swallowed as he crested the hill and saw the approaching army. Nearly a hundred men approached with no flag among them. This was even more men than he had left back at Dunardry. They wouldn't win this battle. Bryce knew the warriors remaining at the castle could fight them off for a time, but he worried they'd lose in the end.

The leader of the other group spurred his horse and came toward them. When he was in sight, Bryce relaxed and scabbarded his blade. "Stand down. It's Dorien."

Bryce eyed the soldiers again, spotting a red coat here and there, but overall they were out of uniform. Paid soldiers.

Lachlan kept his blade at the ready and narrowed his eyes on Bryce. "What have you done to his daughter now that he sends an army to take you down?"

"Nothing," Bryce answered while his mind recalled the things he might have done to displease his father-by-marriage. "I'm fairly sure," he added, not sounding very certain.

"Welcome back to Dunardry," Lach called when he was close enough. "To what do we owe this honor?"

Dorien smiled in greeting, which Bryce took as a good sign. "It was my understanding you wished to have access to the sea through the McCurdy port. And the only way to have it was to take over Baehaven"

"Aye. It was our understanding that your offer of men to help was only available if Bryce came home without your daughter."

Dorien spared a look at Bryce and offered a nod of respect. "I wanted to make sure your heart was pure when you made your decision. You picked her even when faced with losing something valuable."

"I will always choose her," Bryce said honestly. "Always."

Another nod from his father-in-law, this one of approval. "My men are yours on one condition."

"That is?"

"I want Baehaven Castle when the McCurdys fall. And they *will* fall."

Lach spared a glance at Bryce, but nodded. "As long as you'll grant us access to the port."

"My daughter is married to your war chief. I propose an

alliance. This time offered by a man of honor."

Lach agreed and they rode on to the castle. Bryce went ahead, happy to tell Dorie the news of their visitor. She was waiting and worrying in the hall when he returned. "Your father is on his way," he told her after she released him from a relieved and rather passionate kiss.

"My father?" He saw a moment of worry in her blue eyes. "You've not changed your mind, have you? Are you going to send me back?"

"Nay. Never. Your place is here with me. He's here to help us take Baehaven. He apparently wants the castle and the lands for himself."

Her bright eyes went wide, this time in surprise rather than worry. "He plans to move to Scotland and live in Baehaven?"

"I canna speak to what he plans for the place. I only know he wants it in exchange for the use of his men, and Lach agreed. Now, are you coming out to greet the man or no?"

"I am. Do I look a mess?"

"You are beautiful in whatever you're wearing. Or nothing at all." He bent to kiss that soft spot on her neck just below her ear and got a shiver of interest. A smile spread across his lips at her response. "And, I daresay, you're even more breathtaking now with some color on your cheeks."

"Some color?" She rolled her eyes. "I'm probably as red as the evening sun, which is exactly what you planned."

He couldn't help but laugh as he led her out to the bailey. When she saw her father, she picked up her pace and left Bryce behind. He didn't mind. He knew how much she'd missed her new family, even in the short time they'd been back at Dunardry. He would give anything to make her happy. In fact, he'd even considered moving to England for a time so she could visit with them. Although having them come to Scotland was preferred.

As expected, she peppered the man with questions on her siblings and stepmother, asking after their health and happiness. One would think it had been decades since she'd seen them, the way she went on, but Bryce left her to her reunion to go see after the grooms.

There were a lot more horses to be stabled and fed, so some of his men were helping there, while others were at the smithy seeing to the weapons and any repairs needed for battle.

When he paused in the kitchens he noted the organized chaos.

"Do ye ladies need anything?" he offered. After drawing in a few buckets of water and putting a couple of lads on kitchen duty, he moved on to oversee the next thing, and then the next.

He met up with Lach and Cam when he returned to the bailey.

"I think everything is in order," Lach said. "We'll want to be underway in a matter of days so as not to use up too much of our reserve."

Cam nodded and reported on his tasks. "I sent men to hunt. It will give us a few more days at least."

"There's no reason to wait," Bryce said. "The McCurdys do nothing but waste good air by breathing it."

"I canna disagree, but I want to ensure victory. Having the extra men is a step in the right direction, but we'll need a successful strategy, too."

"Riders!" the guard called from his post on the gate.

A moment later the gate opened and a single boy came tearing into the bailey.

"Is it McCurdys?" Lach asked as the lad slid down from his horse to come bow before the laird and offer a missive.

"Nay. Campbells."

"When it rains, it pours," Lach said, looking up at the sky.

Chapter Thirty-Three

Dorie was seated with her father as he shared the latest antics of the twins. Rascal had taken his usual spot at her feet and was the first warning when someone approached. She and her father looked up as Bryce came to stand beside her. While his face was unreadable, his body nearly hummed with excitement.

"What is it?" she asked, nervous because the man got excited over the most dangerous of things.

A small smile pulled at the corner of his mouth. "My father has arrived with more men than planned."

She smiled in relief, knowing what this meant. The more men to aid in the battle, the quicker it would be over, and with the least amount of bloodshed.

"This is good news, indeed."

"Aye. I'd like to introduce my father to my wife." He turned to Dorien. "If you'll excuse the interruption, my lord. It would please me to introduce you as well, since you are also my family."

"That I am," her father said and patted him on the

shoulder.

It didn't take Dorie an introduction to know which man was Bryce's father. A bit shorter and wiry, he had Bryce's good looks. His hair and eyes were different, but Bryce had once told her he had his mother's coloring.

Bryce turned to her with a grin. "Love, this is my sire, Thomas Campbell. Father, this is my wife, Dorie, and her father, Lord Dorien Sutherland, Viscount—"

"Dorien is fine," the viscount interrupted. "It's a pleasure to meet you, sir."

"And you." Thomas turned back to Bryce with a wide smile. "So you went to get her after all? Good for you, lad. I can tell already you made the right choice. She's lovely."

The way the man looked her over made her cheeks heat. Bryce had mentioned how fond his father was of women. Apparently Thomas had no preference as to the age of the woman when it came to flirting, or if she was married to his son.

They all spoke for a few moments, but Bryce was pulled away to take care of the men and horses. Her own father went to help him. Dorie then led her father-in-law inside to see that his men were fed.

"Will ye sit with me for a moment? I'd like to get to know you."

She looked over her shoulder, wanting to go help Kenna and Mari ready available rooms for guests. The hall would be filled with sleeping soldiers tonight. But she couldn't be rude to Bryce's father. She sat next to him and waved over a maid to bring him food and drink.

"My boy seems happy. Far happier than he was when he visited me last." He scratched her dog who had come to sit between them.

"Bryce told me he came straight to England after he left you," Dorie said.

"Ah. Good." The man nodded. His early humor and teasing were gone now. The seriousness on his face didn't sit well, as if he were hardly ever sincere. "Bryce has been haunted by his late wife and child for far too long. It's time he moved on."

"He loved them dearly," she said, defending her husband. She knew Bryce would always love his first wife and their child. Dorie would never begrudge him his happy memories of his previous family. She was only grateful he'd found enough love for her, too.

"True, true. But it's not for a man among the living to send his heart ahead of him into death. I'm glad he figured it out. As soon as you give him a bairn you'll win his heart forever."

The man chatted on and on about his current wife and all his children from his former wives—of which there were many. When he was drawn into conversation with one of the soldiers who had traveled with her father, she took the opportunity to escape.

She spent the rest of the afternoon making beds and setting up pallets for their guests. And occasionally—thanks to the conversation with her father-in-law—she worried about what might happen if she wasn't able to give Bryce a babe.

...

Around a wagon in the bailey, Bryce stood with Lach, Cam, Dorien, and Thomas, planning the attack on the McCurdy fortress. It was determined they would launch their assault at dawn rather than try to keep this many men housed at Dunardry for any length of time.

Most of the lower-ranking men would sleep in the fields beyond the curtain walls, but they would need food, and that would require fires. With the frequency of McCurdy scouts crossing the MacKinlay borders it would only take one of them to see so many men encamped and the MacKinlays would lose the element of surprise.

"If we get all the men settled before nightfall, we can have them rested and ready to leave before dawn," Dorien said. Having been a captain in His Majesty's army, he was skilled in the art of strategy. "Half can circle to the south. From there they can break again and come in from two sides, while the other half comes in from the north and east. The McCurdys will have no choice but to face us or run into the sea."

They had just finished drawing out the plans when the guard on the gate yelled down for the third time that day, announcing riders inbound to the castle. It was a border guard who rode in this time to announce the Stewarts had arrived.

"For the love of all that's holy," Lach muttered, making Cam and Bryce chuckle.

"You said you would not launch an attack until you were certain you would win," Bryce reminded his laird as they looked around the bailey that was still full of horses and men.

The Stewart laird himself rode in with an unhappy Liam riding next to him. They dismounted and joined the other men. "We've come to join forces to take down the mangy McCurdy filth." The laird looked around. "It appears we're not needed."

Dorien came forward and shook the Stewart's hand. "I can assure you, we welcome your swords. Can you be ready to ride at dawn?"

The Stewart laird's smile turned evil. "To draw the last drop of blood from the McCurdys, I would ride tonight." The laird's daughter, Evelyn, had been brutally attacked and held captive by McCurdys.

Both the Stewart and the viscount wanted revenge for the

way the McCurdys had treated their daughters. Their swords would be drawn with the might of vengeance.

The McCurdy didn't stand a chance.

• • •

When a maid came into the hall to announce the Stewarts had arrived, Dorie wanted to weep. There was no more room. Surely by the next day they would run out of food.

Kenna and Mari had joined her in fretting over what to do when Lach came in and drew Kenna into a kiss. "We leave within the hour."

The three women gasped in unison and Mari and Dorie made haste toward the door. Cam met them there and smiled down at Mari. Dorie only heard the rumble of his voice as she passed, knowing the words were for his wife only.

Continuing on, she plowed into Bryce in the bailey as he was rushing toward the hall.

Her heart fluttered when he smiled down at her. Clearly he'd been coming for her. He leaned down and kissed her hard. She felt the excitement of battle shimmering around him when he pulled away.

"The Stewarts have joined us. We have plenty of men. The time has come to put an end to the McCurdys."

Dorie knew it was the way it had to be. Truth be told, she spared only a moment of sadness over the loss that would come to her former family. While she wasn't a McCurdy by blood, Baehaven had been her home for most of her life.

Though it could certainly be argued that it had been a prison rather than a home, she could also remember the castle with fondness—the early years, when she'd played with the children and walked in the fields collecting flowers with her mother. She thought of Rory and swallowed with worry.

Bryce must have seen her reluctance and pressed his

forehead to hers. "Anyone who swears loyalty to us will be spared. We don't wish to massacre the entire clan. Only those who draw their sword against us. The clan leaders will fall today, Dorie. Ye ken there's no way around that."

She nodded in agreement. "I understand. Perhaps if you see Rory—he was at the wedding—a lean lad with a scar across his brow…" She shook her head, knowing how difficult it would be to look for such a small trace. "Forgive me, it's too much to ask. I'll not have you put at risk for a chance he'd change fealty. Thank you for letting me know." She stood taller and forced a smile through her worry. "Ye have a lot of men at your back, but be mindful of your front," she said.

He laughed and kissed her again. "Aye. I'll do so, love."

"Then I'll see you soon."

He kissed her and stepped away, only to come back for another kiss before leaving again. He gave Rascal a pat. "Watch over our woman."

As she watched her husband hurry away, she felt a wave of dizziness. What if he didn't return? She'd never been happier, and now that happiness was in jeopardy.

Kenna and Mari joined her in the bailey, and the women stood watching their men mount up and move toward the gate. Other women gathered beside them until the courtyard was lined with women and children. One by one the men gave a wave as they ducked out of the gate.

When they were all gone, the women remained in silence for a minute or two. Dorie felt them gathering strength.

It was Kenna as mistress of the keep who cleared her throat. "Come now, ladies, we've work to do to put the castle to rights. We'll need to plan a feast to celebrate our victory."

Dorie knew a victory was imminent. That was clear from the sheer size of the army heading toward Baehaven. But not every man who waved goodbye this morning would come home again.

That was the way of war, no matter the odds.

• • •

The ground shook with the thunder of hooves as the four armies moved across the MacKinlay lands as one unit. Bryce felt the energy of the men vibrate the air around them. It was common enough with a smaller group, but the power grew in a gathering of this size. They were unstoppable.

He spotted Liam riding apart from the others and drew his horse up next to him.

"Are you well?" he asked.

The young man—for he was no longer a lad anymore—glared in Bryce's direction. "I see you have your wife back."

Bryce was confused by his reaction. He thought Liam and Dorie got on well enough. She'd given him a bit of trouble when he was guarding her, but Liam hadn't seemed angry about it.

"Do you take offense with my wife?"

Liam's anger slipped away and he shook his head. "Forgive me. I don't mean to take my frustration out on you. It's just that you didn't want to marry and were forced into it, while I *want* to be wed and was refused." Liam frowned in the direction of the Stewart laird who was laughing with Lach and Dorien.

"You offered for the laird's daughter?"

"Aye. He made it clear I'm not important enough to deserve her hand." He winced. "As if I didn't know that already. I don't even know whose blood runs in my veins, and my name is merely borrowed, since I don't know which clan I truly belong to. Still, I thought he would see I would do everything I could to make her happy. Apparently a soldier's pay is not good enough for Lady Evelyn Stewart."

Bryce reached out and squeezed his arm. "Ye are a

MacKinlay. I don't give a damn about your blood or your hair. It is better to be accepted into a clan than be born into it. I speak from experience. There's honor in that. Don't forget it." It was true Liam didn't look like the MacKinlays, who tended toward dark hair. Liam's white-blond hair was even lighter than Bryce's. He stood out as different. The old laird had once said Liam might have been an angel with his hair and icy blue eyes and the way he showed up one day all on his own, no older than four. Lachlan's mother thought he was a fairy child.

"I know. You're right. I'm beyond grateful that the old laird gave me a home. I just wish I was good enough for Evelyn."

"I'm sorry, Liam. When we're done with this, we'll speak to Lach about it. Mayhap he'll be able to help. Don't lose hope."

"It seems strange hearing you speak of hope."

"Things will work out. I believe it." Bryce offered him a smile, and he smiled back. "Let's see this done first."

Liam nodded and let out a fierce battle cry which motivated the soldiers as they marched. Bryce made his rounds through the men to make sure they knew the way and called war cries to bolster their excitement. By the time he returned to the leaders, the men were chanting and ready to charge. The roar of men sounded like hell had been unleashed.

He swallowed down a frown, remembering Dorie's request. It would be nearly impossible to save her friend, but he'd do his best.

Riding up between Dorien and Lach, he explained the situation.

"There's a young warrior on the McCurdy side, a bit smaller than Liam, with a scar across his brow. You may remember him from the wedding. I don't know where his loyalties lie, but he saved Dorie more than once. If it's possible to spare him, I ask for his life so long as you're not in danger for it."

Dorien swallowed and nodded. "I'll not draw against a person who was able to bring any small comfort or protection to my daughter during her time with the McCurdy wretch."

Bryce looked out over the men now that the sun had risen and knew it would be a small miracle if any of the McCurdys survived the day when this army was unleashed upon them.

"His fate is in his own hands," Bryce decreed and nudged his horse.

It was dusk the next night when the armies split off from one another. By dawn they were in position on all sides of Baehaven.

Lach turned to Bryce with a devil of a smile. "Do the honors and lead us to victory."

They clasped arms and then did the same with Cam before turning their horses toward their enemies. Bryce let out a cry that was echoed by the other clans. Even Dorien's Englishmen joined in as they descended on their joint enemy.

Chapter Thirty-Four

Dorie stood dumbfounded as the mistress of the keep rode out of the bailey in breeches atop a giant of a horse. Kenna led a group of hunters doing their best to supply enough meat for the planned festivities.

Dorie couldn't help but think the laird wouldn't approve of his very pregnant wife riding and hunting. She was to deliver the babe in just a few weeks.

Dorie also worried it was premature to plan a victory celebration when they'd not yet heard word if the MacKinlays had engaged or how the battle progressed. For all those left at Dunardry knew it could be McCurdys who arrived back at the castle.

The numbers were in the MacKinlays' favor, but the McCurdys were sneaky and ruthless. Each time Dorie thought of such things she shivered.

"I'm sure our men will be back safely," Mari said with a strained smile as she and Dorie worked on bandages the next day.

"Aye. I've no doubt about it," Dorie lied unconvincingly.

They took turns sharing stories, but it was a futile distraction. They were both worried.

Kenna and Mari needed their men to return safely to help raise their children. And Dorie needed Bryce so they could begin their life together free from the danger of the McCurdys.

"They will all come home soon," Dorie said, her voice more certain this time.

She just hoped it was true.

...

They were winning. Bryce was sure of it. Though the McCurdys were putting up a good fight. Wallace and his crew had run off to leave their laird and the remaining men loyal to him to hold off four armies.

Rory fought beside Bryce. It hadn't been difficult to find him since he'd been camping at the edge of the woods alone, waiting for whoever came to take Baehaven. He took a knee to pledge his loyalty to the MacKinlays and aided in getting them through the lines.

The viscount had wanted to take down the McCurdy laird for Dorie and for her mother. But it was Bryce who faced him first on the battlefield.

And it was Bryce who delivered the blow that dropped him. The older man sputtered and coughed, and eventually laughed when he realized the injury to his chest was a fatal one.

"For Dorie," Bryce said. "My wife."

His eyes locked on Bryce's and he laughed again, a cruel sound that choked off with a wet cough.

"She was never supposed to leave. Damn Wallace for making that arrangement without my knowledge. The lass was supposed to rot away, thinking every day of how thoroughly she'd destroyed our lives. Her ma's and mine."

Bryce looked down at the other man as Dorien stepped closer. It was clear from the expression on his face he'd heard what the old laird said.

"You killed her mother."

"Nay." This time when he coughed, red spattered his lips. "It's true I roughed her up a bit in my rage, but her death... no. She took care of that herself, to spite me."

"You lie," Dorien said. "She wouldn't have taken her own life. Not when she needed to be there for our child."

The McCurdy's eyes narrowed on the Englishman. Even at death's door as he was, it was easy for him to see the similarities between Dorien and the child he'd thought was his daughter for nine years.

"Did she ever tell you of the child?" Blood was running from the corner of the man's mouth and his voice rattled. "She planned to go to you without Dorie because she knew I'd never let her take the girl. When I refused, she took a blade to her own throat." He laughed, blood bubbling from his mouth. "Now I'll see her in hell. And you will never have her." A few ragged breaths later the smile left his lips as life vacated his eyes.

"He lies," Dorien said again.

Bryce didn't know many men who still felt the need to lie when facing death. Generally, they were quick to spill truths until their dying breath. But for both Dorien and Dorie's sake he would let them have their truth as they knew it. Some things were better not known.

With the fall of the McCurdy laird, the remaining men surrendered quickly and came forward to bow in front of them. Lachlan offered them sanctuary in exchange for their fealty, and they were quick to comply.

When everything was settled Lach turned toward Baehaven Castle and nodded to Dorien. "Your castle, my lord."

...

It had taken three days for a messenger to arrive with word of a battle that, by now, was most likely over. The news he brought was outdated, not to mention vague. He had no word specifically of who had fallen and who lived. All he was able to report was that the MacKinlay laird was alive, and the McCurdys had been taken by surprise.

Kenna sent the lad for a meal and gave an encouraging smile to the ladies who'd convened. "They had surprise on their side. I'm certain the McCurdy took one look at the men amassed and laid down his sword in surrender."

Dorie offered a brittle smile and wondered how they were able to sit there without going mad. It took her a moment to see the answer. Each one of them clung to a child. They all had a small piece of the men they loved.

While Dorie had nothing of Bryce.

That night she tossed and turned as visions of her husband being slain in battle taunted her from sleep. It was still dark when she dressed in the messenger's clothing she had washed and mended earlier and made her way to the stable. She'd secured Rascal in their room, knowing the guard would recognize him and know who she was straight away.

She knew it was a foolish endeavor. If the McCurdys had indeed defeated their forces, they could even now be heading her way. But she'd rather face it straight on than wait another second to hear of her husband's fate.

At the gate, she was faced with her first challenge. She had found a cap in the hall and pulled it tight over her hair. Lowering her voice, she announced she was to return to the battle to bring back word. Thankfully, the guard didn't hesitate to lift the gate and allow her to leave.

The sun cast the faintest hint of light on the eastern border so she headed in the opposite direction. It was a simple thing to follow the trail left by more than three hundred horses. As the sun rose higher and she was able to see better, she picked up her pace. She stopped only long enough to rest and water her horse and was off again before dawn the next day.

Rain had settled in and even though it was still summer, she was drenched and shivering in the hills, unsure what time it was since the sun refused to shine. Slogging through the mud made things slower, so she was only at a canter when two men stepped out on the trail, blocking her path.

She turned, but another, larger man had stepped behind her, covered in filth and blood.

"Look what we have found," a familiar voice bellowed. "If it isn't my dear sister, here to aid us."

Chapter Thirty-Five

Dorie tried to steer her horse around them, but the man in front had already grabbed the bridle and was holding her mount as her brother reached up with one hand and yanked her down.

She fell hard to the ground and curled into a ball so he'd not step on her. She anticipated a growl and savage barking, but then she remembered Rascal wasn't with her. He'd not be able to save her this time.

She expected the men would take her horse and go, but a bit of cursing caused her to turn and see that her brother wasn't able to mount.

From the ground she took in the state of the other two men. One was unable to stand as he held a hand over a large gash across his stomach. Dorie swallowed back bile at the twisted bulge she saw him clutching. The man clearly wasn't long for this world with a wound like that.

The man holding her horse hobbled on a leg drenched in blood. When he shifted, she was able to see the makeshift bandage tied around the wound that was also dripping with blood.

Her brother stumbled as he tried again to lift himself to the saddle. He reached to rub his back where she noticed the perfect mark of a horseshoe.

No doubt, if he could get up, he planned to leave them all behind and save himself. If he was able to take her horse, she would be left behind with no food and no way to get back to Dunardry or to go on to Baehaven.

Feeling the dirk still sheathed at her side, she devised a plan. It would take quick work on her part, but her need to see Bryce drove her up to her feet.

In a flash she kicked out, hitting the man holding her horse in the leg, causing him to crumble in pain. Grabbing the reins from her brother in one hand, she came up with her dirk in the other and slammed the blade into his chest.

He gasped and stepped back, a look of shock on his face. She'd spent the last years at Baehaven being as quiet as a mouse. But now she had something worth fighting for. A new, happy life. She'd not let the McCurdys take another minute of it.

"I want to thank ye, *brother*." She said the last word with a sneer. "Ye married me off to the best man possible. I'm now part of a family. I'm loved. And you and your ill-begotten sire will soon be dead and forgotten."

He slumped to the ground and she lifted her leg to mount. He grabbed her ankle, hissing a curse and tugging at her. But he was weakened from his injuries, and she was able to kick at him to gain her release.

Once mounted, she hissed at the pain in her arm. She hadn't even noticed her brother had cut her while she was fighting him. Blood flowed freely from a cut on the inside of her arm and dripped from her fingertips.

She wanted to leave immediately, but she needed to see it done. She waited the few moments it took to see Wallace's chest stop moving with breath.

Then leading her horse away, she hurried toward Baehaven.

• • •

"Bryce, come in here," Lach called from the upper corridor in Baehaven.

When he entered the dim, shabby room he found Dorien weeping. The man brushed by Bryce's shoulder as he fled. Lach wrenched the boards from the window, letting light into the space. Seeing it fully didn't help. Quite the opposite. A broken bed had been pushed in the corner. A small pile of well-worn books sat next to it. The only other object in the room was a wash basin on a stand in the opposite corner.

Cam squinted at the wall. "What the bloody hell…?"

Bryce gasped when he turned to see what Cam had noticed. Thousands of small lines covered the wall beside the door.

Lachlan came to stand next to him. "This room had been barred from the outside. I think this is probably where Dorie was kept prisoner."

"For this long." Bryce stepped closer, noticing the clusters of lines where his wife had kept track of the days, months, and years of her empty existence as a captive in this castle. She'd told him it had been nine years, but knowing that and seeing it broken out by days like this put it all in a different perspective.

He noticed how the lines started a vibrant black but later turned to a russet brown. "Christ," he whispered. "She ran out of ink and started marking the days with her own blood."

Bryce thought he'd be ill. If the McCurdy weren't already dead, he'd take his time punishing him for this. Even if the old laird hadn't known, he should have. And he should have saved her.

Bryce swore he would track down Wallace and end him.

"She's safe now," Lach reassured him. "She's free to live a happy life with you. She'll never have to live like this ever again. Thanks to you."

Guilt over the way he'd treated her at first made his stomach twist even more, but he promised himself he would make sure the rest of her days were spent happy and loved. He knew well enough how memories faded, even when one tried desperately to hold on to them. He would give her better memories so the ones of this place would fade quickly into nothing.

Bryce found his father-in-law outside. The tears were gone but the viscount still looked distraught.

"Are you well?" Bryce asked.

Dorien offered him a strained smile. "My life wasn't the way it should have been. I should have brought her with me. We could have raised Dorie together. My daughter never would have been punished for having my blood and held prisoner in that wretched room."

Bryce sighed. "My life isna the way it should have been, either. If Maggie and Isabel had lived, my daughter would be almost fourteen years. We would have gone on rides, talking of her dreams." He smiled and let that life drift off in the breeze. "But this life is going to be great as well. I have Dorie. She makes me happy. Mayhap we'll be blessed with children. I'll never forget the ones I loved before, but I've been given a second chance for happiness. I'll not let it get away."

"I married Harriet while my heart was still here in Scotland. It was impossible not to notice all the ways she wasn't like the woman I'd loved. It wasn't fair to her. She's an amazing woman who's borne me four wonderful children. I do love her. I see that now. I wish she were here now to ease my sorrow over Dorie. Harriet deserves better. I vow to do better by her."

"There's still time," Bryce said. "Not many people find happiness at all. We should be grateful for finding it twice."

They stepped out into the sunlight. A beautiful day for new beginnings.

At first Bryce thought his eyes were playing tricks on him. It would explain the reason he saw Dorie riding toward them on a horse, her gown covered in blood. When Dorien gasped next to him, Bryce realized the viscount saw her, too.

"Is she really here?" Bryce asked.

"Dear God, let her be all right," Dorien said, then took off running with Bryce right behind him. Bryce passed Dorien and got to her faster. Just in time for her to topple from her horse into his arms.

"Dorie? Dorie!" He pressed a hand to her pale cheek, his fingers finding the pulse under her chin. It was weak and thready. Bryce carried her into the castle and checked her over, calling for a healer.

A reluctant woman came forward and Bryce begged her, "Please help my wife. I canna lose her. Please."

The woman took a deep breath and nodded. Bryce and Dorien kept close watch over the woman to be sure she didn't treat Dorie as an enemy. But the woman stitched up the gash on Dorie's arm and dressed it with clean linen.

"It's good to see her free," she said, and gently brushed Dorie's hair back from her face.

"You know her?"

"Aye. It's been many years since I've seen her, but I remember her as a little girl. She's been trapped for so long. In a way, we all have."

"You're all free now," Bryce assured her.

"Are we? Or are we just giving our freedom to another?"

In truth, Bryce didn't have an answer to her question. The castle belonged to Dorien now, per his arrangement with

Lach.

"I can assure you, your next laird will be more than fair," Dorien cut in with a smile.

Did the man plan to stay on as laird? What did he want with a castle in Scotland? At the moment, Bryce didn't care. For just then Dorie opened her eyes and looked up at him.

• • •

"You're alive?" she whispered, her voice rough.

"Aye, and so are you." He smiled and kissed her forehead. "Why on earth did you come all this way?"

She looked away nervously. Would he be angry to know she'd risked her life for nothing more than worry? She sat up, wincing at the tightness in her arm. "We'd had no word," she explained. "And I couldn't wait any longer. I needed to make sure you were alive and well."

He looked at her for a full minute, his expression unreadable. It seemed he didn't know what to say. Eventually he shook his head. "I want to scold you and tell you how foolish you were to put yourself in danger just to check on me, but I can't. Not when you're here with me, alive and smiling. All I want to do is kiss you." He held her cheeks in his hands and pressed his lips to hers in a fierce kiss.

They were interrupted when her father cleared his throat. Lachlan and Cam had entered the hall and were standing next to Dorien with smiles on their faces. Even Rory was off to the side with a grin in place. Liam stepped around Cam. Thank God. They'd all survived. She relaxed, knowing the women waiting back at Dunardry would be happy.

"What's going on?" Bryce asked curiously. He must have noticed something was afoot as well. They were all up to something, it was clear enough.

She looked toward Lach, but it was her father who spoke.

"As you know, I requested ownership of Baehaven when it fell, and it has indeed fallen."

A cheer went up around them. Even some of the McCurdys seemed pleased with the outcome.

"As I understand it, you married my daughter without a dowry. In fact, your laird had to pay the McCurdy, and then you didn't even get what you were promised."

Bryce smiled down at her and winked. "I'm not complaining. I got more than I'd hoped for from the bargain."

"And it's for that reason that I am giving Baehaven to you."

The smile on Bryce's face turned to confusion as her father came closer to kiss the top of her head.

"You've proven yourself to be a fine husband for my daughter, and I'm making you laird of the remaining clan and any who care to join you. With the understanding that the MacKinlays may dock their ships in your port."

Dorie reached up to push Bryce's jaw shut when his mouth fell open in shock. "But I'm the war chief—"

Lachlan held up his hand. "Liam will make a fine war chief. And I'll leave Rory here for you." He came closer to clasp arms with Bryce. "We both know we'll be better off with each of us ruling our own lands. You're not very good at following orders."

Bryce laughed and hugged his cousin. "Maybe if your orders weren't shite." It was clear Lachlan took no offense to the jest.

Dorie hugged her father tightly. "Oh, Father. Thank you."

"I hope you will be happy here. I know this place holds a lot of bad memories." He frowned.

"We will make new memories. Happy ones. It will be a true home, and you and the rest of the family will always be welcome."

"We'll visit often," he promised with a smile.

"A laird!" Bryce laughed again as if still in disbelief. Then the smile turned to worry. "Bloody hell. I don't know how to be a laird."

Lachlan laughed. "You're a fair man. You'll make a fine laird. Besides, ye don't have to do much to be better than what these people had before."

Rory nodded in agreement, and Dorie squeezed Bryce's hand. He pulled her into his arms, whispering in her ear. "Can I do this?"

"You'll do it so well," she assured him.

"Can you be happy here?" he asked, sharing the same concern her father had voiced. When she was imprisoned in her room here, she had dreamed every night of escaping this place and being free.

But as she looked around at the sunken faces of the women and children who had also been trapped in this place, she wanted to make it better for them as well. She'd seen what could become of a place where love ruled. The people thrived.

"Let's make this a home for ourselves and for everyone here."

He pulled her into his arms and kissed her hair. When he finally backed away, he was smiling. "Welcome home, wife."

"Welcome home, laird."

Epilogue

One year later

Bryce balanced himself on the edge of the Baehaven battlements for a few seconds longer before stepping back. The sound of laughter rose up from the bailey where the McCurdy children chased after Rascal who was clean for once, in anticipation of the festivities.

He turned toward the ocean, breathing in the salty sea air and the scent of summer in the Highlands. The MacKinlay ship, the *Davinna*, sat at the dock still under construction. Dorie's father's ship sat next to it.

The castle was filled with family. His cousins and their wives were visiting, along with some of the Campbells.

In a few hours, the remaining McCurdys would be pledging their loyalty, and everyone in his motley clan would be taking the name MacKinlay.

"I knew I would find you up here," Dorie said as she came up behind him.

"I can't get enough of this view. I feel so alive here." It

was a huge change from the times he'd spent atop the walls of Dunardry, when he'd allowed his pain to bring him to the edge.

"Are you ready to become Laird MacKinlay of Baehaven?"

"I am. I feel I've always been more a MacKinlay than a Campbell, having spent much time with my mother's family. It's time to make it official."

When his wife shivered, he led her below, out of the brisk spring air.

"Be careful on the steps," he warned, going before her to lead her down the tight stairs. "I don't know how you see past that lump."

"Are you calling our child a lump?" she accused as she rubbed her stomach affectionately.

He turned and placed a kiss where their child grew. The expected arrival was the other reason their family had gathered.

"Before we go down for the celebration, there's something I want to show ye," Bryce said, feeling nervous. "I have a surprise. I hope you'll like it."

In truth, he wasn't sure how she might feel about his efforts. She followed him down the hall to stand near the room that had served as her prison for part of her life.

When her father had first suggested renovating the castle, he worried how they would ever make it a home when it held so many bad memories. But Baehaven was a beautiful castle and as the changes were made, they found ways to fill it with light and happiness.

But this room had been the hardest. At times Bryce wanted to wall off the door and never look upon it again. But in the end he'd found a way to make it a place of peace. At least he hoped so.

"Are you ready?" Bryce asked as they stood by the

doorway. The door to the room had been removed so it would always be open.

Dorie nodded and stepped into the space that had been her life for those years after her mother died. She let out a quiet gasp as she spun around, taking it all in.

Bryce and her father had transformed it into a library.

The windows, previously boarded up, were now exposed, with cheery curtains pulled open to let in the light. The sun cast bright spots on the floor, adding to the warmth of the room.

The wall where Dorie had marked the passing of time now held shelves filled with books.

The ratty bed had been removed. Pretty chairs now sat in groupings around the different windows.

"I wanted this to be a place where you could feel comfortable. I didn't know if we could make Baehaven our home as long as the memories still haunted you." Bryce wrapped his arms around her as she stood by the window looking out over the harbor.

"It's beautiful. And I will enjoy spending evenings with you here, reading to our children."

He placed his hand on her belly.

"You're not afraid?" she asked.

There'd been a time when he hadn't wanted the risk of a child or a wife. He'd lived through a great loss and his pain haunted him. Together, though, they were moving forward.

"I might not have been held captive in this room like you, but I was trapped all the same. Imprisoned by my fear of caring for or loving anyone. I'll not let my fear hold me in its bonds again. Living without you might have spared me pain, but it was not a life worth living. Now we'll face each day together."

"I like the sound of that." She reached up to kiss him.

Feeling his wife's lips on his neck sent a shiver of

excitement through his body. They were living this life and growing their family together.

With a groan, he led her toward their room and closed the door.

She giggled as he unfastened her gown. "But we'll be late for the celebration!"

"They'll wait for their laird and lady." He kissed her, feeling the fullness of his mended heart. Stronger than ever. "Besides, they should get used to us being late. It's sure to happen often."

About the Author

One very early morning, Allison B. Hanson woke up with a conversation going on in her head. It wasn't so much a dream as being forced awake by her imagination. Unable to go back to sleep, she gave in, went to the computer, and began writing. Years later it still hasn't stopped. Allison lives near Hershey, Pennsylvania. Her contemporary romances include paranormal, sci-fi, fantasy, and mystery suspense. She enjoys candy immensely, as well as long motorcycle rides, running, and reading.

Don't miss the Clan MacKinlay series...

HER ACCIDENTAL HIGHLANDER HUSBAND

Also by Allison B. Hanson...

WITNESS IN THE DARK

WANTED FOR LIFE

WATCHED FROM A DISTANCE

Discover more historical romance…

THE HIGHLANDER'S UNEXPECTED PROPOSAL
a *Brothers of Wolf Isle* novel by Heather McCollum

A lass begging to marry him tops the list of "oddest things to happen," but Chief Adam Macquarie is desperate. And he's not above lying to get what he needs. Lark Montgomerie is thrilled the brawny chief agrees to save her from her father's machinations of wedding her off to the first fool that agrees. Nothing will dampen her spirits. That is, until she arrives and realizes things are amiss…

TWELFTH KNIGHT'S BRIDE
a novel by E. Elizabeth Watson

To help her starving clan at Christmastide, Lady Aileana pilfers vegetables. Except the bastard Laird James MacDonald shows up and demands marriage as recompense. She's able to negotiate a severance on Twelfth Night, but that's still two weeks in enemy territory. James needs to marry in order to inherit his fortune. He might as well handfast with the spitfire Aileana. He'd get his money, and a bonny lass he can't help but admire. If only she'd give him a chance.

THE SINFUL SCOT
a novel by Maddison Michaels

Constance Campbell, the Duchess of Kilmaine, once believed that all she needed in life was a duke. But everything unraveled when she realized her perfect husband was a perfect monster. Now broken beyond repair, she hides her misery behind a perfect Society mask...even from her childhood friend, Alec. But when the Duke of Kilmaine is murdered in cold blood, with Connie sleeping right next to him in bed, Alec and Connie must set out on the run together. Finally unencumbered, Connie feels a freedom she only ever dreamed about, and an unexpected attraction to the man who is keeping her safe. But even if they can win her freedom and clear her name, could she ever open her heart up to someone again?

HIS REBELLIOUS LASS
a *Scottish Hearts* novel by Callie Hutton

When Lord Campbell inherits a Scottish beauty as his ward, it's his job to marry her off. Easy. Lady Bridget will have plenty of suitors. But Bridget has plans for that fortune and she refuses to help her handsome guardian find her a husband. Bridget and Cam are on opposite sides of a war that neither one plans to lose. Even if neither can deny that they set each other's heart afire. And then Cam makes a bold proposal...

Printed in Great Britain
by Amazon